"You're [...] now. You're my wife."

The teasing light warmed in her beautiful eyes, and he felt a thrill over assessing her correctly.

He stopped. She faced him and a long, silent moment filled the energy between them. Lifting his hand, he caressed her cheek with his thumb.

"You're going to make a great mom."

Her slow blink told him she received his comment favorably, in opposition to her choice in profession. Maybe he'd overgeneralized. Women could take on any type of career and be great moms. Jocelyn's case differed in how she'd come to her decision. It didn't matter. She fascinated him.

Without any thought over why he shouldn't, Trevor leaned in and kissed her.

* * *

We hope you enjoy this preview of The Coltons of Texas: Finding love and buried family secrets in the Lone Star State...

* * *

If you're on Twitter, tell us what you think of Harlequin Romantic Suspense! #harlequinromsuspense

Dear Reader,

Welcome to the last book of Part 1 in The Coltons of Texas series! I love writing these stories. They are full of action and intrigue. Never a dull moment in the characters' lives!

With a copycat killer on the loose, the trail picks up right here in *A Baby for Agent Colton* and Trevor Colton is the man for the takedown. Lead profiler on the case, he has a lot of work to do and Jocelyn Locke isn't making it easier on him. Rookie though she may be, she brings out the protector in him, and his ongoing battle with his desire for her is more difficult to control. It doesn't help that she'd like to settle down and raise a family.

What led both of these characters to become smart, brave FBI agents plays into their attraction for each other and is what I enjoyed most about writing this book. Well...that and the suspense!

After you immerse yourself in Trevor and Jocelyn's story, look for Part 2 of this series. There's more action and love to come!

As always, happy reading!

Jennie

A BABY FOR
AGENT COLTON

———

Jennifer Morey

HHARLEQUIN® ROMANTIC SUSPENSE

Special thanks and acknowledgment to Jennifer Morey
for her contribution to The Coltons of Texas miniseries.

ISBN-13: 978-0-373-27991-3

A Baby for Agent Colton

Recycling programs
for this product may
not exist in your area.

Printed in U.S.A.

www.Harlequin.com

Two-time RITA® Award nominee and Golden Quill Award winner **Jennifer Morey** writes single-title contemporary romance and page-turning romantic suspense. She has a geology degree and has managed export programs in compliance with the International Traffic in Arms Regulations (ITAR) for the aerospace industry. She lives at the feet of the Rocky Mountains in Denver, Colorado, and loves to hear from readers through her website, jennifermorey.com, or Facebook.

Books by Jennifer Morey

Harlequin Romantic Suspense

The Coltons of Texas

A Baby for Agent Colton

Cold Case Detectives

A Wanted Man
Justice Hunter

Ivy Avengers

Front Page Affair
Armed and Famous
One Secret Night
The Eligible Suspect

All McQueen's Men

The Secret Soldier
Heiress Under Fire
Unmasking the Mercenary
Special Ops Affair
Seducing the Accomplice
Seducing the Colonel's Daughter

Visit Jennifer's Author Profile page at Harlequin.com, or jennifermorey.com, for more titles.

For Allie, my adorable, smart,
loving Australian shepherd, who always knows
when to paw me for attention!

Chapter 1

"It's not her." Trevor Colton strolled around the body lying on blood-soaked carpet next to the bed.

Evidence of a violent fight for life cluttered the scene, a tipped-over lamp and chair, broken picture glass and the item that had prompted the call to him. A red permanent marker lay on the floor where a pen and pencil jar had fallen from a small desk crammed next to a dresser. That, in addition to the first letter of the victim's name, had alerted him and his team that this could be the work of the Alphabet Killer. As soon as Trevor saw the scene, however, he didn't agree.

When his most promising agent didn't respond, he turned to see Jocelyn Locke staring at the body, one arm folded against her ribs, the other propped on top, fingers curled at her lips.

Since when did she get queasy at crime scenes? The

bloody body and overall gore surrounding what had once been Jane McDonald would shock anyone not familiar with this line of work. Jocelyn was a trained FBI agent, still a rookie, but this wasn't her first murder case. Trevor enjoyed training her, molding her into an excellent detective. He ignored the little voice that taunted he liked something else about her, too.

She noticed him scrutinizing her. Lowering her hand, she asked, "What?"

Whatever had her disturbed abruptly disappeared. He decided to let it pass for now. They had work to do.

"Our subject didn't do this," he said. "Someone who once loved her did this. A man. Husband. Lover." He pointed to the stab wounds. "See how many times he stabbed her? Twenty or twenty-five times. Look at her chest. It's shredded."

Jocelyn's curled fingers went back to their previous pose. She stared at the body again.

"Jocelyn?"

Dropping her hand, she glanced at him with a sickened swallow and then headed for the door.

Startled, Trevor trailed behind her. What had gotten into her? Maybe he hadn't noticed her queasiness until now. This had to be the worst reaction she'd had. Concern rose up, more than he should have for a fellow agent.

Most of the time he concentrated on the investigations. Paying too much attention to her would only lead to trouble. Jocelyn had one of those slender, hot-in-skinny-jeans bodies that drew a man's eye—and heart—away from tasks at hand. And she talked about babies a lot. Why she'd become an agent, he never guessed.

She struck him as more of a stay-at-home mom, albeit an armed one.

Outside, he watched her take several deep breaths under a streetlight, late on a warm June night in Granite Gulch, Texas.

He stopped beside her. "Are you all right?"

Her long dark hair swung in a ponytail as she turned. "Yeah. Yeah. I just… I don't think I'll ever get used to that."

Crime scenes were never easy to see. "You have to learn to detach yourself. Your goal is to help the victims and their families. That's your job, your duty. You bring them justice." He jabbed his thumb toward the ranch house where the murder had occurred and a neighbor had called to report screaming. "That in there is just a body. You don't have to feel sorry for it. Feel sorry for the life that left it. And get motivated to avenge her."

Jocelyn nodded a few stiff, short times. "I know. I know all of that. It's just…"

"Hard, yeah. It is. Just stay focused on your job."

With a strange look at him, she nodded slower, closing her eyes and letting out a final, deep breath.

Why had she looked at him like that? She looked at him that way every time he made references to work. Things they had to get done. Deadlines. Facts of a case. Did he use the phrase too much? *Stay focused.*

"Staying focused keeps it from getting too personal," he said.

As she recovered from her nausea, Jocelyn's eyes took on a familiar, teasing glint. "And we all know you don't get personal."

What did she mean by that? She turned this onto him. "Not when I'm working."

"We aren't working all the time. We do have personal conversations, you know. Like right now, for example."

"You think this is personal? You just said I don't get personal."

"You shared advice with me that isn't related to the job." She pointed to the house. "To that."

"It's advice that will help you be a good agent."

Her brow lifted. "By shutting everything and everyone out?"

"Distractions won't catch killers."

"And you're the best at controlling distractions?"

Her teasing had taken on a sarcastic note. "I didn't say that."

With an exaggerated sigh, she started walking toward his SUV. "Don't be getting any ideas that you're better at this than me just because I got sick to my stomach in there."

First she accused him of not getting personal and now she thought he outdid her. Why? Because he stayed professional? "You're a rookie."

"Best rookie you'll ever have." She smiled over at him.

Damn if she didn't have a way of turning on the charm. "I can see you've recovered. You're back to your cheery self."

"You should try it sometime." She slid him a playful glance as she came to a stop at the sidewalk.

He grunted, used to her teasing, which at times could be crass. "You're saying I'm a downer?"

"You're serious."

Dead people had a tendency to take humor out of the day. He took in her slender form, curving in the right places in dark jeans and an FBI jacket over her white

T-shirt. Maybe her femininity did distract him. But she reported to him. He morally disagreed with intimate relationships with his employees.

"You own a cat," he said.

She laughed, breathy evidence that she enjoyed the way they poked at each other. Trevor had trouble deciphering whether she meant everything she said. Did she really think he was serious? Too serious? He wasn't all the time...was he?

"Having a cat doesn't make me serious. You're a guy. Guys don't like cats."

"Only guys who have dogs."

She laughed outright at that.

She had a great laugh, one of many things he'd begun to like about her.

Big smile still sparkling all over her face, she tapped him with her finger. "The Alphabet Killer might be trying to throw us off. Remember, she's copying Matthew Colton's methods. Don't discount her as a suspect in this murder. Wait for the DNA testing."

She may have a point. The evidence told the truth. But he'd investigated a lot more crimes than she had.

He didn't comment. Any other detective, he'd have argued, but not with her. He encouraged her to offer theories. She learned when wrong and he preferred she figured that out on her own.

"My two o'clock," she said. "We have company."

He covertly turned and spotted a car parked on the side of the road. Illuminated by dash lights, a man sat inside, watching. The car still ran.

"Did our subject come back to see the fuss his handiwork caused?" Jocelyn asked.

Killers sometimes did return to the crime scene.

Parking down the street displayed boldness. Or in this case, maybe guilt.

"I thought you were convinced this was the Alphabet Killer."

"Not convinced, just open to possibilities—including this killer being who you suspect."

Trevor covertly looked over at the car. "Could be someone who's just curious."

Reaching his black Yukon, he started to open her door for her.

She swatted his hand away. "Stop doing that."

Ever since they'd first met, he felt compelled to treat her like a lady. Sometimes she talked like a man and kept him at a distance like a man. Except when she teased him. Then he wasn't sure if she flirted with him. But she had a certain femininity about her, a sexy heat that burned just below the surface. Like now, denying him while her eyes and the way she moved said something different.

He walked around to the other side as she got in, seeing the way she watched him while checking on the person in the other car.

Maybe she felt the same as him, attracted but uncomfortable with that. She might complain about his professionalism, but she had the same standards.

Starting the engine, he checked the rearview mirror and saw the car hadn't moved.

"Buckle up."

"Stop doing that," she said again.

"Doing what?" How did asking her to buckle up resemble treating her like a lady?

"Being so…attentive."

Or…attentive. He'd go with that. "I'm being attentive

by making sure you wear a seat belt. Okay. Would you rather I let you go through the windshield if we wreck?" He drove into a U-turn and approached the other car.

"I was going to put my seat belt on, just not in your time frame." She connected the belt with a firm snap.

"You get grouchy when you're tired and hungry, you know that?"

"So do you. I'm not grouchy. Are we fighting? It started out okay, but it seems like it graduated into a fight." Her face crimped into a befuddled frown.

"I get grouchy?" Trevor realized he *was* hungry as he stopped beside the parked car and Jocelyn rolled her window down, gesturing with her other hand for the man to do the same.

The stranger gaped at them, a deer-in-headlights stare, and then jerked into action. He yanked the gear into drive and tires squealed as he sped off.

"Not a curious onlooker." Jocelyn closed her window as Trevor whipped the SUV into another U-turn.

The big engine easily caught up to the car, a green Prius. He flipped on the flashing lights along the top of the windshield.

The Prius turned right. Trevor followed, turning on the siren. The Prius didn't stop. Instead, the driver drove toward Main Street. Late at night, traffic didn't concern Trevor much, but his luck ran against him when a moving truck pulled out from a side street. The Prius dodged the front end and Trevor veered to miss the rear.

The Prius crashed into the front of a liquor store, shattering glass and tearing down the front wall. Screeching to a stop, Trevor jumped out, drawing his gun. Jocelyn did the same and he wished she wouldn't.

The man had gotten out of the Prius, the crunched

driver's door left open. Trevor jumped over debris and ran to the back of the store. The man kicked open the metal back door and ran into the alley.

"FBI! Stop!" he shouted.

The man ran down the alley toward the road, and to Trevor's horror, Jocelyn appeared from around the corner. As he saw the subject aim his gun, Trevor's blood left his head. But Jocelyn ducked back around the corner of the building just before a bullet hit the concrete.

He gained on the running man.

Jocelyn peeked out from her hiding place and aimed her weapon. "FBI! Stop!"

The shooter fired in answer, hitting concrete again as she leaned out of sight.

A man who'd shoot at a law enforcement officer was a dangerous one. Trevor put all he had into his run. The man glanced back as he veered to the left, away from Jocelyn, and sprinted down a busy street. He toppled a few chairs in front of a café. Trevor leaped over those and saw the man shove a middle-aged woman out of his way. She sprawled to the concrete sidewalk.

Trevor veered around her, quickly assessing her to make sure she was all right before charging after the heartless man who'd plowed into her.

He gained some more on him. The man glanced back and swung his gun, very poor aim. He fired and Trevor feared for innocent lives along the way.

Closing the gap, Trevor grabbed a hold of the subject's shirt. The man rolled onto his back, gun waving as he tried to steady it for aim. Trevor knocked his wrist and then punched his eye.

The subject's head jerked backward, and Trevor almost wrestled the gun from his grasp, still holding on to his own gun, but the man moved his arms and legs in a practiced way to throw Trevor off. He knew how to fight. Trevor should have anticipated that. His hold loosened just enough for the man to escape. Trevor got to his feet just as a blur of a shape passed him. Jocelyn, running at full speed.

Stumbling into a run, Trevor took up chase behind her, cursing his mistake of overconfidence.

The man ran into an Indian food market, located in a strip mall. He tipped over a display of spices. Boxes and containers scattered over the floor. Jocelyn jumped over most of the mess but smashed one of the boxes in her chase. Trevor cleared the spices in one easy leap. The man ran down an aisle, pushing a shopping cart and the woman behind it. She bumped back against the shelf of jars, knocking some of those, one breaking when it fell. At the end of the aisle, the man twisted and fired haphazardly. Jocelyn shot back, not aiming to kill. She wanted to talk to him as much as Trevor did. But she missed.

Bursting through swinging double doors, the man ran into the back of the store. Jocelyn and Trevor followed.

Trevor put his hand on Jocelyn's arm to make her stop. He peered around the wall and ducked back in time to avoid being shot. Shouts of workers echoed as they scurried to get out of harm's way.

Peeking around the wall, Trevor saw the man running for the open overhead door, where workers had stopped unloading a delivery truck. The truck still ran.

Jocelyn must have thought of the same thing, because she headed for the driver's side.

Trevor reached the side of the truck just as the man opened the truck door. He would try to get away in the delivery truck. Hauling the driver out, the man climbed up into the truck while the driver sprawled to the ground.

Seeing the gunman turn and aim his weapon at Jocelyn, Trevor felt another moment of dread. Jocelyn would be shot!

He dived for her. Tackling her to the ground, he heard the bullet ping a nearby Dumpster. The gunman shut the truck door.

Trevor shot at the front and rear tires as he scrambled to his feet and ran for the driver's door.

"Out of the truck! Now!" Trevor had the man's head in aim.

The man looked from Trevor's gun to his face, his own gun not raised enough to fire with any accuracy. His hands had been occupied trying to drive away, and now he was caught. Trevor knew it. The gunman knew it.

After a brief stare-down, the man held up his hands, making sure Trevor saw that his fingers were off the trigger. Trevor stepped forward and opened the door.

"Step out of there," he said. "Nice and easy."

He backed up as the man complied.

"I didn't do it."

"Nobody said you did."

Jocelyn appeared next to him with cuffs. "Turn around and put your hands on your head."

The man did.

"You're under arrest for assault with a deadly weapon," Jocelyn said. "You have the right to remain silent. Anything you do or say may be used against you in a court of law. You have the right to consult an attorney before speaking to police and to have an attorney present during questioning now or in the future. If you cannot afford an attorney, one will be appointed for you. Do you understand?"

"I didn't kill my wife."

"Nobody said you did," Trevor said again.

The man turned his head and looked at him over his shoulder. "Then why are you arresting me?"

"You ran from us after we approached you and then shot a gun at us. Is there anything about that you find questionable?" Jocelyn asked, her sarcasm shining through.

"I knew what you'd think. Everyone always thinks the husband did it."

"Let's talk about that at the station." Jocelyn took him by the arm and guided him back toward the store.

"I want an attorney."

Trevor followed them back through the store, past several people recovering from fear, stepping back and out of the way. He called in the arrest. A few minutes later, a car arrived in front of the store and two other officers took the gunman away.

Now standing on the sidewalk with a crowd of on-lookers, Trevor turned to Jocelyn. "Don't ever do that again."

She faced him in genuine question. "Do what again?"

She really didn't know? "Go after somebody who has a gun."

"I had a gun." She held up hers in front of him, barrel up as she flipped on the safety.

"You were almost shot back there."

With an indignant twirl, she started up the street beneath the watching crowd. Ignoring them, he caught up to her. Obviously she didn't take criticism well, not about her detective work. He always found that intriguing. There had to be a reason.

"What made you join the FBI, anyway?" He let himself enjoy another look down her body, lingering on the glimpses of her perky breasts moving with each of her steps. "You aren't the type. I mean, you're tomboyish enough, but…"

She glanced over and caught him admiring her breasts.

"Stop while you still can, Agent Colton."

Stop getting personal, she meant. He ignored her comment. "Why not get married and raise kids?"

"I seem like the housewife type to you?"

He looked straight ahead because looking at her while they talked like this would get him in trouble. "Not the way you're thinking."

She gave him an indignant look. "You're talking personal."

He ignored her again, preferring not to analyze that right now. He was getting personal, going against his rule. But one thing nagged him.

She wouldn't make a good housewife. She'd make a great *wife*. A man wouldn't be able to get enough of her. He'd have lots of kids with her because of that. And that filled him with both fantasies and foreboding. The foreboding had him shoving the thoughts back.

They reached his SUV. Facing her with his hand on the handle, he watched her angle her head with lifted eyebrows. Why was she so touchy about this?

"No wonder you're still single," she said.

Had he managed to rile her? "Because I treat women chivalrously?" He opened the door for her and stepped aside.

"No." She fought back a smile as she got into the SUV.

The almost-smile didn't throw him off. He watched her profile a few seconds before going around to the other side of the SUV. Something about being treated like a woman bothered her. What could that be? Maybe it wasn't so much how a man treated her that bothered. Maybe it was him doing the treating.

"I don't feel like going home." Jocelyn looked over at Trevor, dreading her quiet condo. "Let's go grab something to eat."

Trevor looked surprised. "It's three o'clock." And not in the afternoon.

"We haven't eaten yet. We got that call at seven." Dinner hadn't mattered with the issues of the day, but that wasn't her reason for wanting to eat out.

"Let's just grab something and go to your place. It's closer than mine."

"My place?" Why her place? Had she not imagined his earlier flirtation? No, surely she had.

"We've been working together long enough. Come on. It's late. I don't want to be in public. I'm tired. And I probably smell by now." He lifted his arm for a mock sniff.

For such a serious man, he did show signs of a sense of humor. What harm would it be to let him stay? They'd had a long day and night. Besides, she didn't want to be alone. His crack about her cat kind of drove home that point. She loved her cat, but the animal only needed her for food and shelter.

Entering her two-story condo felt strange with a man, especially Trevor. Tall, dark-haired and lean, he took on a new persona now that they weren't working. She saw him the way she repressed herself from seeing him—as a great-looking man with intense, smart dark eyes and thick lashes.

Leaving the entry, she led him into her open living room, aware of how he surveyed her big-screen TV across from a gray sofa with yellow-and-white throw pillows. Varying shades of stacked gray rock with a few yellow for accent made up the wall behind the sofa, and a vase of yellow lilies on the coffee table tied the room together. Top-down, bottom-up window coverings were set halfway up for privacy on a row of three tall square windows.

Her black cat meowed, walking leisurely toward her.

"Sigmund, meet Trevor Colton. Trevor, this is Sigmund."

Sigmund lifted green eyes to her and then Trevor.

"Sigmund, it's a pleasure." He crouched as the animal moved toward him. When he began to pet him, Sigmund let him.

Jocelyn dropped her jaw. "Wow. He doesn't let just anyone pet him. He likes you." Sigmund had a keen judge of character. She looked up at Trevor as he straightened, amazed and awed, seeing him even more as a man—an attractive man. That disconcerted her a bit. She didn't mingle with sexy coworkers who didn't want to get personal with her.

"I had a dog growing up."

That announcement appealed to her awe, kept it going. "Of course. *Boy.*" She covered her mouth, widening her eyes in exaggeration, reminding him of their earlier banter.

He chuckled. "Plato. I named him."

That sobered her. "You were into Plato as a child?"

"No. I thought his name was cool. You were into Sigmund?"

"No way." She walked toward the kitchen, remodeled with light gray tile, stainless steel appliances and granite countertops.

"Nice place."

She smiled as she saw him look over her vaulted ceiling open concept living room and kitchen. "Thanks. I did all the work myself." She'd painted the kitchen cabinet white and installed the brushed chrome hardware.

"I can see the tomboy in you here," Trevor said.

Astonished, she looked where he had, trying to see what he saw.

"Other than the lilies, there are no personal touches. No pictures. No candles…"

She'd allowed the architecture to provide the ambience. But now that he'd mentioned it, she had to agree. She had no decorative touches, another product of her upbringing, she supposed.

"Do you like Mexican?" She went to her refrigerator.

"I like anything right now."

"Have a seat."

He sat at her kitchen island and she went to work reheating a green chili and beef mixture. Moments later, she had steaming burritos ready, depositing the plates on the island.

She went to a wine cooler tucked neatly into her kitchen cabinetry. "I like a glass of wine after nights like tonight. It helps me sleep. Want one?"

"No, go ahead."

She sat and began eating, too aware of him and glad for the lulling effect of the wine.

"You never talk about your family," he said.

Why was he curious? Her lack of pictures? Putting her fork down, she contended with the weight of his question.

"I don't have family anymore. My dad and brother both died in the line of duty." She hoped he wouldn't dwell on it.

"Really?" He leaned forward, his forearms on the counter as he looked closer at her. "They were cops?"

She nodded. "Both of them. Narcotics." She averted her face, the reminder of that time gripping her.

"My God, Jocelyn. I had no idea. I'm so sorry." He reached over and put his hand over hers.

She looked down at his bigger, masculine hand touching her so tenderly and then lifted her gaze to meet genuine sympathy.

"When did that happen?"

"They died two years ago. When I was in college." She looked away, not wanting to talk about this now. She never liked talking about it. Their faces came to mind as vividly as if they were still here, and the painful knowledge that they never would be again crushed her.

"What was your major?"

She turned back to him. "Hmm?"

"Your major in college? What was it?"

Why did that matter? Maybe it didn't. Maybe he'd just changed the subject. For her.

Her heart warmed. "It was education. I was going to be a schoolteacher."

"And then you changed your major."

"Yes." She eyed him, wondering why he probed there. Maybe he hadn't changed the subject.

"Now I understand why you do what you do," he said.

He'd ruined a nice moment. Snatching her hand out

from under his, she snapped, "You say that as if I don't belong on your team."

"I didn't mean that. I think you carry a torch you don't need to carry." He breathed an ironic laugh. "I always thought you crusaded more than necessary for the job. I couldn't put my finger on why or even what struck me as off about you."

Did he have to be so insulting? "You're not making this better."

"Are you going to sit there and tell me this is what you want for the rest of your life?"

How the hell had he gotten to know her so well? They never talked about personal things. Now, all of the sudden, they were.

She stared across her kitchen. Lately she had been thinking her line of work was getting to her. Living alone, working long hours, spending so much time with other agents, all of it had begun to take its toll on her. Before her dad and Nathan had been killed, she'd dreamed of finding a nice man to marry, raise two or three kids and have birthday parties and barbecues. Teaching junior high kids would give her a good schedule.

"How did they die?" Trevor asked.

He had on his investigator hat now.

"A drug raid went bad and my dad was shot. My brother was shot trying to help him out of the building."

Sympathy darkened his eyes. "That's terrible. Are their killers in prison?"

"For the rest of their worthless lives." Jocelyn drank a hefty sip of her wine.

"Maybe it's time you let them go," he said. "Do what you want to do with your life. Do it for *you*, not them."

"Why are you so interested in what I want? Do I not do a good job?"

"You're one of the best. But I can see your heart isn't all the way in it. It's my job to analyze. Don't take any of this personally. It's just an observation, that's all."

"What do you want out of your life? Why are you an agent?" If he could ask her all of these things, he'd better be willing to share his side. "Was it because of your father?"

"All of us do what we do because of Matthew Colton. I consider it a privilege to work on homicide cases. It's my honor and my duty to protect people from monsters like him."

"Then we have that in common, Agent Colton. It's my honor and my duty to protect my fellow officers from monsters like the ones who killed my dad and brother."

He met her gaze, a deep discovery of kinship warming the energy between them.

"What would you have done with your life had your father not murdered your mother?"

She knew all about his past because of the case. The serial killer copied his father's technique.

"I don't know. Justice is all I've ever craved."

Craved. One of the sexiest things about him was his drive and determination, his ambition to catch killers and his finesse in doing so. She'd learned a lot from him.

Had she just thought the word *sexy* about him? And then she realized the word had come up before now. She eyed her near-empty glass of wine in suspicion.

"A family of my own would be nice someday."

He shocked her with that announcement, so mirroring what she'd left unspoken.

"But I think that's a dream and not a reality, not for me," he added.

"Why do you say that?" She felt the same way sometimes. Her life would never settle down. The hours and demands of her days took too much out of her. But most of the time, the rewards outweighed the regrets.

"I think you know."

His intelligence and smooth, friendly way of talking tickled her softer senses. She'd never felt more drawn to him. There had always been an underlying attraction, a physical one. This meeting of minds had only occurred on the job.

"I'm thinking about making it my reality," she said.

Never had she revealed this to anyone. Why Trevor? Why now? Sure, she talked about babies, but they were always other people's babies.

She sat close to him, with his dark eyes giving her a rare glimpse of a softer man behind a hardened exterior. Did he want what she wanted but think he couldn't have it?

The fantasy of having a more peaceful, happy life fell over her. She let it engulf her, no darkness interfering, only light and joy. The excitement in entertaining the possibility of drastic, pleasing change gave her temptation. With none of the restraints of work in the way, her new knowledge of him warmed an intimate place in her heart. His handsome face captivated her. She allowed herself the luxury of taking in every detail.

She leaned closer, propping her chin in her hand. "Who would have thought that a family man lurked behind the dark eyes of the great, intimidating Agent Colton?"

"You like to tease me."

She smiled, intoxicated with attraction. "You think I'm teasing?"

"When you talk like a poet, yes."

"I'm just surprised, that's all. Pleasantly."

His eyes lowered, bestowing her lips an invisible caress. When his gaze lifted, she felt heat roar to life.

Not giving it a second thought, Jocelyn stood from her chair and swiveled him to face her before taking his face between her hands and pressing her mouth to his.

Chapter 2

"What are we doing?" Trevor asked.

Jocelyn had shut her eyes and seemed to drown in a heavy dose of passion.

"Getting personal."

He smiled against her lips and she took his lower one between hers for a sensuous taste, stirring answering passion in him.

"I got that part."

Her mouth trailed over the rim of his upper lip. "I love your mouth." She kissed him as though taking a soft, juicy bite out of a peach. "It's so full." She moved to the corner of his lips. "Manly."

"Just say what you mean." His heart slammed with excitement. She'd made him hard with the first kiss. And now she coaxed logic clean out of his head.

"I love something else about you, too." She climbed

up onto him, straddling his thighs and rocking herself over his hardness. "That."

"How can you love it? You've never done this before."

"I've seen it. In your pants."

"You have not."

She smiled, sexy and alluring, rocking and rolling her hips in slow gyrations.

"Why are you doing this?" Some logic still remained in him. Why and how had this sudden desire reared up tonight? Or was it sudden? Maybe it had been building ever since they started working together.

"I don't know. It's just happening. It feels good."

"Yes." She felt amazing on him.

She pulled up his shirt and tossed it onto the floor. That invited him to do the same to her. She raised her arms to allow him and then looked right into his eyes as she unclasped her bra.

He stopped a thought that she worked with him. Right now, she didn't work with him. Right now, she was a woman he desired intensely.

He cupped her breasts. "You're so beautiful." He kneaded her and thumbed her nipples. "I knew you would be."

"So are you." She kissed him again and ran her hands down his chest to his abdomen, her fingers dipping beneath the waistband of his jeans. Trevor thought he would die of exquisite torture. Reaching for her ponytail, he tugged the band and slid it off. Silky strands of long dark hair slipped free and fell forward, tickling his chest. When she withdrew from a long kiss, he slid his fingers into her hair and looked into her sultry hazel eyes.

She rocked on him again and he reached the threshold

of his restraint. In a smooth motion, he stood with her and walked down the hall off the living room, finding the master bedroom and taking her to the platform bed. Depositing her there, he unbuttoned her jeans and took his time pulling them off. Then he removed his while she watched with hot anticipation.

When they were both naked, Jocelyn scooted back on the bed and lay on her back. He crawled over her, nudging her knees apart.

She slid her hand down to his abdomen and beyond, encircling his hardness. He clenched his jaw in a fight to slow his urge to push into her. He reached for her soft wetness, sinking his finger inside. Her mouth parted with a passionate gasp.

He continued to caress her, gritting his teeth at the silkiness against his rougher skin.

"Trevor," she whispered.

Her quick readiness intensified his mind-numbing rush of lust. He shook with the effort to keep from shoving into her in one hard thrust. Inch by inch he sank inside her. Fiery sensation swallowed him. When she surrounded him fully, he paused to catch his breath, unable to stifle a groan.

After a moment he moved as slow as he could manage without dying inside. She moved with him, grinding, unabashed in pursuit of her pleasure. She was a dream lover. He kissed her hard to show her his appreciation.

Her hands glided over his shoulders and biceps, then down his back to his rear. She pulled him closer as he moved. Sweat glistened on his skin as he obliged her. The sound of their breathing filled the room.

"Jocelyn," he managed to say. "Are you with me?"

Her neck arched and her eyes closed as her head pressed back into the pillow. "Yes."

He took her hands in his and stretched them above her head as he moved.

"Oh, yes." A deep, throaty moan slipped free from her. And then louder, she cried out, "Trevor," as she came.

He cursed with the eroticism of her response to him. Unbearable. Intense. She brought him to sweet oblivion.

The sun had risen a good way up the sky when Jocelyn woke. She stretched with a long sigh. Before any analysis of what had occurred spoiled her fluffy cloud, she reached over and put her hand on Trevor's arm and then rolled to her side, propping her head on one hand. She ran her hand over his chest, marveling over how incredible his body could make her feel.

His eyes opened.

She gave him time to wake up, eyes blinking sleep away and turning to her. With a soft, sleepy smile, he rolled to his side, forcing her onto her back. Then he kissed her.

Sweet heaven.

His thumb brushed her nipple, making her gasp against his mouth. He kissed her harder. She angled her head and he devoured her.

Abandoning her breasts, he moved down her ribs to the curve of her waist, pushing covers off her as he went. Then he withdrew from the kiss to look at her. She felt exposed, deliciously so. He intensified the sensation by coaxing her to open her legs.

Heat pooled low in her abdomen as his hands slid

up her thighs. When he reached the apex, she ground back a moan.

He took her mouth in a hard kiss and got up onto his knees and then between her legs.

She could feel his erection against her, thick and hard. It numbed her to anything but building want. He began to probe and she dug her head back in ecstasy.

He slid deep, stretching her, filling her. When he started to move, he took her to the stars as he had before, touching a place no other man had. He braced his hands on either side of her and began to push in and pull out faster. He swore softly and closed his eyes.

Jocelyn came hard and fast, gripping his muscular biceps. With a long groan, he sank deep into her once, twice and a third and last time.

"Oh. So, it was real," she breathed when he collapsed on top of her.

He regained control of his breathing and lifted his head. After his smiling eyes met hers awhile, he kissed her.

"Good morning," she said.

"Almost afternoon." He reached over for his phone. "We better get going. Coroner's office called."

"Back to work." Jocelyn's mood slipped a notch.

"I'll run home and shower and change, then come back and pick you up."

"Okay." Would it really be this easy to fall back into a coworker role? A bothersome instinct said no.

Trevor led Jocelyn out of the coroner's office, not convinced Jane McDonald's murder correlated with the Alphabet Killer. The case had ground to a stop and showed no signs of moving forward anytime soon. He thought about going to visit his dad again. Not Dad. Trevor called him Matthew now. Matthew was no father of his, not beyond the biological. Even being biologically related to that man made him ill. What kind of DNA would he pass along to any kids he had?

He glanced over at Jocelyn when she came into stride beside him. She'd been watching him ever since he came back to pick her up. He'd had time to think about what had happened.

The sex had been phenomenal. The reality of it was something entirely different. Trevor dealt in reality. The flames of their quick passion had dulled any thought of consequences. He forgave himself for that. Jocelyn couldn't have resisted any more than he could have, after working together for so long, fighting their attraction the whole time. He might have fooled himself that he could control it, but obviously he couldn't. They'd been swept up in the moment, both of them tired from a long, grueling day at work. It was no wonder they didn't stop and think about what they were doing.

But he had a feeling she didn't see it the same as him. She'd gradually gotten more and more bristly as the day progressed.

"We need to talk." He stopped at his SUV. Her car was still at the FBI residency office in Fort Worth, where their marathon day had begun yesterday. He'd drive her back now and then go for another visit with Matthew, if his stomach could handle it.

"Right. Talk." She faced him, hand on her hip, revealing her badge clipped to her black pants. Above that, her Glock 22 stuck out from a shoulder harness holster. Looking stealth in her outfit, black everything.

Black T-shirt, black boots, black hair in a ponytail. Sexy as hell.

Without her FBI jacket, Trevor noticed her body a lot more than he would have otherwise. Or maybe he just noticed it more now because he knew what she looked like naked.

"Um…" He felt uncharacteristically awkward. "I'm not sure how we ended up in bed."

"I kissed you and you took it from there. Remember now?"

Her anger took him aback. What had her so mad? Did she expect more from what happened?

"Yeah. Hard to forget. It's just… I didn't expect it to happen."

"Neither did I, but it did."

Trevor couldn't decide how to say what needed to be said without hurting her. Her defensive reaction told him what last night meant to her. More than it did to him.

"It's not that I don't care about you, I—"

"Oh, cut to the point, Trevor. Don't plant me a daisy garden. You regret having sex with me. You think it was a mistake. Ya-de-ya-de-ya."

"'Mistake' is a little harsh. I don't regret having sex with you." No, the sex had been memorable to say the least. He'd revisit that night over and over, even when he didn't want to. "I never mix work with…pleasure." Did he really have to use that word? No other described it better.

"I don't put restrictions on who I sleep with. Generally, if a man attracts me and I'm turned on, that's a Go sign for me. It's simple. Much less complicated than you make it."

Nothing like being blunt. He let out a tense breath.

"Can we at least agree that what happened was unplanned?"

"Very unplanned." She folded her arms, defiant over what she must know was coming.

"You didn't expect it. I didn't expect it." He began talking with his hands. "We had great sex, and now we need to maintain a professional relationship."

"What I'm hearing is that *you* need to maintain a professional relationship."

Trevor ran his fingers through his hair. No surprise that she'd make this difficult for him.

Dropping his hand, he said, "These kinds of relationships never last. Affairs in the workplace are just… wrong."

Now she lowered her hands, and her eyes grew less confrontational. "You sound as though you've had firsthand experience."

"I do. I have." And he avoided the subject whenever possible.

Her head straightened with that revelation. "You've had an affair in the workplace?"

"Yes. Five years ago. She was another agent."

Jocelyn's eyes widened with the sardonic lift of her brow. "Another agent, huh. So, I must be exactly like her."

He grunted a laugh. "No. Oh, no." He shook his head. "You're nothing like her. You're not quiet. You say whatever's on your mind. And…you're not afraid to…" He regretted including that last part.

"Not afraid to what?"

"Go after it in bed."

"Go after it in bed." She nodded slowly, folding her

lower lip under her upper and sliding it free with her agitation.

All he'd succeeded in doing was pissing her off. "Jocelyn, all I'm saying is—"

"That I'm a coworker and therefore no one you intend to pursue in a relationship."

"Right. Yes. It's that simple."

"But I'm okay to go after in bed."

"No. That was a mistake. A careless one on my part. I should have stopped you when you kissed me."

She said nothing for a while and he thought he'd made it through the talk.

And then she said, "Tell me about this woman you had an affair with."

"Look, I understand if you're hurt—"

"What happened between the two of you?"

She wouldn't let it drop. "She slept with me to get even with another agent. She lied. And when she and the other agent patched things up, she kept sleeping with me."

"The scorned heart. You have trust issues, then."

"I don't want to see anyone I work with outside of my professional relationship with them." By his tone, she should know he wouldn't back down and he didn't appreciate her attack mode, trying to pin his reluctance to mix work and pleasure on a past relationship.

Her eyes lowered and lifted, long enough for her to regain control of her emotions. "It's okay, Agent Colton. I'll respect your wishes. I wasn't looking for anything long-term anyway."

Her cell phone rang just when he would have asked her why she felt the need to say that. It sounded—no, *felt, rang* like a lie. She just got nauseated from a crime scene. Rookie reaction? Or had she not found her true calling?

"Agent Locke." As she listened, her eyes flashed to him, and then she snapped her fingers. "I need a pen."

Trevor took out his small notebook and a pen from inside his jacket. She took the pen and he held the notebook in his palm while she wrote some information down on a woman named Caressa Franklin.

"Thanks." Putting her phone away, she turned to Trevor. "Caressa Franklin knew Erica Morgan. Apparently they had a falling-out a year before the murder. Caressa moved to Fort Worth a few months ago. She didn't know about Erica."

"Estranged, how?"

Jocelyn held up the paper and gave it a little wiggle. "That's what we're going to go find out."

"How'd you get that info?"

"Contacts are key." She smiled, wily and charming. Disarming, more like.

"Good work. Who's your contact?"

He watched her debate over whether to tell him, as though his rejection made her distrust him more now. But they were part of a team. This had nothing to do with anything personal, and the investigation mattered most.

"A private investigator I know." She sounded blasé in a staged way.

"You contacted a PI without telling me?" She could ruin evidence for them.

"I just asked him to look into Erica for me, see if he could find anything new that we may have missed. Just our luck, he did." She walked around the vehicle as he went to open the driver's-side door.

"How do you know the PI?" he asked when he got behind the wheel, hearing his own forced idle tone and refusing to call it jealousy. He caught her noticing.

"I dated him a couple of years ago. He'd still like to get together. I use him every once in a while on cases."

She didn't have to include all of that information, but he knew she had because she savored his reaction. "You used him?"

"I pay him. I knew Erica."

Why hadn't she ever mentioned her handy PI who got information she needed? "I didn't realize she was that close."

"Her mother was my mother's friend." She turned her face away as though more than Erica's death troubled her. "My mother's friend stayed in touch with my dad after my mother died. And then after my dad died, she stayed in touch with me. I got to know her and Erica fairly well."

"You were close to them? Erica?" Closer than she'd let on.

Dropping her elbow from its perch on the window frame, she looked over at him. "We met for lunch a few times after my dad and brother died. They aren't what I'd call close friends. Erica's mother talked about my mother a lot. I feel like I wouldn't have known my mother as well as I do. Not that I know her the way I would have if she'd been in my life the whole time. But if it hadn't been for her, I wouldn't have known as much. For that, I'll always be grateful." She sighed forlornly. "I didn't know until after Erica's murder that her mother was killed in a car accident. She never told me. We sort of fell out of touch."

She talked as though she'd never met her mother. "What happened to your mother?"

Jocelyn turned away. "She died shortly after I was born."

Trevor took a moment to ponder all the tragedies that had befallen her. She had no family. They were all dead. Even the friends of the family had gone, one who'd given her a precious gift. Her father must have told her things about her mother, but a friend could give her another perspective. Jocelyn could envision the person who had been her mother. He could see how that would motivate her to find Erica's killer. He could also understand her fondness of her mother's friend. Even with all her losses, though, Jocelyn had drive. Optimism. Or the outward appearance of those attributes. What lay underneath? And how had they shaped her decisions up until now? How different would her life be, had she not lost those closest to her?

Caressa Franklin wasn't expecting them, but Jocelyn had agreed with Trevor that surprise might work in their favor. Her PI friend hadn't revealed the FBI's involvement in Erica's murder investigation and hadn't revealed any details of the Alphabet Killer case.

The midforties woman didn't answer her front door even though they'd seen her through the side window.

"Must have pegged us for solicitors," Jocelyn said.

"Let's hang around until she goes somewhere."

A little more than an hour later, Caressa did leave her house. They followed her to the parking lot of a grocery store and walked to intercept her on her way to the entrance.

"Caressa Franklin?" Jocelyn called.

The woman looked back as Trevor moved to block her path to the grocery store and Jocelyn stood in her way back to her vehicle.

Jocelyn exposed her badge clipped to her belt on her Sleek Agent pants and Trevor dropped open his wallet.

Caressa looked at both and then up at their faces with her jaw dropping. "What happened?"

She seemed stiff to Jocelyn. Cornered? No. Shocked. Why shocked? Almost…expecting. Had she *expected* them to show up? Jocelyn watched closely.

"We're here to talk to you about Erica Morgan," she said.

Caressa regained composure. Yes, this is what she'd expected, someone to come talking to her about her friend. "Really? Why?"

"Why didn't you answer your door earlier?" Trevor asked.

Now cool, masked eyes turned to him. "I never answer my door to strangers. I live alone."

Jocelyn bought that.

"I haven't seen Erica in years," Caressa said.

"A friend of hers said she came to see you two days before her murder. Would you tell us about that?" She hadn't told Trevor that piece she'd gotten from the PI. Maybe she wanted to punish him at least a little bit for turning last night into a one-night, scandalous affair. She'd thought for sure they'd see each other for a while. She hadn't expected anything from him other than to explore where such great sex would lead. She felt him glance over.

"I refused to talk to her." Caressa averted her gaze a moment. "I turned my back on her."

Erica had come to see her and she'd ignored the

knock or doorbell. What had caused their falling-out? "You were friends, right? How did you know her?" Erica had never mentioned her. But then, Jocelyn had always felt closer to Erica's mother.

"She was a friend of my sister's. We started out fine. Great, in fact. We had a lot in common. She was always so nice and talkative. A good person…or so I thought." Caressa lowered her head and seconds passed while she went into her own world. Guilt. Regret.

Jocelyn wondered if this woman was ever happy. She didn't have many laugh lines around her eyes. And while anyone would feel bad about an old friend being murdered, Caressa seemed to exaggerate her reaction, or maybe some other reason warranted that extreme. Or maybe guilt over rejecting her friend's attempt to see her made her seem flighty.

She stole a glance at Trevor, who hid his analysis of Caressa's reaction to them questioning her. He must have noticed, though.

He caught her look and winked, a playful reassurance that tickled her feminine side, especially when a gentle breeze ruffled his dark hair.

Why did he do that? Preserving a work relationship? Keeping the peace? Or was he taken by her and couldn't control his actions?

"Am I a suspect?"

Caressa put her back in check. In an instant, Trevor could stir her senses, take her right out of a moment, even one as important as this.

"We're trying to piece together her last days," Trevor said. "You were one of the last people to see her alive."

Caressa scoffed. "I saw her through the window beside my front door, a small window." She covered her mouth, choked up with emotion. "My sister tried to call me and I didn't answer because I thought she was going to argue with me over it. I didn't know Erica was murdered until…until I finally answered one of her calls." She breathed through a threatening sob and moisture glistened in her eyes. "I didn't know."

Clearly, Erica's death had devastated her. She'd known she was one of the last to see her estranged friend alive and the estrangement could give her motive to kill. She'd feared that.

"We're very sorry for your loss," Jocelyn said.

"Why were you estranged from Erica?" Trevor asked before she could. And the way he asked impressed her, so unassuming…and yet right to the point.

Caressa's face sagged with hurt. "She had an affair with my husband. My marriage was in trouble, I admit that. It gets hard to keep the relationship together if you aren't made for each other. You don't realize these things until you can look back, get out of the stagnant routine and see the big picture. But I just could not believe my closest friend would betray me."

Jocelyn didn't know. Stagnant routine? What was that? She supposed people got complacent with their life situation, lulled by false security. No change felt safer. Caressa probably knew in her heart things weren't right between her and her husband, she just hadn't faced it until she was forced to. Jocelyn never wanted to live like that, settling for mediocre. But she could definitely understand the betrayal.

A car drove by at a slow speed, turning at the end of the parking lot lane just as a couple emerged from the market. Caressa turned to look as Trevor took out a picture of Regina Willard, their prime suspect in the case.

Trevor held the picture in front of her. "Do you recognize this woman?"

Caressa looked at the photo and then shook her head. "No. Who is she?"

She didn't know Regina. Or recognize her. Jocelyn had hoped she would.

"Did Erica ever mention anyone named Regina Willard?" she asked on a long shot.

Caressa shook her head.

Jocelyn nodded to conceal her disappointment. "Are you sure?"

"Yes. She never told me about anyone named Regina." She looked down at the photo and asked again, "Who is she?"

"If you've watched the news, you've likely heard of the Alphabet Killer," Trevor said. "One of the victims positively identified Regina Willard before she died. While we have no evidence to prove it yet, we believe Erica was one of her victims."

Caressa drew her head back in something of a flinch. "But...that can't be. Erica didn't know anyone named Regina Willard. You have to be wrong."

"We don't believe so," Jocelyn said.

"What about Josie Colton? Isn't she the one you should be looking for?"

"Josie Colton is innocent," Trevor said.

"The perfect cover for murder."

"Josie Colton is Agent Colton's sister," Jocelyn said. When Caressa gave her a blank look, she glanced over at Trevor. "Him."

Caressa's eyes widened and she faced Trevor. "Oh, my goodness. I'm so sorry, I meant no disrespect to you, it's just, all the talk around town and..."

Trevor held up his hand. "No need to apologize. But it's Regina Willard we're after. Most of the victims appear to have encountered her in a restaurant. We believe she works as a waitress under false identities."

Caressa absorbed that a moment and then said, "You have no idea how upset I am over her death." Ravaging sorrow drew her mouth down.

Jocelyn reached over and touched her arm. "You had no way of knowing. She tried to contact you. That means she wanted to try to earn your forgiveness. She cared."

"Yes." She struggled to subdue a sob. "But she died believing I wouldn't forgive her."

Jocelyn lowered her hand. Caressa would have to work through her regrets on her own. What the living thought or felt regarding the dead no longer mattered. They were dead.

"Is there anyone else Erica might have talked to about Regina?" Trevor asked, getting the conversation back on track. "Your sister, perhaps?"

"No. I would remember that." She paused as though something dawned on her. "My sister did mention Erica had an ex-boyfriend. She kept him secret, which I found odd."

That seemed off to Jocelyn. Why keep a secret ex-boyfriend? She could think of a few possibilities. Drugs. Infidelity. Disapproval from her family and friends.

"I have a photo." She ducked back and retrieved her cell phone from her purse and began navigating to find it, eager to help find the killer of her lost friend.

Jocelyn caught Trevor's familiar silent look that said they may be wasting their time.

Caressa showed them the photo.

"I think we have enough for now," Trevor said. "We appreciate you talking to us."

"Thank you for your cooperation," Jocelyn added. Trevor must have decided this was going nowhere.

"Wha…"

"We'll let you know if we learn anything new." Trevor turned and headed back for their vehicle.

"Why did you do that? The boyfriend might know something," she said quietly, still too close to Caressa. A glance back confirmed the woman watched them walk through the parking lot.

"Ex-boyfriend. Male." His eyebrows lifted in skepticism.

"Right. Doesn't fit the profile." They'd established that without words. The boyfriend wasn't the Alphabet Killer.

"Hey, that's *my* job."

Smiling big at the sexy sound of his voice and the easy way of communicating they had, Jocelyn said, "But we should check out the boyfriend. He may have seen Erica before she was killed and may be able to tell us something about Regina."

"And that's *your* job," Trevor said with his grin still in place. "Thinking like a smart detective."

Jocelyn walked beside him, disconcerted that the charming man she'd never known before sex interested her more than the dead end in their case.

Chapter 3

Trevor looked on the bright side of going to see Matthew Colton in prison. A, he had some time apart from Jocelyn, and B, he might be able to extract more information. Matthew enjoyed his visits. He enjoyed the game. He enjoyed his kids' desire to find their mother's body, the power he held over them by drawing out when and how he offered clues. A clue in exchange for a visit from each of his kids. Josie was the last to get her clue. She'd gone once and Matthew had toyed with her without giving her the clue. Now she refused to go back. Going the first time had been too much for her. She wasn't ready to try again. Maybe she never would. Trevor couldn't blame her. Visiting Matthew made him sick to his stomach.

"Hey, Trevor."

Trevor turned to see Mac approach, the corrections

officer who'd taken him to see Matthew the other times he'd been here. "Mac."

"Come with me. We've got him in the room just as you requested."

Trevor walked beside him down a white, windowless hall. An eye-aching row of rectangular lights reminded him of the painted lines on highways. "How's he been?"

"He was treated for dehydration after some chemo treatment he received. He's recovered from that, though. Doing all right, considering."

Considering he was dying of cancer. Trevor felt no sympathy for the man. "As long as he can talk."

The officer chuckled. "He loves to do that." He opened the door to the round communal room. "Just let the guard know when you're ready to leave."

"Will do. Thanks." Trevor entered, seeing Matthew sitting at one of the tables in the overcooked-pea-green-painted room. It just so happened Trevor had come during visitor hours. There were three other tables with inmates meeting with loved ones. He'd been offered a private room to talk, but he'd declined. Maybe meeting around other people would ease the discomfort of having to face his murderous father.

"To what do I owe this pleasure?" Matthew asked.

"The pleasure is all yours." Trevor sat on the other side of the table.

"You should be nicer to an old man who only wants to help you." Matthew had lost a lot of weight with his illness. His skin sagged and had a ghostly pallor, and those evil, beady eyes seemed to have sunk into his skull.

"Feel like talking about Regina Willard today?" Trevor asked.

"Any admirer of mine is worth discussing. Besides, what else do I have to do in here?"

"Have you received any more letters?" That any woman would send letters to a killer like Matthew befuddled Trevor. Matthew knew something about the killer, and Trevor suspected it had something to do with the letters. But so far, Matthew refused to reveal anything.

"What do I get in exchange if I did?"

"A clear conscience?" Trevor couldn't keep his sarcasm out of his tone. Matthew was always looking for leverage.

He sat back as he observed Trevor. After a long study, he finally said, "You were a wild kid. I remember when you ran off while we were at that amusement park and I had to go to the lost child booth. You remember that?"

Trevor did. He had run off to get away from his dad, tired of his weak ego and smart mouth. The way Matthew had spoken to their mother had gotten Trevor in trouble more than once. He'd often gone toe-to-toe with the man, who'd shut him down with his bigger size. Matthew, though smart, had needed too many compliments to feel like a man. And he had never responded well to criticism.

"Now you think you're some hotshot FBI profiler." Matthew scoffed. "Hell, you can't even find your own mother's grave."

Anger simmered low and hot. "You insult her memory by calling where you dumped her a grave."

"Your mother was a good woman up until the end."

She'd put up with Matthew, loved him, even. To the public he'd appeared normal and even likable. But living with the man had revealed a lot more. He'd kept his murdering ways hidden up until Saralee had discovered what he'd been doing. That had gotten her killed and had led to Matthew's arrest.

"Tell me," Matthew said. "What's your profile of me?"

Matthew actually wanted him to say? Trevor would take pleasure in this.

"You're insecure and that insecurity led to your first murder. You never measured up to Big J Colton. He always made more money than you."

Matthew's face began to color, the most life Trevor had seen in that skin so far.

"You never got over him buying you out of the family ranch. You felt he gave you no other option. You were never going to feel like a man living in Oklahoma, where Big J lived. So you ran off to Texas, where you were still never able to measure up."

"You always were a smart-mouthed kid. I should have beaten you more, taken you down off that high horse you like to ride so much."

Trevor grinned, taunting. "You hated Big J. That's no secret. It's what drove you to kill those men. They reminded you of him. You compensated your weakness by killing your brother over and over again. As long as you killed, Big J stayed dead."

Matthew liked that analogy. Trevor watched him go back in time to his kills, relishing the experience of killing his brother over and over, because to Matthew, each victim was his brother.

"Except now you can't kill anymore," Trevor said. He would not allow this monster to enjoy his crimes. "You can't kill Big J. In fact, Big J is doing just fine in

Oklahoma. Richer than ever. Successful rancher. Happy as can be. Nothing you've done has changed that."

Matthew started to stand. "You son of a—" The security guard took a step forward, his hand on his gun. Matthew saw this and sat back down, glaring across the table at Trevor.

"You asked me to profile you," Trevor said, checking his phone for the time. "I've got to go. You've wasted yet another of my visits."

"Wait." Matthew's temper cooled. He didn't want this visit to end, this escape from everyday prison routine. "You convince that daughter of mine, Josie, to come and see me?"

"She already came to see you." It had been a brief visit. Josie had given up and left.

"If you want another clue, bring Josie to see me."

Trevor wasn't sure he could convince her. "She thinks you're bluffing. You don't give out information easily." He'd refused to give Trevor any clues. Maybe because Trevor came to see him the most. He knew Trevor would come to see him. Josie was more of a challenge. But Josie had been through a lot. A person could only take so many doses of evil at a time.

"You can give me her clue," Trevor said. He'd tried every time to get information.

Matthew scoffed. "What fun would that be?"

Matthew didn't consider Trevor a challenge. He also despised him for what he represented. Law enforcement. FBI profiler. And though Matthew would never admit it or say it to Trevor's face, he knew he was good at what he did.

"Give me Josie's clue. You'll find peace knowing your wife will have a respectable burial."

"Peace," Matthew sneered. "You left that part out of your profile. I am at peace."

He would not bend. He would not hand out any more clues until Josie came to see him again. Killing all those people, Saralee included, didn't bother him.

"You want to know where your mother is buried, you'll do as I say. No more clues until I see Josie."

That put him in a bind. Josie didn't believe Matthew would give a clue. She also struggled with the drama. Going to see Matthew would be painful for her, bring up old memories she didn't welcome. None of them did. He couldn't blame her, but he wished she'd at least try to get the clue, go see Matthew more than once if that was what it took, even if he never divulged what he owed them all.

When Trevor arrived back at his office, the visit at the prison had left him emotionally drained. He sighed and tipped his head back, shutting his eyes and trying to block the image of Matthew Colton from his mind. His grayish pale skin. Empty eyes that only livened up when he felt in control. His frail body. On the drive back here, Trevor had actually felt a tinge of sympathy for the man. He'd die in prison. Cancer would be the weapon to do the job. Justice.

Why or how he could feel any sympathy for his murderous father confounded Trevor and upset him. As he examined his feelings, he supposed the sympathy came from the basic fact that Matthew was his father. A biological fact. He mourned the loss of a real father, one who didn't kill and hold a psychotic grudge against his brother.

The justice, however. Ah, the justice. Trevor smiled

a little at that. Matthew was where he belonged. Cancer would take him from this world, and Trevor and his brothers and sisters would never have to see him again.

A knock preceded Chris Colton saying, "Must be good. Did you catch the Alphabet Killer?"

Trevor lowered his head and sat forward. His younger brother's sharp blue eyes crinkled in a half smile. Tall and muscular with dark blond hair, he made an imposing presence. He'd gone into private investigation, something Trevor had always been proud of, especially the similarity to his job. Except he'd seemed reserved around him since they'd reunited, more collateral damage that cancer would hopefully remove from their lives.

"Chris." Trevor got up. "I'm surprised to see you." Chris didn't come to his office much, if ever.

"Yeah." He moved into the office and closed the door.

Trevor stopped. A closed-door meeting? What was this all about? Chris didn't talk much about his feelings, but Trevor sensed that was what had brought him here.

"There's something I need to ask you."

"Sure. Fire away." He walked closer to his brother.

"It's okay, however you answer. I just need to know the truth."

This sounded serious. Since Chris had the most easygoing personality out of all the Colton kids, Trevor went on alert.

"I'll tell you the truth. What is it?"

Chris hesitated, as though not sure he should hear the truth.

Trevor put his hand on his little brother's shoulder. "Hey. Whatever it is, we'll figure it out, okay?"

Chris relaxed in his easy way, a genuine smile lighting

his face. "I'll hold you to that." After the brief levity faded, he said, "I need to know why you tried to adopt Josie and not me. Not the rest of us."

That took Trevor aback. "I tried to get custody of her and the rest of you." Trevor lowered his hand. Why did Chris think he wouldn't?

"You tried?"

Trevor grunted in disbelief. "Of course I tried."

"How much? Once? Twice?"

"Chris." He couldn't believe his brother doubted him. "How long have you thought I wouldn't try to get us all together?"

"It couldn't have been that hard to get custody of us. You could have. Why Josie?" As he spoke, his voice rose and his hands went to his hips.

Wow. He was really upset over this. And he'd never talked to him about it before now. Why had he kept it all bottled up? Trevor took his arm and guided him toward the two chairs before his desk. "Sit down, why don't you. We have a lot to talk about, it would appear."

Chris shrugged out of his touch and sat down, looking like his younger brother again, during one of their fights. Trevor's heart wrenched. Damn Matthew. Damn him to hell.

"We were fostered out through different private agencies, Chris."

"I know that."

"Social workers prefer other relatives above siblings adopt or take custody. They look at lifestyle and economic standing. Where I lived, whether I was married or had a girlfriend. I had neither. And I moved a lot."

As Chris's face smoothed, he got his answer.

"The court felt we had the best chance at a normal

childhood in separate homes. They allowed visitation, but it wasn't enough. I made that argument over and over. But it didn't matter. I couldn't show financial stability at the time. I was in college and I didn't have a steady job. Having to deal with different agencies didn't help." Trevor raked his fingers through his hair, agitated all over again with the frustration of hitting wall after wall. "Social workers moved or quit. Files were misplaced or lost. And then they didn't want to talk to me once they saw I was a single college student. They saw me as young and irresponsible, even though I told them I was going to college to gain stability. You have no idea the headache I went through."

Trevor put his hand behind Chris's neck, coaxing, wishing he hadn't doubted him at all. "I never gave up trying to get us all together."

Chris nodded a few times, leaning over with his elbows on his knees. Did he truly understand or did he still have doubts?

Rage for his father intensified. Ever since he'd reunited with his siblings, the negative fallout continued to emerge.

"Do you believe me?" Trevor asked.

The burden he'd carried for so long took a while to ease, but eventually, after thinking it over, Chris turned his head, at an angle with his position, and a grin curved his mouth. "Yeah." He sat up. "I believe you. And I should have thought to check the rules. I should have known Matthew would ruin any chance we had."

"We're together now. That's all that matters." That and burying both the Alphabet Killer and Matthew.

"Josie said you had a new murder that could be linked to the copycat," Chris said.

"Yeah, but the DNA will take some time to analyze. According to Jocelyn, we have to wait before we eliminate the suspect in Jane McDonald's murder as the copycat killer."

"You don't think her killer is the Alphabet Killer?"

Trevor shook his head. He didn't think there'd be a link and hoped something else would break the case open.

"But Jocelyn says we have to wait for the DNA test." Trevor smiled fondly.

"Jocelyn, huh? How are things going with you and your hot new partner?"

Did he have to call her hot? Since when had his little brother noticed how hot Jocelyn was? "She's not my partner. She's on my team and she's a rookie."

"I wasn't talking about your team. I've seen her. She's hot. Don't tell me you haven't noticed." He elbowed Trevor with a smile and a "Huh? You've noticed, haven't you?"

This man-to-man banter was new to Trevor and he liked it. However, he didn't like the romantic connotations. Only Chris's laid-back way made it bearable. Somewhat.

"Yeah. I've noticed." But that didn't mean he could act on his baser instincts. He had a job to do.

Even as he thought that last line, he could hear Jocelyn jumping at the chance to tease him. *And what job is that, Agent Colton, being a professional stick-in-the-mud?*

Trevor chuckled and Chris misunderstood the cause, laughing with him. A glimpse of the eleven-year-old boy flashed in his brother's eyes and all the lost time taken from them made Trevor all the more determined to solve the Alphabet Killer case and put Matthew underground and out of their lives forever.

But first he had to find Regina Willard.

Chapter 4

Three weeks later the DNA results came back on Jane McDonald and they did not match DNA found at other Alphabet Killer crime scenes. The DNA did, however, match the DNA sample they'd taken from Jane's husband, the man who had claimed not to have killed her.

"Told you," Trevor said, liking how Jocelyn's head pivoted, her beautiful hazel eyes more green in the light.

"A good detective doesn't jump to conclusions. She waits for the evidence to confirm suspicions."

"She?"

Jocelyn smiled. "You're a profiler."

"Still a detective. And for the record, I had the husband pegged all along."

Jocelyn wrinkled her nose at him, all in fun and with a cute smile that had him smiling back.

Another agent tapped the open door of Trevor's office. "Your sister Josie is here."

"Josie?" Trevor hadn't expected her to stop by. She'd been avoiding him ever since he'd confronted her about going to see Matthew.

"Send her in." He dropped the printout onto his messy desk. Books lay sideways and upright and this way and that on the bookshelf that ran along one wall. He had two uncomfortable chairs on the other side of his simple but big wood desk.

Jocelyn sat down on his comfortable desk chair and leaned back, thinking about the case, no doubt. He had to admire her tenacity. Despite his opinion that she'd be better suited at an ordinary job with a husband and a few kids—maybe a dog instead of a cat—she also made a good agent. He respected her for that. But he didn't like thinking of her married. Why, he'd stop himself from wondering.

She looked up and caught him watching her and smiled. He felt pinned to where he stood, her beauty and light stunning him with a powerful zap of sexual chemistry.

Josie appeared in the doorway, a serious set to her smooth-skinned, striking face. And long dark hair. "Hey."

"Josie." Trevor moved around the desk and hugged his sister. He'd already spent a fair amount of time with her since her return from witness protection after witnessing a drug lord kill a man—a drug lord, who also happened to be the brother of her foster father.

He could see what the experience had done, how it had changed her. She was still recovering. "You remember Jocelyn?"

Jocelyn got up briefly to shake Josie's hand over the desk.

"Yes, of course." Josie looked back at her brother. "Anything new come up in the case? Sam said you got the DNA results from the latest murder."

"Yeah." He gestured to the DNA report. "No match."

Josie slouched a bit, dropping down onto one of the uncomfortable chairs. "Damn. Are we ever going to be able to put Dad behind us?"

"Right now. He doesn't matter anymore." He felt Jocelyn's assessment when he said that.

"Is he still playing that stupid game, saying he'll give out clues when someone goes to see him?" Josie bobbed her crossed leg, arms leaning elegantly on the chair armrests.

"Yes. He says he'll give you one. You should go see him again. Maybe he will this time."

"Clue to what?" Jocelyn asked.

Trevor hadn't yet told her about Matthew's toying. He didn't like talking about the man.

"He's been dropping clues to where he left our mother's body," Josie said. "When he feels like it."

Jocelyn leaned back on the chair, her investigator hat going on. "What kind of clues?"

Trevor leaned back against the bookshelf and let the girls talk.

"Texas, hill, the letter *B*, peaches and Biff," Josie said. "Those are all we've gotten so far."

Jocelyn lowered her hand and moved forward. "Wait a minute. He only gives clues when someone goes to see him and those are what he's revealed?"

"Sam went to see him and Matthew told him *Texas* was his clue. Ethan went and he gave him the word *hill*.

Ridge got the letter *B*. Annabel got *peaches*. Chris got *Biff*. We've tried to piece it all together. She's some-where in Texas, on a hill in a city that starts with a *B*. Biff was the name of our mother's childhood golden retriever. The best we can tell is Dad buried her on our maternal grandparents' property in Bearson, Texas. It's an old house on a hill, really remote. There's a peach tree in the backyard and that's where Mom's golden re-triever was buried."

Josie's frustration came out in her tone and the way she folded her arms and had to stop talking, lest she begin to shout. His sister had plenty of fight in her.

"We've all been over that property a hundred times. We can't find any sign of a grave," he said.

"Why don't you go see Matthew?" Jocelyn asked the sensitive question. "Keep going until he gives you the clue."

Easier said than done. Trevor watched his sister struggle with that, hoped she wouldn't blame herself.

"I've already tried. He won't give Trevor a clue, ei-ther. He lies and leads us on to get visitors."

"But if there's the slightest chance…"

Josie began to get upset, the reason Trevor never pushed her. Maybe she'd go again in her own due time. Nothing would bring their mother back, so waiting made no difference.

"You don't know our father," Josie said.

"He's dying," Trevor said. "I think some part of him needs to reconnect with his kids before the cancer kills him, but he has a warped way of going about it."

Josie said nothing, just lowered her head as the idea of facing her father settled over her. She rubbed her hands together, slow and something to do to ease her tension. She still needed time to recover.

Trevor pushed off the shelf and went to his sister, standing beside where she sat. "He has no empathy for what he put us through." He put his hand on her shoulder. "It's okay, Josie."

"What if he did give you a clue, though?" Jocelyn asked, steepling her fingers over the desk, oblivious to Josie's discomfort, or the degree of it. She zeroed in on the investigation, hunting answers. She didn't understand what the separation had done, in addition to their father's crimes.

"You could find out where your mother is buried," Jocelyn said. "I don't understand why you wouldn't do anything to do so."

"Jocelyn," Trevor warned gently.

She glanced up at him, seeing his face and realizing she'd pushed a boundary. Lowering her hands, she rested them over her forearms.

"I don't ever want to see him again," Josie said in a defensive tone. "And what good are those clues anyway? They mean nothing. When I went to see him, he dangled that clue over my head without ever telling me what it was. I don't think he ever intends for us to find our mother. I don't even think she's on that property." A shudder racked Josie's shoulders. "Just seeing him made me nauseous." She looked up at Trevor. "To think he could actually kill Mom." She shook her head and lowered it again. "He's evil."

Trevor gave her shoulder a squeeze and then removed his hand. "We'll catch his copycat killer. Having her running free isn't helping any of us put the past behind us."

Jocelyn's eyes softened as she saw the exchange and listened. Trevor knew she had great sympathy for Josie and him. As a detective, she had no illusion over the kind of man who'd killed Saralee, but she backed off in questioning when necessary. He appreciated her for that. She was a good detective, insightful and smart. And beautiful. He couldn't stop from acknowledging that. The longer he worked with her, the more difficulty he had keeping on track with this investigation. No wonder he'd lost his willpower and had to have her. He took in her breasts and the trim curve of her hips and thighs in her pants. Hair draped over her shoulder, hazel eyes sparkling with responding warmth.

He turned and saw Josie watching them. No longer upset, she appeared to have taken this distraction with hearty welcome.

"You two have been working together awhile now, haven't you?" Josie asked.

"Awhile, yes." He tried to sound nonchalant, but pleasure came out in his voice. He did like working with Jocelyn. He was just afraid he liked working with her for the wrong reason.

Realizing he'd turned to Jocelyn as he answered, he saw a renewed surge of sultry yearning come over her eyes. Another night with her in bed tempted and enticed, even though it went against his moral code. She did that to him. Wrecked him.

"Are you…" Josie waved her finger back and forth between them, not having to finish with, *sleeping together*.

Trevor stuffed his hands into his pockets and moved a step back from Josie and the desk, where Jocelyn sat, hoping his sister would drop it.

Blinking and lowering her head, Jocelyn tapped her fingers on the desk, doing a poor job of acting as though nothing revealing had just transpired.

"Are you two sleeping together?" Josie asked outright.

Sleeping together implied an ongoing activity. Trevor glanced at Jocelyn and she met the awkward, telling look.

Josie's mouth dropped open. "You are!" She gaped from Jocelyn and back to Trevor. "How long has this been going on? You work together. I heard you don't mix business with pleasure."

"Let's stick to the point here," Trevor said. He did not want to talk about his work ethics.

"What point?" Josie asked. "I'm not going to see Matthew. I'm not ready for that."

No one knew what that felt like more than Trevor, as many times as he'd gone to see him. He needed a shower after each visit to wash away the filth. "I told you that's okay, Josie. When you are ready, I'll go with you. You don't have to go alone."

Josie visibly softened. Matthew Colton had caused all of Trevor's brothers and sisters too much pain. "I'm being irrational, I know. I'm sorry. Of course I should go see him for the clue. I just…"

"You've been through a lot," Trevor said. "We all have."

"I'm sorry," Jocelyn said. "I shouldn't have grilled you. I know what it's like to lose family members to murder."

Josie turned to her with new interest. "You do?"

Trevor wanted to fast forward through this conversation. Two women connecting—no, *Jocelyn* connecting with his little sister. That disconcerted him.

"My dad and brother were both killed in the line of duty. They were policemen."

"Oh." Josie reached across the desk and Jocelyn extended her hand. "I'm really sorry."

They held hands briefly, silently communicating the grief.

Jocelyn had a history that complemented Trevor's. While his went over the top in drama, they both had lost people they loved to murder and had been driven into law enforcement as a result.

"It's changed us all." Josie glanced over at Trevor as she leaned back. "Trevor is so serious and chained to his work, for example."

"I've noticed." Jocelyn leaned back, too. "And he accuses me of owning a cat."

Josie laughed. "He's obsessed with his work."

"That isn't true," Trevor said. "Not completely. And I'm right here."

Jocelyn continued to speak as though he wasn't in the room. "Is that what makes him shy away from serious relationships?"

Trevor sat on the corner of the desk. "Do we have to do this now?" Although Jocelyn teased in her usual fashion, this broached an uncomfortable subject.

"I think foster care did that to him," Josie said, sobering. "I mean, I've been away a long time, but Annabel told me he went through a rebellious stage. And he's never gotten over what our dad did. Well…none of us did, really. How can we? Our father is a serial killer."

Trevor heard and felt all the years of suffering she'd endured—all the years of suffering they'd all endured. If the state hadn't decided it wasn't in their best interest to stay together, he could have found his brothers and sisters sooner. Chris wouldn't have come to him with the doubt that had plagued him all these years.

"Are you any closer to catching the copycat killer?" Josie asked Trevor. "It's Jesse Willard's half sister, right? That's so unbelievable."

Ah, much better ground. "Regina Willard is a suspect."

He'd like nothing more than to put Matthew behind him once and for all, but this copycat killer prevented that. He could talk about the case much easier than he could about foster care, how bitterness had ruled, how he'd blamed Matthew—and still did—for taking his normal, stable life from him, life with a family. But all of that had been an illusion. Did normal and stable really exist for biological organisms? He kind of doubted it, since biological organisms all came to their inevitable, unwanted, terrible, dark deaths. Some died worse than others, like his mother. She'd been murdered by her own husband when she discovered what he was doing.

"She probably works as a waitress and that's where she encounters her victims," Jocelyn said in his lapse, filling Josie in on what they knew so far. "Women with long dark hair trigger something for her, women who upset her, maybe rude diners. It reminds her of something from her past, sets her off."

"A man?" Josie asked. "Scorned woman syndrome?"

"She could be going after women who remind her of the one who stole her man," Trevor said. "Or it could be her father, women her father chose. Maybe they treated her poorly, according to her code." All that had gone into his profile notes.

Jocelyn sat back against his office desk chair, making him wonder what thoughts were going through her head right now. He could tell when she started to have ideas in a case. What idea had struck her now?

The three fell into silence for another moment. Rather than talk the case with Jocelyn now, he turned to Josie. She leaned forward as though weighed by her own thoughts, head bent, brow low.

"You okay, Josie?" He had to admit to some over-protectiveness toward his little sister.

She looked up and seconds passed before she responded. "Someone's been following me. I don't know if it's my imagination or not. I'm so used to looking over my shoulder that it's hard to stop. I'm not quite used to living with a sense of security."

This, Trevor hadn't expected. Someone was following her? Who? Why? She hadn't come out of hiding very long ago. She needed time to adjust. Maybe she had imagined someone following her, but what if she hadn't? It alarmed Trevor.

"You're not sure?"

She opened her hands in frustration. "I saw him, but…no, I can't be sure. I don't want to take any chances. Are you sure Desmond Carlton is in prison?"

"Locked away and won't be let out. Yes, I'm very sure." He'd reassure her, but if Carlton hadn't been the one who followed her, who had?

"What did the man who followed you look like?" Jocelyn asked, getting a notepad out from Trevor's center desk drawer.

"I didn't get a good look at him," Josie said. "I didn't recognize him or his car."

"It was a man?" Jocelyn probed, taking out a pen next.

"Yes."

"Anything strike you about him? His hair? Maybe a hat?"

Josie shook her head. "He was too far away. Short hair, not thick. Sunglasses."

Jocelyn jotted down the information. People remembered more than they thought when they were being questioned by police. "Close-cropped hair?"

"No, just thick and not long."

"Okay. Good. How high did he sit in the seat?"

Josie sat straighter, eyes narrowing as she searched her memory. "Not high. Not low, either."

"So average build, you'd say?"

Josie nodded. "Yes."

"Where were you when you saw him? Is that the only time you saw him?" Trevor asked.

"When I came out of the market about a week ago. And again outside my house, except he drove past that time and didn't seem to notice me." She looked from Jocelyn to Trevor, clearly worried. "Can I trust the word of a reporter that everyone associated with the kingpin is either dead or in prison?"

Trevor didn't want to frighten her. "Not the word of a reporter, but I've seen no indication that you should be concerned."

Josie's eyes closed briefly and she sighed. Then she waved a hand and stood. "It's nothing. I'm being paranoid."

Trevor let her go to the door. He may not have given her cause for concern, but he'd keep a close eye on her.

She smiled back at them. "I'll leave you two love doves alone now."

He'd make sure his brothers were aware of this and

put an agent on her. As for her parting comment…he'd just forget she'd said such a thing.

Jocelyn couldn't stop thinking about Josie's visit earlier today, what she'd made her begin to ponder. The sounds and sights of the busy and brightly lit diner outside Granite Gulch faded away. Of course Trevor would have a hard time as a fourteen-year-old whose father had murdered his mother and been thrown in prison as a serial killer. She hadn't considered how that might mar his ability to maintain relationships. She'd thought he'd want what he hadn't had—a family. But he didn't. He may fantasize about having one, but he didn't embrace the reality. He consumed all of his time with work. He'd dedicated his life to his profession as an FBI profiler. She'd always understood why, or she'd thought she did. His father, of course. But why did he shy away from close relationships?

Workaholism bandaged his insecurity. Jocelyn almost blanched with the word in her head. The weakness didn't fit the man. But he kept his insecurity hidden, even from himself. His affair with another agent supported her theory. The woman must have welcomed her ex back after seeing the hopelessness of investing her heart in a relationship with Trevor. He must have distanced himself from her—as he'd done with Jocelyn.

She respected his flaw. She did. Who could deal with a murderer as a father? She would stumble and perhaps fall, too. Few could handle that without emotion, and if they could, Jocelyn was sure something was wrong with them, too.

But even rationalizing all of that didn't ease the trepidation creeping over her. He didn't want to be involved with her because of his father. Mass murderer. Killer of his mother. Mind game player.

That had to mess with a kid's head.

Did he have no sense of family? That had to be it. What glimpse he'd had of a family unit had to have been unusual. His father must not have been home much, and he had to have had interpersonal issues. Serial killers were renowned for their intelligence. Matthew Colton may have personified himself as a normal, even charismatic man, but no one would have known him like those who shared his house.

Did she care that much? Yes. She worked with Trevor. She'd had sex with him. And then the matter of her feelings compounded the rest.

"Something on your mind?"

Jarred from staring across the room, realizing a woman sitting with a man glared at her for doing so, thinking she'd been staring at the man, Jocelyn lowered her hand from her chin, leaned back and contemplated Trevor.

Rather than take up that discussion with him now, she broached something she'd been thinking about lately. "I want to pose as bait for Regina, see if we can draw her out."

Instantly, Trevor's brow dived for his nose. "What? Where did that idea come from?"

She leaned forward, elbows on the table. "When your sister Annabel pieced together that the victims frequented restaurants, I got to thinking. I have long dark hair. Regina doesn't know me. She doesn't know I'm an FBI agent. I'm a rookie. I'm in the background in this investigation. So are you. We haven't been in the media."

The Alphabet Killer would pay attention to the news. She might even enjoy hearing about her work.

"No way." Trevor shook his head. "No."

She slapped the tabletop. "Trevor, stop trying to protect me. You've done that ever since I started working with you."

"Because you have *long dark hair* and your name starts with a *J*. Really? You'd risk your life for this?"

"Wouldn't you?" She shook her head, shaking off what he insinuated. "I won't be a risk until I agitate her. We need a plan, a surveillance plan and a cover story. We're getting nowhere. We need to move in, get closer and catch her!"

Trevor sighed long and hard, glancing over the diner, seeing everything. The man didn't miss a thing, even when something distracted him like this. At last his eyes returned to her. She felt their dark intensity.

"What did you have in mind?" he asked. "Because I can tell you've thought about this in detail."

She smiled. How did he, and when had he gotten to, know her so well?

"I could create a fake identity and start going out to all the local restaurants." She looked around. "This one. All the others in town, and any outside the area. That's something we need to research. We can't limit the locations, but we should start with a perimeter and work with that set of establishments first."

"What fake identity?" he asked.

"A real estate agent. There's a vacant building at the edge of town. I contacted the owner. We can lease it."

"What if Regina checks your background?"

She'd encountered a few criminals in her rookie days. She knew where to go to get a fake ID. But her cover had to be good. She needed Trevor and the rest of the task force on her side. He'd persuade the rest of the team to set up a sting operation. She didn't respond. He wouldn't agree, not easily.

He rubbed his fingers over his jaw, having shifted his position "Jocelyn." He lowered his hand and she saw his sincerity. "This is a dangerous killer."

"Really? I didn't know that."

He put his hands up as though to calm her down. "I'm not trying to be condescending." And then his expression changed as something struck him. "Hold on a second. Why did you say *we*? Do you want the whole team involved?"

What else did he think? Or better yet—*why* did he think involving the whole team was so far-fetched? What was with him? "I'm part of this team. You're the only one who's against me."

"I only mean to keep you safe—not do something foolish like put you in the path of a psychotic killer."

"It's not foolish. You're being overprotective of me. Let me do my job."

He stared at her for long seconds. "You expect me to convince them to set up a sting operation?"

"I'm an agent. Just like you. Why do you think they'll be so hard to convince?" He was starting to make her really angry.

His lips flat-lined, assurance his patience waned. "I won't let you pose as bait."

"It's not your decision to make."

"I outrank you."

Jocelyn had had enough. She stood, planting her hands on the table and leaning over, furious. "Damn it, Trevor, stop being so pigheaded!"

"I won't let you do it."

She felt like throwing something. How could she get through to him? She wouldn't. He wouldn't allow her to pose as bait.

Now deflated and so angry she could spit, all she wanted was to retaliate somehow, to poke back at him.

"Yeah? Well, you let me get pregnant easy enough."

Trevor's face turned to stone. "What?"

She wasn't a hundred percent sure, but…

"I'm late. And I'm never late." Regretting the outburst, she straightened and turned, walking briskly toward the exit, aware of the table next to where she and Trevor sat, watching her. They'd heard her.

Ah, entertainment.

Outside, she walked up the sidewalk, her leather work shoes soundless. She heard Trevor come up behind her. Of course he'd come after her.

Walking beside her, she felt him looking at her profile. She refused to look back.

"You're making that up."

She wished she was. "Nope. I'm late."

"That doesn't mean you're pregnant."

That made her look at him. He was in denial if he believed that.

"Have you been to a doctor?"

"I don't need a doctor. Not for that." She was pregnant. She just knew it. And, like him, she'd been in denial for about a week now.

Chapter 5

*S*unlight warmed the ground. A breeze brushed tall grass. Birds chirped, soft and Beethovenian. An old ash tree shaded a spot by the barn. She walked there, letting her hand trail through the feathery tops of grass, tipping her face up to the clear blue sky to savor the lovely summer day. Passing the barn, she walked and walked, through endless, swaying grass.

The landscape didn't end. Fields of beautiful grass extended as far as she could see. The land rolled, down a hill and then back up. She had the sense that she'd get nowhere like this.

Her mood shifted. Foreboding began as a harmless shadow and grew, steadily intensifying as she walked. Except now she didn't seem to be walking anymore. Floating. Skimming over the grass. She wanted to turn *around and go back to the ash tree, where she'd felt safe and at home.*

A force pushed her from behind. She had to keep going. Reaching the top of the hill, she saw a fence, painted as blue as the sky. White daisies moved to the breeze. The grass had been trimmed here.

The fence began to blur. Clouds gathered overhead. The air cooled.

Danger.

She tried to turn and run, but something pulled her down to the ground. Her feet locked into place among the daisies. The sky darkened. She struggled to free her feet.

Then the daisies began to wilt. Their petals turned black and their stems lost their leaves and bent over. The cold wind whipped and swirled around her. She'd be swept away in this eddy of horror that shouldn't be horror at all. The once peaceful place had come under attack by some strange and ominous force.

A paintbrush dripping with blue paint morphed into a sword. Blue paint changed to red. Blood dropped to the ground. The face of a man emerged just before the rest of his body. He now held the bloody sword, his eyes black and evil. He raised the sword for a swing...

Hearing her own muffled cry, Josie sprang up on her bed, sweating, breathing fast and in tempo with the frantic pace of her heart.

A dream. It had only been a dream.

"Damn you, Trevor." All that talk about Dad had spooked her. That and whoever had stalked her...

With the pregnancy test long ago thrown in the trash, Trevor paced from one end of the living room in Jocelyn's condo to the other. She sat on her gray sofa before the stacked gray rock wall, a fresh vase of yellow lilies on the coffee table, reminding him that her chosen profession missed the mark. What hit the mark was what had him pacing the room. Her. Pregnant. Raising babies in a warm, inviting home like this one, in a gated community with a pool and clubhouse, or in a house with a backyard.

He knew what he had to do. He just couldn't believe he actually would.

Without hesitation, he stopped pacing in front of the sofa, looking at Jocelyn over the tops of cheery lilies. "We have to get married."

That blunt announcement removed her annoyed observation of him digesting the unsavory idea of his impending fatherhood. Just the opposite. Now shock rounded her eyes and parted her lips with a grunt.

"Will I be at gunpoint?" she finally asked.

Beyond her sarcasm, he knew she felt at least a little like him, forced into having a baby. She'd accepted her situation a lot quicker than he had. Maybe as a woman that came naturally. But what would she do? Have the baby without him? He couldn't fathom not being involved in his own child's upbringing. He'd lived through that as a young teenager. Despite not being ready to take this on, his resolve would not bend.

"Love isn't important right now," he said, knowing he came on strong on this point. "The baby is what's important. No child of mine is going to be raised in a broken home."

She stood up. "Nothing's broken in *my* home."

She kind of went low on that one. His home was broken. Did she mean him or his dad? Both, probably.

"I won't get married just because I'm pregnant," she said. "I want love. Love is important to me, equally as much as this child." After a beat, she added, "And I thought you didn't mix personal relationships with your professional ones."

"I don't, but a baby changes everything. I won't be my father. I won't tear apart a family and destroy the lives of my children. I'll give them support and the best chance at a good life as I can."

He'd do anything, go to any length to avoid turning out like his father. He was no murderer. He had sanity. And he was on the opposite side of the law from his father. That was where he'd stay.

"You're a piece of work," Jocelyn said, walking around the big square coffee table to face him off. "We have sex and the next day you spout off about keeping our relationship professional and now you want to race off to the altar."

"There's a baby involved now. An innocent life will be our responsibility in less than nine months. That cancels out professional relationship options."

She took in his face and registered his words. And then something changed in the way she regarded him.

"I can see how this would be important to you, with your dad turning out to be a cold-blooded killer and all, losing your mother the way you did and going into foster care at fourteen, but what about me?"

She needed some major convincing. He wasn't doing a very good job of that, bulldozing with his determination to do right by their baby. "All of my brothers and sisters were sent to different foster homes. Our family ceased to exist after our mother was killed and Matthew was arrested. I know it's rushed. I know we only had sex once and before that we were coworkers. But do you really want to share custody and swap our child back and forth for eighteen years? Think what that will do to the kid. Think of the child, Jocelyn."

When she only stared at him, disbelieving and undecided, he put his hands on her upper arms. "We hit it off that night, I think you'll agree."

After several seconds, she tentatively nodded, hazel eyes lifted up warily to meet his, long dark hair shiny. Just looking at her made talking about this easier.

"That's something, isn't it? I'm not saying we'll have a relationship based on sex. I mean…at first it will be that way, since we haven't been seeing each other intimately and regularly, and we haven't been involved in a serious relationship." He was really botching this. "That doesn't matter. All I'm saying is that if you don't want to have sex with me, that's okay. I won't sleep with anyone else. I'll be a faithful husband and a good provider and I'll always be around for the child. It means too much to me to be a good father."

As she studied him, he couldn't tell what she thought or felt. But he saw when she'd made up her mind. Her eyes narrowed and she fixed him with a hard look. "All right, Trevor. I'll marry you, but on one condition."

"Name it."

"We marry without any disillusionment over the reality of our relationship. The marriage, although legal on paper, will be a farce. We may look like a family and act like a family, but we will not be a family in our hearts. You'll love our baby. I'll love our baby. But there will be no *we* in that equation. The only *we* in it is when we talk about our own individual relationship with our child. You think you can just marry me and presto we're a family. Well, it takes love to make a family. So, until you actually love me, and I you, if that ever happens, this is a fake arrangement, done solely for the baby."

Could she be more pessimistic? She painted a dismal picture of their future. They might as well be room-mates and split everything right down the middle. "No. I can't agree to that. We will be a real family."

"Take it or leave it." When she stepped back, out of his reach, he knew there'd be no swaying her. Fine. Let her go on thinking that way. He'd never consider this a fake arrangement. Forced, maybe, but not fake. Having a baby was real.

"Deal."

She smiled and he caught a glimpse of what lay ahead for him. "I'll make the wedding arrangements."

Jocelyn stepped out of the cab feeling wily and secretly happy. Trevor had no idea what he'd gotten himself into. He blindly thought marriage was the answer to all his problems. Well, she'd show him that impulsive actions had consequences.

Thank God for annulments.

That was where this would end up if they didn't truly love each other, and she was 99.9 percent positive he would never love her. His warped thinking would never allow him. Holy cow. His decision to marry a woman he didn't love proved that, didn't it? And he carried his family tragedy like lead-filled luggage.

Trevor came to stand next to her as she admired the grandeur of the luxurious Menaggio casino and hotel off the Las Vegas Strip. Pale beige stone rose thirty-six floors and jazz music played from hidden speakers. A bellman took their luggage from the back of the cab—

not much, just two carry-on bags. There would be no honeymoon after this wedding. They'd head right back to Texas tomorrow. She'd arranged everything in a day. The most important props were the costumes.

So far Trevor had indulged her despite how seriously he took this. He seemed to approve of the hotel, although he'd told her Italy would have been better. She'd responded with "Only for weddings that include love."

Vegas suited this wedding just fine. And…checking the time, they'd have just enough to get ready for the ceremony. She'd planned on this being a quick trip. Shotgun wedding. Get married and get home, no time for generating special memories that would give her false hope for this false marriage.

Up in their suite, she entered ahead of Trevor into a marble-floor foyer that opened to a spacious color-splashed living room and dining area. Double doors opened to a large master bedroom. The elegance almost ruined the staging of this event. A secret part of her had deliberately splurged. This would be her wedding night, after all.

Moving into the bedroom, she smiled when she saw the costumes hanging in the closet. They'd go as *Mr. and Mrs. Smith*.

Trevor went to them, inspecting his and then running his gaze down hers. Hot, smoldering eyes met her when he finished. Seared by him, she experienced a moment of doubt. Maybe these weren't the best costumes. She'd meant for them to be somewhat normal in attire. The gray suit and white shirt for him, and a black dress for her. She'd thought black the perfect color for a fake wedding. But this Mrs. Smith spaghetti strap number had a slit up one side and fit snug to the skin. The garter-like gun holster did add some fun, though.

"I'll dress out here. You take the bathroom." Trevor took his suit.

She took her dress and closed the door behind her in the bathroom, a sinking feeling accompanying her that there'd still be enough time for special memories.

Trevor waited for Jocelyn in a small circular courtyard overlooking a lake on the casino property. A stone railing enclosed the marble-bedecked space, the trellises of fragrant flowers and the lights of the Strip behind him. He'd greeted the minister. Jocelyn hadn't mocked that part of this wedding. They'd be well and truly married in less than an hour. He broke out into a sweat and not from the June heat.

She appeared and Trevor stopped breathing. She'd done her hair and wore makeup. Thick dark hair cascaded silkily over her shoulders. She seldom wore it down like that, not while she worked. The dress revealed a slender leg with each of her steps, the black gun strap showing. She'd worn the damn plastic gun, and her breasts looked as though they'd pop right out of that bodice.

He felt the minister glance his way.

Trevor stood stiff with tension. This might have been a bad idea, not the right solution. Maybe he'd jumped a little too quickly. Jocelyn might be more than even he could handle.

She smiled that cat-got-the-mouse grin as he offered his arm. Sliding hers through the opening, she rested her hand on his forearm and burned him with just a touch.

They faced the minister, who eyed them a little longer,

searching Trevor for what had to be another plastic gun before clearing his throat and beginning.

"I've been instructed to make this quick and to the point," he said, glancing at Jocelyn.

"Thank you," she said.

The minister cleared his throat again. "The vows you are about to exchange will be among the most significant in your lives. This kind of union is based on mutual respect and love." He looked up at each of them. "Not to be made fun of, but to be taken to heart."

Trevor held back a spark of hope. Jocelyn had chosen a real minister and now he sounded as though he were admonishing them.

"Your lives will change, your responsibilities will change and joy will come only if you are sincere and honest with your pledge to one another."

Now Trevor thought she had planned this speech— for him.

"Trevor Colton, will you have this woman to be your wedded wife, to love her, comfort her, honor and keep her, and forsaking all others, keep you only unto her, for so long as you both shall live?"

Sweat ran down the back of his neck. "I do."

The minister turned to Jocelyn. "Jocelyn Smith—" He cleared his throat again. "Pardon me, *Locke*. Jocelyn Locke, will you have this man to be your wedded husband, to love him, comfort him, honor and keep him, and forsaking all others, keep you only unto him, so long as you both shall live?"

She hesitated.

Trevor turned to her and saw her stark face, eyes wide and on this man of God. He put his hand over hers on his arm. She tipped her head up and blinked a few times, then something smoky softened her eyes.

"I do," she said in the sexiest voice he'd ever heard.

He started to get hard.

Bad timing. He looked at the minister, who hadn't missed the exchange.

He smiled and continued. "Hold hands and repeat after me."

Jocelyn removed her arm from the hook of his and he took her hand.

"Face each other and take both hands," the minister said.

Trevor was certain that wasn't part of his script. He faced Jocelyn, so beautiful and looking at him with that heat.

"I, Trevor Colton," the minister said.

Trevor began repeating what he said. "I, Trevor Colton, take you, Jocelyn Locke, to be my wedded wife, to have and to hold, for better or for worse, for richer or for poorer, to love and to cherish, from this day forward."

"Very good," the minister said, clearly enjoying what had appeared to be a debauchery of marriage but now showed signs of promise.

"Now for the lady," he said. "I, Jocelyn Locke…"

"I, Jocelyn Locke, take you, Trevor Colton, to be my wedded husband, to have and to hold, for better or for worse, for richer or for poorer, to love and to cherish, from this day forward."

"Is there a ring?" the minister asked.

Trevor tried not to notice his anticipation. "Yes." Now he wished he'd have bought a different ring. Something a little plainer. But no…

He took out a labradorite band with a one-carat diamond in the center and smaller blue rose-cut stones tapering away on each side. It was something she could wear every day, even with her job.

As she stared at it, he began to fear she didn't like it.

"Please place the ring on the bride's finger and repeat after me," the minister said.

Trevor took Jocelyn's hand and slipped the ring halfway onto her finger. Then he looked into her eyes and said, "With this ring, I thee wed." He pushed the ring all the way on.

"Is there a ring for the groom?"

Jocelyn reached into her bodice and pulled out a silver ring with a hammered texture. She'd put some thought into his ring, too.

He held up his hand and her soft skin touched him as she slipped the ring on.

"With this ring I thee wed," she said, repeating the minister.

When she finished, the minister said, "Let these rings be given and received as a token of your affection, sincerity and fidelity to one another. By the authority vested in me by the state of Nevada, I now pronounce you husband and wife."

Jocelyn lifted her eyes, still with his hand in hers, stunned, probably as much as him.

"You may kiss now," the minister said.

Forget how they'd gotten here. Trevor slid his arm around her waist and drew her against him. He placed his other midway up her back as she rested her hands on his shoulders.

Lowering his head, he touched her mouth. As before, an instant inferno roared. Chemistry would not be their problem. As a man, nothing should make him happier. Except this ceremony, no matter how much Jocelyn had tried to subdue the significance, held more realness than either of them had anticipated.

Jocelyn wasn't finished with Trevor yet. They'd already had sex. She was already pregnant. The damage had already been done. What did she have to lose?

Inside the posh, top-level hotel suite, she went into the bedroom, pretending not to notice him go into the living room, removing the jacket and unbuttoning the top of the dress shirt. Before closing the bedroom door, she looked back to see him sit with knees apart on the sofa, remote in hand.

She'd felt the ceremony more than she'd anticipated, and she had seen the same in him. But if he thought he'd spend their wedding night flipping channels, he was in for a big surprise.

She changed into the teddy she'd brought for this very purpose. A black, sheer confection that dipped low in the bodice and pushed her breasts up, the bottom fastened to stockings, and the underwear wasn't really underwear. Although they appeared to cover her, they left her crotch bare. When she'd made this purchase just a couple of days ago, she'd considered it a perfect representation of the kind of foundation that had caused this marriage. Now she didn't know if it was appropriate.

Did a fake marriage have to be consummated? No, but Trevor needed to understand what he'd done. The sooner he did, the sooner she could walk away. Because he also needed to understand that she would not settle for a loveless marriage. Maybe enticing him with sex would backfire on her, maybe it would mean too much.

Or maybe a deeper part of her hoped it would mean too much to him.

Taking a deep breath, giving her hair a toss, she turned off the bathroom light and opened the bedroom door.

Trevor had leaned back on the sofa. His back to her, he didn't see her approach. He had some kind of documentary on, something about a mama bear and her two cubs. The narrator's voice drifted to the background as she made her way to the front of the sofa and his head lifted and turned.

He went still as his gaze ran from her face on down her body, lingering at the top of her thighs. Did he know the underwear was crotchless? After a slow foray down her legs and back up over the eye candy, he met her eyes.

"What's this?" he asked.

He hadn't moved.

She walked to him, moving slow and smooth, deliberately stretching her strides like a sexy model, even though she never saw herself that way. The ploy worked. Trevor seemed to grow nervous as she stood before him.

"Our wedding night," she finally answered.

One of his brows lifted higher than the other. "We don't have to…"

"Consummate the wedding?" she helped him out.

"Uh…"

Desire and hesitation did battle in him. "If we don't, it's not a marriage. I could go to the courthouse tomorrow and have it annulled." That wasn't the most romantic thing to say, but would he actually reject her when she'd put on this getup for him?

"You want it annulled?" He stood with another glance down her body.

"I told you I want a real marriage."

He stepped toward her. "Yes, but that doesn't mean you have to have sex with me tonight. We can ease into that."

Ease into the role of husband and wife? What did that mean? Would they wait until they grew accustomed to living together and therefore comfortable enough to graduate to sex? Love would make sex a natural instinct. A benefit. A beautiful thing. They didn't have love.

"What makes you think I feel like I have to?" she asked, trying to ignore the tight pull of disenchantment.

"I don't. I… It's just…" He ran his fingers through his hair, messing the strands up and making her wish she didn't want to be the one to do that.

"This needs to be right," he said. "Between us."

Rushing off for a shotgun wedding didn't qualify as right. "We had great sex." Raunchy though it may be, the sex had been right between them. Dead-on. A blazing, hot fireball of rightness. But she wouldn't point that out to him now.

He lowered his hand and a slight, one-sided grin emerged. Up until now she hadn't been able to read him. "Can't argue that."

Progress. But did she still want what she'd intended with this teddy? That knot of apprehension twisted.

He moved to her, stopping close and putting his hand on her arm, giving her a soft rub.

The feeling in the pit of her stomach intensified, a sense of wrongness.

His other hand came up and touched beneath her chin. He tipped her head up a bit and she met his dark, burning eyes. They startled her with passion and, in the next instant, doubt of its authenticity. Or, no, its origin. Not from love. From sex. Great sex. It wasn't enough. Why did that bother her so much now? It hadn't bothered her the first time they'd had sex.

He bent lower and kissed her. The tingle of passion collided with anxiety.

Putting her hands on his chest, she pushed and stepped back. "You're right. Maybe we should ease into this." Or get an annulment first thing tomorrow morning. She'd been crazy to think she could pull this off. Why had she agreed to marry him?

Turning, she walked hastily back into the room. She began to remove the teddy, beginning with the belts, when she heard him at the doorway. She hadn't closed the door. She hadn't thought he'd follow. More like, he'd be relieved she'd stopped tempting him.

"Are you all right?" he asked.

"Fine." She felt ridiculous in the teddy, belts hanging down. It may as well be Halloween.

"I didn't mean to move so fast. You just…look so… beautiful."

Sexy. Lustful. Seductive…

Slutty.

Had one of those words crossed his mind before he replaced it with *beautiful*?

He stuffed his hands into his pockets, awkward and needing her to forgive his male instincts to ravage her.

She found this gentlemanly side of him endearing. He disarmed her. "Let me change into something more comfortable." Something more *her*.

His gaze passed down her body almost regretfully. But then he turned and went back into the living room.

Jocelyn put on her knee-length pink-and-blue-polka-dot cotton nightgown with an animated print of Sid, the ground sloth from the movie *Ice Age*, on the front. It was too early to go to bed, or she'd have contemplated not rejoining him. But she went out to the living room, where Trevor had turned the channel to an action film.

She went to a chair.

"Come here." Trevor patted the sofa cushion next to him.

Wary, she didn't move.

"Sit next to me, wife." His mouth curved in a lop-sided grin.

Curiosity made her go to him. Tingles sprinkled through her as he looked her up and down, taking in the nightgown with humor lighting his dark eyes. She sat and eyed him in question.

"That thing is almost worse than the teddy."

She hadn't expected him to say that. He liked her in this very nonsexy nightwear.

He leaned back and stretched his arm along the back of the sofa as though making an attempt to cool the moment.

She leaned back with him and watched the television, too aware of him to pay any attention to the story playing out.

"This is a real marriage, Jocelyn."

Surprised he'd said that now, she turned to him with another silent question.

"You make a mockery of it by dressing in sexy lingerie." When she would have argued why, he held up his forefinger. "I can't wait to see you in it again, but I'd prefer it if you wore it for me and not to prove a point."

"Then you'll be waiting a long time," she said.

His mouth tightened briefly. He knew what she

meant. "We can make this marriage work, Jocelyn. We can be a family and live a good, happy life."

Could they? Did he really believe that? More like he'd done some heavy-duty convincing to himself.

"I want to talk to you about work," he said.

She predicted where he'd go with this and grew irritated. "No."

His brow lifted. "You haven't even heard what I have to say."

"You mean what you're going to propose? That I don't work?"

"How did you—"

Incensed, she stood and faced him with her hands on her hips. "Oh-my-God. You were actually going to suggest I quit my job?" Flashes of her dad's and brother's faces ran through her mind.

"Jocelyn." He stood and faced her, looking down at her defiant stance with a little too much appreciation. "You're going to have a baby anyway. You can't work once you do."

"Why not?"

"Don't you want to stay at home with our baby?"

Oooo…he masked his true intent with that dangling carrot. They had a long time before she'd give birth.

"The baby isn't born yet. I'm working until I go into labor." He ought to know her better by now. She was not the type to quit anything, especially when her dad and brother died in the line of duty and she was all that remained of her line. Her honor alone would keep her working.

After looking at her for several seconds, Trevor sighed long and ran his fingers through his hair again.

"Jocelyn, please. I don't think we should work together as husband and wife. You'll distract me from the case."

"I'll *distract* you?"

"I need to know you're safe," he said.

"No. Let's address what this is really all about, Trevor. This reminds you of your failed relationship with that woman—that coworker of yours. You're afraid I'm right and this won't work out."

When he hesitated, she wondered if she was in fact right, or if she'd only touched the surface.

"You're the one who mentioned an annulment," he said.

She'd have to be careful not to bring that up again. "If this doesn't work out, it'll be because you forced me to marry you."

"I didn't force you."

She leaned her face closer to his. "You coerced me."

He leaned closer to hers. "You agreed."

Planting her hands on his muscular chest, she gave him a frustrated shove. He didn't budge.

Jocelyn pivoted and stomped toward the bedroom. At the doorway, Trevor took hold of her wrist and tugged. In one smooth movement, he gently spun her, taking her other hand and pulling her against him. His arms slid around her and she stared up into his intense eyes, determined and flaring with passion. Instant awareness of her body pressed to his softened some of the shock over his bold action. Her soft breasts against his hard torso. Her hips to his thighs.

The tightness around his mouth softened as he grew aware of the same.

"What are you doing?" she asked, breathless.

"I'm consummating this marriage."

Dizzy with that raspy declaration, Jocelyn melted against him as he slid his hand up her back and sank his fingers into her hair. She gripped the front of his shirt as he brought his mouth down to hers. She had no time to prepare for this sensual onslaught. The baser part of her remembered how good they were together. Like invisible tentacles seeking his heat, the core of her responded to his every touch. Each soft movement of his mouth on hers, each stroke of his tongue and his hand on her rear blew oxygen into the flames of her passion.

He became the center of her consciousness. When he moved forward, she naturally backed toward the bed. Everything he did, climbing on top of her, stripping her, drowned into the background of sweet sensation. His kisses took her away from reality and into a magical world. His skin against hers and his roaming hands only perpetuated the dreamlike state. Sparkles lit the fantasy when he penetrated her. An expert lover, or an expert lover only with her, he moved to a slow, intimate and drugging rhythm. As her eyes met his at that pinnacle moment, she knew he'd been carried away as much as her.

Trevor woke to a quiet hotel room. Bright sunlight beamed through the wall of windows beyond the foot of the king-size bed. But it was the mass of long dark hair all over his chest that got most of his attention. Jocelyn lay with her head there, an arm slung over to the other side of him, and one slender leg doing the same to his hips. The covers had fallen half off the bed and none covered them. What the hell? What had happened to him last night? He felt as though he'd dreamed it all. Maybe he had.

He should welcome the explosive chemistry they mixed. He had a chance to make this a real marriage. Instead, a wave of apprehension swept him. What was a real marriage? Had he ever seen one? Because most people put on a damn good face in an attempt to convince the world they'd gotten it right, that they'd found the ever elusive True Love. The only truth Trevor believed was that kind of love was rare, if it existed at all.

Control slipped out of his reach. The powerful emotion Jocelyn stirred with just a touch and a look last night disconcerted him. He didn't feel himself. Who was that man who'd made love to her that way?

One that would take him straight to a broken heart, that was who. Both people in a relationship had to feel the same, exactly the same. Equal levels of love, and a lot of it, for it to qualify as True Love.

When he'd discovered how easy it had been for his ex-girlfriend and agent, Christy, to get back together with the other agent, Trevor only grew more convinced. He'd had real feelings for her. He wouldn't go so far as to say he'd fallen madly in love with her, but he'd thought they had a chance, a real chance. But, no. Once again, having faith in finding that kind of love left a person cold and alone.

He hadn't thought about when he'd give love a try again. He hadn't even thought about dating. Sure, he'd taken women out over the past five years and even slept with a few of them, but none had inspired him to start a relationship. Jocelyn inspired. And that was what had him on edge.

Carefully, he eased out from under her, replacing his chest with a pillow. She moaned and adjusted her position and then sighed as she fell back into deep sleep.

Trevor pulled the sheet over her naked body. Marrying her for the sake of a child had seemed like the right thing to do, but falling in love hadn't been part of the plan. At least, not this soon. Maybe he had hoped they could have done what he'd suggested—ease into it. Or just have a nice, uncomplicated companionship while they raised their child. Hell, he no longer knew what he'd been thinking. Right now, he felt as though he'd made a big mistake.

Chapter 6

Jocelyn sat in the meeting room at the Granite Gulch FBI satellite office. The task force met regularly to discuss the case. Chief Jim Murray stepped into the room, tall and trim and not bad-looking for a man in his fifties. Unlike many men his age, he also had a full head of salt-and-pepper hair. He was her new best friend. She'd spoken with him prior to this meeting while Trevor had gone to the restroom, and he supported her idea. He'd let her present it to the task force today.

She glanced over at Trevor, sitting beside her as her husband and boss for this case. He wasn't going to like this.

He caught her glance and she smiled.

He eyed her strangely, suspicious of what thought had put that smile on her face.

"Stop being so serious," she said.

"What are you so chipper about?"

He'd been surly all the way back from Vegas. The flight back to Granite Gulch had been awkward—for him. Jocelyn inwardly celebrated the connection they'd made. She didn't need an annulment if this turned into something good.

At four in the afternoon, their schedule had been tight to make this meeting. The busy pace had helped her to avoid analyzing the magic of last night too much.

Chief Murray took to the podium in the cramped room. Other officers and agents sat on uncomfortable folding chairs. They were a team of about twenty, working diligently to catch the Alphabet killer.

"Thank you for coming this afternoon," the chief began. "I'd like to announce a possible change in our strategy. Up until now, surveillance and other methods of investigation haven't worked in our favor. One of our FBI agents came up with an idea I'd like us all to discuss, and if we have unanimous agreement, we've got a plan to start implementation tonight."

Jocelyn felt Trevor turn his gaze on her. She didn't have to see him to know he was angry.

"Jocelyn?" Chief Murray invited her to take the podium.

She got up.

Trevor got up, as well. "Wait just a minute."

She kept going.

"Jocelyn."

"Just hear her out, Agent Colton," the chief said. "This is a team effort."

Trevor remained standing, an intimidating presence as she took the podium.

"We know Regina Willard works at restaurants and that's most likely where she meets her victims," Jocelyn began, gaining strength as she spoke. "We think she's a waitress. We know what she looked like before she began her crimes. She changes her appearance and her identity to escape detection. Because she goes after women with long dark hair, I propose to pose as bait to lure her out."

A flurry of murmurs spread through the room.

"There's a vacant building at the edge of town that I propose to use as a real estate agency. My real estate agency. I'll have business cards ready in the morning, and my false identity will be arranged once I have approval to move forward."

"How do you plan to lure her out?" one of the seated officers asked.

A glance at Trevor confirmed he'd like to hit the man for asking.

"I'll go to the restaurants as a patron and behave rudely. No waitress likes condescension. One who kills will like it even less."

"It's too dangerous," Trevor said. He moved to look at the faces in the crowd. "We can't put one of our own at that kind of risk."

"I think it's a good idea," an officer in the back said. "She's got long dark hair and her name starts with a *J.*"

"I agree. It might work," an agent on the right said.

"Are you crazy?" Trevor roared. "She could be the next victim!"

"You could go with me, Agent Colton." Jocelyn tried to calm him. She already knew he wouldn't stand for her going alone.

"And do what?" he snapped. "Pose as your husband?"

"There wouldn't be much posing involved," she said,

loving how that curbed his temper and put him in check. "Would there?"

Everyone in the room turned startled eyes to Trevor. They hadn't made the announcement yet that they were married.

"Out in the hall. Now." Trevor began to turn.

"Wait. Let's take a vote," Chief Murray said.

Trevor stopped short and bestowed the man with an ominous look.

"Who's in favor?"

About 80 percent of the room raised their hands.

Jocelyn beamed a smile, eager to get to work and catch a killer. Trevor, on the other hand, would take some convincing.

At the edge of town, Trevor looked around for any suspicious movement while Jocelyn unlocked the front door of her new pseudo office. Inside, the older building smelled dusty and stale and the previous tenants had left a mess behind, but the sturdy construction made up for that. Messes could be cleaned.

"Looks like we have a lot of work to do," Jocelyn said.

She walked through the front room with white-trimmed windows and redbrick walls. A broken table in one corner, a dirty towel nearby, a checkout counter with the display glass in pieces all around and more. His feet scuffed along a wood floor that would gleam with a little love.

"I'll get a cleaning crew over here in the morning," Trevor said.

"Movers will be here any minute."

She'd been busy. "You had this all planned, didn't you? From the moment you mentioned it that first time."

She smiled. "I had faith in you."

"Me?" He lifted his brow.

She walked over to him, putting a hand on his chest with a pat. "I knew you'd come around...*husband*."

"I still don't approve of you posing as bait." He wouldn't tell her she'd come up with a smart plan, that he'd have raised his hand along with the rest—had she been anyone else proposing to take such a risk.

"I've been around law enforcement my entire life," she said. "I've trained for this. I'm an agent, Trevor. Just like you."

Not just like. "You're a rookie."

"I learned from my dad and brother." She dropped her hand to put it on her hip, a sexy hip that he'd like to have his hands on again. "I've been shooting guns since I was twelve."

"You have not." What father would let his twelve-year-old daughter shoot a gun?

"I started with toy guns."

He chuckled.

Then more seriously, she said, "Real guns when I was sixteen. I'm a good shot. Take me to the range—I'll show you."

She didn't need to show him. He'd seen her shoot before at the practice range. She was a natural. "Okay, Ellen the Gunslinger."

Jocelyn laughed. "Just don't start calling me *The Lady*."

"I go with you at all times," he said. "I don't want you to get into any situations where you have to use your gun. Leave that to me. You draw Regina out, and I'll take care of the rest."

"Why are you so protective?" She started to clean up.

He found a broom and began to sweep. It was almost as though the previous tenants had left in the middle of cleaning the place before leaving.

"What makes you that way?" Jocelyn asked when he didn't answer.

No one had ever asked him before. No one had ever told him he was protective, either. He certainly wasn't like this with other agents. He trusted them to do their jobs. Jocelyn...

She'd become an agent for a noble reason, but this wasn't her calling. He glanced over at her stomach, which would soon begin to show signs of her pregnancy. He stopped sweeping.

"You're going to have a baby. It's not only your life that's at stake anymore. I'd still like you to take a leave or quit. And, yes, I am being protective when it comes to that."

"I wasn't pregnant before and you've always been protective. I'd like you to stop. I'm a good agent."

"What's wrong with not wanting you to get hurt?"

"Nothing." She threw some papers into a full trash can. "But it kind of goes against your rule not to mix personal matters with work. I can't figure you out. You don't want to get personal and yet you married me."

That did come with some angst. He maintained professionalism at all times while working. Ethics mattered to him. Affairs or inappropriate behavior didn't feel right. He'd learned the former the hard way.

He resumed sweeping. "Getting married was the right thing to do."

Jocelyn sighed out a long breath, exasperated as she picked up other items from the floor. "You didn't want to get married before you found out I was pregnant."

No. A baby changed everything. He'd said that already. Didn't she understand? Maybe she did but dreamed of a perfect wedding, in love with her groom. He'd like the same with a bride, but they both had to take responsibility for their carelessness. Now an innocent life would come into this world, faultless of any lack of caution on their part.

"In fact," she went on, busily tidying up the place, "I thought you were like that because you *didn't* want to get married."

"I'd have married if the right woman came along."

"I'm not the right woman."

"It's too soon to tell. Stop overthinking this." He'd rather not consider how good they were together physically. While that might lead to a deeper relationship, it was all they had for now.

She stopped tidying and looked at him, incredulous. "I don't think it's possible to overthink rushing into marriage just because I'm pregnant. What if I miscarry?"

The possibility bit into his conscience. Once again, he stopped sweeping. He hadn't considered that in his haste to do the right thing.

"Are you afraid of ending up like your dad?"

What did Matthew have to do with this? "A serial killer?"

"No. I don't mean that. Maybe you lost your way after he was arrested for your mother's murder. Maybe that's what's kept you from marrying until now."

"I'm not that old." He had plenty of time for a family, and he wanted to be a good father. He wanted his kids to grow up in a solid family unit. Yeah, maybe he wanted that too much. He did worry he wouldn't succeed, especially with Jocelyn treating their marriage as a sham.

"Did you and that agent talk about having kids?" she asked, busy picking up things left behind and organizing them in one area.

"No. We didn't get that far."

"How long did you see her?"

"A few months." Long enough for him to contemplate something more lasting. The thought of having a family, one full of love and laughter, had enchanted him. It had also seemed too good to be true. As it turned out, it had been. She'd revealed herself to be artificial. She needed thrills. Excitement. In hindsight, that was why she'd become an FBI agent. She'd never be the type to slow down.

"I know you said you wanted a family, but did you ever really see yourself settling down and raising a family?" she asked. "Or did you become an agent to devote your life to catching criminals like your father?"

He had thought about settling down. Yes. Except he'd never planned on when. Maybe some part of him did second-guess his ability to parent. Maybe that was why he'd rushed into marriage with Jocelyn. He knew if he thought on it too long, he'd hesitate and not follow through.

"Movers are here."

Through the front windows, Trevor saw the truck pull to a stop in front of the building. Good. He'd have plenty to get his mind off what Jocelyn had put to seed in his head. And then she shot down that glimmer of hope.

"Let's go out for dinner."

* * *

While the movers—who were part of the team working the case—set up the real estate office, Jocelyn insisted they grab a late dinner. Why not start the sting operation now? Trevor had fought her, wanting to help the movers set things up. She sensed his reason wasn't so Samaritan, especially when she dressed for her part as bait. Tight jeans, cowboy boots and a sexy low-cut top complemented her made-up face. Jealousy would intensify Regina's reaction to her rudeness. And Jocelyn would enjoy pushing Trevor with his idea of marriage for the sake of their baby and not love.

Ever since the team had agreed to let her pose as bait, he'd fallen into moments of distant, pensive thought. She suspected he had doubts over his decision—not over supporting their child. She didn't doubt he'd always do that, but marriage in general. Maybe he was in shock over the realization that he was, in fact, married. That he was, in fact, going to be a father. He'd been so determined to seal the deal, though. Why did he second-guess himself?

Jocelyn swayed her hips with a little more verve than usual as she entered Blackthorn County All Night Diner. Her jeans had beads on the back pockets and flared just enough at her ankles. Trevor held the door for her, and his gaze didn't miss her hips. When he lifted reproachful eyes to hers, she winked at him.

Inside, she scanned the diner, picking out the restaurant staff. Most were women. Young and older. Two blondes, a dark-haired woman and a redhead. The dark-haired woman could be Regina. She resembled the photos they had of her.

The dark-haired woman waited on a booth next to a vacant one.

"Can we sit over there?" Jocelyn asked the hostess.

"Of course."

Seated at the booth, Jocelyn patted the space next to her, stopping Trevor from sitting across from her.

"Newlyweds sit next to each other," she said.

He sat with another reproachful look and then picked up the menu. "I'm actually really hungry."

She was, too. She leaned close and read the menu with him.

He turned his head.

She smiled at him, putting on her best smitten face. "People will think you don't love me if you keep doing that."

Abandoning the menu, he touched her under her chin and shocked her by kissing her. Soft, smooth, he moved over her lips like an expert lover. When he drew away, she had to catch her breath.

"That should dispel any doubt," he said in a raspy tone.

He wasn't immune to their chemistry. She had that, at least.

The waitress approached with a slight smile as she noticed their exchange. Jocelyn didn't see any animosity, but a serial killer could mask how they truly felt.

"My dad and brother took me hunting with them. And when we went to the amusement park, they took me on all the scary rides. You know the one that drops straight down from way high up?" She laughed with the memory. "They had to talk me into going on rides like that and soothe me if I cried, but by the time I was a tween, I wasn't afraid of anything."

"I'm not sure that's a good thing."

"You wouldn't, Mr. Overprotector." She leaned in close and rested her head on his shoulder for a second, just to make it look good to anyone watching, flaunting her left ring finger.

"What can I get you two?" the waitress asked with a hint of laughter in her tone, pen ready over a notepad.

"I'll have your cheeseburger, but it has to be cooked well and I want the top bun on the side—and make my fries crispy," Jocelyn said.

"I'll have the same, medium-well. Don't worry about where you put my bun." He turned with an affectionate look at Jocelyn.

The waitress eyed Jocelyn with less affinity but said, "And to drink?"

"Water. No ice."

"Iced tea. Ice is fine." Trevor handed her the menus.

The waitress smiled at Trevor and took the menus. Then she turned and went to put their order in.

"What do you think?" Jocelyn said. "Is it her?"

"I'm not sure. She resembles the photos, but her hair is a little dark. In the pictures she's more of a dirty-water hair color."

"Dirty water can be black."

"Mousy brown, then."

"Are you trying to be mean?" Why not? Regina had likely killed all those other women. All the way up to the letter *I*. *J* was next, which explained a lot of Trevor's overprotectiveness. But not all of it.

"I have anger issues over someone copying my father's method of killing," he said.

Although he sounded sarcastic, he must really have issues over that. Seeing the waitress return to check on the table next to them, Jocelyn said to Trevor, "I'm sorry, honey." She leaned over and planted a kiss on his cheek. "I never want to upset my lover, my one and only, my true love."

Trevor fell into his role. "You didn't, my love. Nothing you say upsets me. I love you."

"Aww." She put her head on his shoulder. "I love you, too."

The waitress moved to their table next, holding a tray of drinks. She put down the iced tea and the water—no ice.

Jocelyn sipped as the waitress began to turn. The water was cool.

"Wait a minute," she called to the waitress.

The woman turned, wary over her tone.

"Why do you think I asked for no ice?" Jocelyn asked harshly.

"Uh… I'm sorry. Is something wrong with your water?" She reached for the glass, distressed over an unhappy customer—or pretending to be. Jocelyn couldn't tell.

"Ice makes the water cold," Jocelyn spat. "This water is *cold*."

"Oh. Goodness. I'll get you another." The waitress took the glass and hurried to comply.

"Would Regina have reacted that way?" she asked when the waitress was far enough away.

"Let's see what she does when she comes back."

They didn't have to wait long. The waitress quickly returned with a new glass of water.

Jocelyn sipped while the waitress wrung her hands and watched. The water was room temperature.

"That's perfect. Thank you."

The waitress visibly relaxed. "Good. I'll bring your food right out."

"I don't think it's her," Trevor said. "She's too worried about pleasing you." He turned to her. "You're playing a really good mean lady, by the way. I'm almost embarrassed to be with you."

Jocelyn couldn't repress a laugh. "We need to be sure. Do you think she's wearing a wig?"

"I don't know. You could pull her hair to see. Get into a cat fight." He had his elbow on the table, looking over at her in playful sexiness.

"Why do cats get such a bad rap with that?" she asked. "Sigmund doesn't get into fights."

"Some cats do. Your cat is more like a dog. He likes to be petted. Does he come when he's called?"

"No. He's his own entity."

He grinned. "He takes after you."

"He's my family." She leaned back with a soft smile, missing her cat. She'd arranged for her neighbor to take care of him while they did this sting.

She and Trevor hadn't had time to talk about where they'd live now that they were married. She liked her condo and Sigmund was accustomed to living there. She didn't want to uproot him. Well, maybe she wouldn't have to worry about that for much longer. This marriage wouldn't last if she and Trevor didn't have real feelings for each other.

Would Trevor ever have feelings for her? Would she have feelings for him? She feared she already did. She remembered the first time she met him. Her first day on the job. He'd been in his office, wearing a suit and tie, the black straps of his gun holster and the shiny gold of his badge clipped to his belt making him look like a secret agent. His dark, sexy eyes and hair. He'd had faint signs of stubble growing on his so, so handsome face. She'd stared and gotten all hot just seeing him. The way he moved, a saunter, a confident one, a strong one. Oh. She felt the same pitter-patter of attraction as she had then.

And then he'd spoken in that deep voice, totally professional and giving no sign he'd felt anything in return for her.

She'd closed off her reaction to meeting the man of her dreams, at least physically. From that day on she'd had to smother her attraction. But every once in a while a glimmer of something would emerge. A look. A change in his tone. The touch of his hand on her lower back.

But she could never be sure if he felt anything toward her, not until they'd tumbled into bed almost a month ago. Then all the hotness he'd unleashed in her at first sight exploded.

He'd reverted right back to professionalism afterward, having that talk with her. Even after they'd gotten married, he still reverted back to that professional act.

It had to be an act. And Jocelyn had a burning need to know why. What made him do that?

"What was it like growing up in a foster home?" she asked, having a hunch all of his issues stemmed from that. "I know it must have been awful after you found out what your father did. You don't have to get into that. But what was it like? Were your foster parents good to you?"

He shrugged. "They were good to me, but they were strangers."

And he'd been alone. All of his brothers and sisters had gone to different homes.

"I didn't have long to wait to leave, either. As soon as I graduated from high school, I went to college."

Jocelyn pondered how to ask what she really needed to know. He must have felt lost as a teenager. What family he'd known had been torn apart.

"I also started tracking down my brothers and sisters. By the way, Josie said she told them we were together. We're going to have to tell them we're married and are going to have a baby."

He seemed to dread that. Again, his actions contradicted the man.

"Trevor, why did you marry me if you don't want to be married?"

"We've talked about this."

"For the baby. Yeah, that's an excuse." She needed him to be honest right now. "If I hadn't gotten pregnant, would you ever have gotten married?"

After meeting her face and what her eyes must convey—imploring for him to tell her—he stared off across the restaurant. He couldn't answer right away. He must not have given it much thought. Yet another red flag as far as Jocelyn was concerned. Who didn't think about getting married? The oldest son of a serial killer?

At last he faced her again. "I might have married Christy."

Christy. "The agent you slept with?"

"It was more than that."

How much had she meant to him? Or had he walled his heart off with her as Jocelyn sensed he'd begun to do with her?

"Did you love her?" she asked.

"No. I thought I did. Maybe I would have fallen in love with her. She didn't give me the chance to find out."

His honesty came as a wave of freshness. "Do you ever see yourself getting married, Trevor?"

He grinned. "I married you."

He tried to hide his feelings with that grin. Humor from an otherwise serious man. But Jocelyn would not be deterred. "No, you didn't. You married the mother of your child." Her earlier assessment hung like heavy fog. He held back in love and the cause of his rebellion at fourteen had caused it.

"Why are you afraid of ending up like your father?" she asked.

"I'm not a serial killer. And I've thought about what you said before. I'm not afraid of being a father. Of course I want to be a good father, but it's more than that. I want to be a good husband, too. I want to make a good family."

That sounded like a step in the right direction— in the direction Jocelyn wanted to go. "Do you doubt you're capable?"

"I don't even know what a good family is. I've never had one. I've seen other families, but what are they like when no one else is around? Are they like mine?"

His family hadn't always been separated. When he was young, surely he had to have had some kind of exposure to what made a family work.

"I didn't have a close relationship with my father," he said as though reading her thoughts. "But I do think he did love my mother. I remember them together. Up until the end, they got along well. I just don't remember much interaction from my father. He worked and came home for dinner most nights. Except when he was out killing men who reminded him of my uncle Big J Colton."

Then he had learned something from seeing his parents together when they were in love. Trevor was a gentle lover. He treated women with respect and kindness. Fatherhood and family would come naturally to him. But he didn't believe that.

Jocelyn's reticence over this fake marriage intensified. He didn't believe they'd make it as a family. He didn't believe he had what it took to give his child a loving home. He didn't believe he'd ever love her.

Feeling his hand on her forearm, Jocelyn realized she'd looked off across the restaurant with those despondent thoughts.

"I haven't given up on this marriage, Jocelyn. We have something between us. While I hope it grows into more, I do worry about what kind of message I'll send my son or daughter if we don't fall in love. Maybe my father has tainted my confidence. Sometimes I wonder if the good memories I have are based on a lie, and being a dad scares me." He touched her chin as he had before. "But I want what you want, Jocelyn. I want a family. I want us to work. For real."

She melted on the inside. He did care. She did mean something to him. And she believed him.

When he kissed her this time, she lost awareness of everything but him. She felt his caring all the way through her. It rang with truth.

She moved back when the waitress arrived with their food. Jocelyn had to shake herself free of the drugging effect of Trevor's kiss—and his words.

I want us to work. For real…

She saw the waitress eyeing her warily but Trevor with a tiny smile. She'd seen him kiss her again. Had Trevor done it on purpose?

That kiss had not felt staged. Even if he'd planned for it to seem that way, he must have felt it as much as she had.

Back to acting her part as a terrible patron.

"That took way too long," Jocelyn said to the waitress. "What did you do back there? Kill the cow? This burger is probably too cold now." With jerky movements, Jocelyn used her knife to cut into it.

The waitress wrung her hands again, nervous and apprehensive.

Jocelyn slammed the knife and fork down. "This is medium-well. I asked for well-done. Take this crap away from me." She shoved the plate down the table.

Other diners turned their heads in their direction.

"Ma'am, I—"

"What's the matter with you?" She shot daggers at the woman with her eyes, wondering if she was overdoing this. Maybe she should have tried to become an actress instead of an FBI agent. "Don't you know how to do your job? Waitressing isn't that difficult. Get rid of this gross food and bring me what I asked for."

Tears sprang to the woman's eyes. Jocelyn saw, instantly horrified. With a sob, the waitress ran toward the back of the restaurant.

"Oh my God." Jocelyn stood, feeling terrible that she'd obviously upset the wrong woman. Regina would not have burst into tears like that.

Trevor let her out of the booth and she hurried after the woman. Going through the swinging double doors, she entered the kitchen, stopping short when she found herself in the kitchen and a cook had his hand on the waitress's back.

"I'm sorry," the waitress said to the cook between gasps for air and sobs. "I've had such a bad week. My husband left me for a younger woman and my mom just told me she has cancer last night. There's a customer out there who isn't happy with her meal. Will you deal with her, please? I think I need to go home."

Jocelyn felt two inches high.

The cook saw her. "Is that her?"

The waitress wiped her face and smoothed her apron as she turned. "Someone will cook your hamburger the way you like it."

"Oh." Jocelyn walked to her. "Screw the burger. I am so sorry. So very sorry." She dug into her back pocket and retrieved her badge. "I'm an FBI agent. I'm here with my partner doing a stakeout. All of that." She waved toward the dining area. "Was all an act. You look like the subject we're trying to find. But you're obviously not her."

"W-what?"

Trevor appeared next to Jocelyn. He showed the woman his badge. "We didn't mean to upset you."

"You didn't." The waitress pointed slowly to Jocelyn, confused. "She did."

"We're posing as husband and wife to draw our subject out," Jocelyn said.

"You pretended to be married?" the waitress asked, looking from Trevor back to Jocelyn, not believing.

Had they acted that well? Maybe they hadn't acted at all…

"Well, no, not really," Jocelyn stammered. "I mean,

we are married. We work together and we're married. We just got married. This week, in fact."

The waitress looked from her to Trevor, not understanding. Why had they said they were pretending?

"Anyway," Jocelyn said. "We're sorry to have upset you."

"Who are you trying to find?"

Revealing too much may tip off Regina. If word spread that two agents had posed but not really posed as a married couple to try to draw out a serial killer, they might damage their sting operation. The damage may already be done, but no way could Jocelyn leave without making things right with this woman.

"Thank you for your cooperation." Trevor took her arm and guided her toward the exit.

Chapter 7

Trevor watched Jocelyn light a tall candle in the center of the table in their second-story apartment. On a slim budget, the bureau had put together a cozy place for them. The two-bedroom apartment had an open living room, the biggest room, with a kitchen island and a small rectangular table—just enough to seat two. Jocelyn sent him another of her side glances. She'd been looking at him that way ever since the restaurant. He had encouraged her too much. He didn't want to mislead her, not when he felt so mixed up.

Life had swept him up onto a fanciful sled and now he careened down a slippery slope. No control. No way of predicting the future. He'd never felt this way before. And he didn't like it. One day he'd been going through his days as every other, working, investigating, no doubt as to where he headed, and the next his whole world had flipped inside out.

Jocelyn had cast a spell on him. He couldn't pinpoint when or how…well, how he had a pretty good idea. Especially when she leaned down to put a plate of steaming spaghetti in front of him. That low top enticed him. Those flashing eyes and upturned mouth.

"What has you so happy?" he asked.

She put her own plate down and sat. They hadn't had a chance to eat at the restaurant. He was starving. But if she kept this up, he wouldn't be hungry for anything except her.

"You," she said.

Away he went on his slippery slope again. He'd told her he wanted her and this family—for real. He'd spoken the words but felt conflicting emotions. The truth was, he wasn't at all sure about this. Leading her to believe anything else would upset her, though, so he hadn't explained.

"Don't worry, sweetheart." Jocelyn twirled her fork in the juicy spaghetti and lifted it to her mouth. "You'll get the hang of this." She put a bite into her mouth.

He'd made his declarations and she knew he was still out of sorts over their marriage, the baby. She may have the wrong idea, may be too confident in her assessment of his feelings. Love didn't describe his inner turmoil. Or fear of it. He wasn't sure what did.

Her beautiful eyes sparkled, flirting and content. He couldn't look away.

She amazed him. And magnetized him. Drew him into her, faster than he was comfortable.

He decided to let her be happy. He liked seeing her that way. Her happiness would cultivate a good family. Their child would have a healthy home.

He grew disconcerted when Jocelyn put down her

fork and pushed her chair back to stand. She moved to him. The look in her eyes spelled trouble.

When she reached his chair, she straddled him and sat.

"What are you doing?"

She looked down at his mouth, where the words had come out raspy. "Playing your wife."

He didn't understand. But when her mouth touched his, fire roared to life and he understood. She kissed him once, and again. Then raised her head.

"You can't tell me you don't feel that."

"Oh, I feel it." That wasn't the issue.

Putting her hands on each side of his face, she said, "That's all we need for now."

Trevor wished he felt as sure as her.

The next morning, Trevor got a lead on where to find Hershel, Erica Morgan's ex-boyfriend. They'd tracked him to Houston, where he'd gotten a job as a controller at a start-up technology corporation. He'd been there a few months and several years at his previous place of employment. Steady at work. Married once for ten years, but not since. He seemed a decent guy, but appearances could be deceiving.

Trevor and Jocelyn followed him to a nearby pub, where he went to the bar and sat alone. Professional worker who partook in happy hour on a regular basis. Finance could be stressful. So could women.

Jocelyn stood on one side of the man and Trevor the other, each showing him their badge.

Hershel looked from her to him, alert and apprehensive. A well-dressed, neatly trimmed man, he'd loosened his tie a bit and his face looked a little drawn beyond his surprise.

After some quick introductions, he asked, "What do you want with me?"

"You were seeing Erica Morgan before she was murdered," Trevor said, tucking his wallet back into the inside pocket of his jacket.

Jocelyn clipped hers to her belt.

"Yeah. So? Do I need a lawyer?"

He was awfully defensive. And he knew not to talk. Experienced criminal? He had no priors.

"We're just here to talk," Trevor said.

"How'd you find out about me?"

"Caressa Franklin gave us your name," Jocelyn said. "She and Erica were friends. But I'm sure you knew that."

Trevor saw how he looked sharply at her and then returned his attention to his beer.

"How do you know Caressa?" Jocelyn asked.

Pride rose up in Trevor when she thought to ask that question. Hershel might expect them to ask his association with Erica, but not so much Caressa.

"Erica talked about her, but I don't know her. She said she was going to go see her and try to patch things up."

"She told you about their estrangement?" Trevor asked.

He shrugged and drank a gulp of beer. "Yeah. It bothered her, especially toward the end."

Trevor caught onto the way he added the last part. "What happened toward the end?" The end of what?

"Ah… I just mean…before she was killed."

Trevor wondered if that was all he meant.

"Weren't you two split up? You and Erica?" Jocelyn asked. "Toward the end?"

He loved how she tagged that onto her well-planted question.

"Yeah, but we still talked," Hershel said.

"Did she break up with you?" Trevor asked, forcing himself to concentrate.

"She needed space."

Wasn't that what they all said when they just wanted to get away? Jocelyn looked over at Trevor. He'd said pretty much the same to her after they'd had sex the first time.

"Were you upset about that?"

Hershel smirked at Trevor. "Why? Do you think I'd kill her for breaking up with me?"

Trevor said nothing.

"When is the last time you saw her?" Jocelyn asked.

The man still seemed apprehensive, nervous, as he searched his memory. Then he said, "I met her at that all-night diner a day or two before she was killed."

"Which was it? A day or two?" Jocelyn probed.

"I can't remember," Hershel answered, irritated. Or was he defensive?

"Why did you meet her?" Trevor asked.

He turned to him. "I picked her up after she met a woman there. She said her name was Josie Colton." Hershel's gaze roamed down to the pocket where Trevor had put away his badge. He'd seen his name.

Jocelyn's brow twitched. Trevor felt the same confusion.

"Erica met with Josie?" A glance at Jocelyn told him she didn't believe this, either. Josie hadn't returned to Granite Gulch until after Erica's murder.

"Are you sure it was Josie Colton?" Trevor asked. "Did you meet her?"

"Yeah, I'm sure. Erica introduced me to her before we left."

"Why did you pick up Erica if you'd broken things off?" Jocelyn asked.

Herschel adjusted himself on the stool as though to get comfortable. "Erica and I have always been on and off. We split up, but we stayed in touch. We were friends." Regretfully, he looked away and Trevor could see he told the truth. "That's why we never gave up, not completely."

"Why did you break up?"

"Like I said, she needed space." After a bit, he shrugged again and added, "We fought a lot. Couldn't seem to find common ground." He looked up at Jocelyn. "But I wanted to try."

If he felt so much for Erica, why lie about Josie? Hershel may not know the FBI had a strong suspect in Regina Willard. For some reason, he feared implication. Did he know something about Erica's murder or was he lying to throw them off? Why else bring up Josie Colton?

"Where were you when Erica was murdered?" Trevor asked.

"I was home." He shifted his gaze to Trevor, holding up his beer. "I was home," he repeated before taking a long drink.

Not a detective to leave any suspect uninvestigated, Jocelyn asked, "Would you come to the station to give your statement? Maybe provide up a DNA sample? We'd like to eliminate you as a suspect."

"I have nothing to say to you. And you don't need my DNA. I didn't kill Erica. I loved her." He dug into his pants pocket and opened his wallet. Dropping cash on the bar, he stood up, making Trevor take a step back.

"Josie Colton couldn't have killed Erica," Jocelyn said.

Trevor didn't think her last attempt to keep him from walking out the door would work.

"She was in witness protection," she went on. "Living in another city at the time of Erica's death."

Hershel stopped and faced her in disbelief.

Trevor removed his wallet once again, this time to take out a business card. He handed it to the man. "In case you change your mind and decide to come talk to us some more."

Snatching the card, Hershel turned his back and headed for the door.

"What do you think of that?" Jocelyn asked.

"I think something has him spooked."

The flash of blue jolted Josie awake. The book she held dropped to the coffee shop tabletop and she realized she'd drifted off into one of those half-asleep nods. She'd hoped the light, action-packed story would distract her enough to relax, forget the years she'd spent looking over her shoulder. Rubbing the back of her neck, she picked up the book and noticed the sun had set. Well, at least the book had been good enough to give her an escape for a while.

Outside, a warm breeze carried the remnants of a hot Texas day. She walked toward the street where she'd rented a redbrick colonial town house, passing beneath the bright illumination of streetlamps and through the darkened spaces between. Turning off Main, she headed down a side street, noticing her porch light had burned out. As she drew nearer, though, she saw the light had been broken.

She stopped, breath catching, heart jumping into flighty beats.

Nothing moved in the shadows. A car passed on the street. Just one. The otherwise quiet night seemed peaceful, but foreboding sent her on high alert. Approaching the porch, she saw broken glass from the light fixture scattered on the wood planks. It had been fine this morning. Who would do this? Someone who wanted her porch dark for when she arrived home?

Stepping back, she took out her phone and called Trevor. Turning to hurry back toward Main, she glanced back in time to see a figure taking shape in the shadows on her porch.

"Just who we need to talk to," her brother said. "Where are you?"

The dark figure raised a gun. Josie screamed and ducked behind a tree as the first shot exploded. If she ran toward Main, she'd be in direct line of fire. Looking the other way, she could take cover at the side of her building and make a run for the strip mall.

"Josie?" She'd lowered her phone but heard her brother's yell.

She lifted the phone, checking on the figure and seeing it move to the steps.

"Someone is shooting at me!" She ran for the side of the building.

Two more shots cracked through the night, one hitting the building just as she reached the side.

Trevor swerved around the turn onto Josie's street and screeched to a stop at the curb in front of her town house. They'd been on their way here when she'd called. He caught sight of something disappearing around the next street corner. Josie's complex took up a block, flanked by other houses and some commercial businesses.

Readying his pistol, Trevor alighted from the SUV, leaving it running as he ran toward the corner of the building. Passing Josie's porch, he saw the broken light fixture. Someone had planned to wait for her, to attack. The broken light would be enough to tip off most. Whoever had done it hadn't planned well. In a hurry? Or not the best criminal?

Jocelyn ran with him, gun drawn, as well. At the corner of the building, he paused to check for whomever he'd seen. No movement, but clouds made the night inky black.

Where was Josie? He kept his fear in check as he searched the darkness.

The explosion of gunfire made him duck for the cover of brick siding. Jocelyn leaned against the stone beside him. He wished she had stayed in the SUV, but he also knew the request—no, the demand would go unheeded.

Things settled down early in this neighborhood. No one walked the street. A car drove by and another turned into the parking lot of the strip mall. Screams followed by a gunshot coming from the pizza restaurant turned him in that direction. The woman who'd pulled to a stop in front of the place got back into her car, cell phone to her ear and reversing to get away. She'd call for help.

Jocelyn ran beside him, gun drawn and aimed at the ground for now. He ran ahead of her so he'd reach the entrance first. More screams spread as the diners saw them.

"FBI! Stay down!" Trevor shouted, more to calm them down than to protect them. He saw right away that the shooter wasn't there anymore.

He ran through the dining area and into the kitchen. Cooks and waitresses cowered behind stainless steel counters and appliances. The back dock door was open.

He jumped down and turned to help Jocelyn, but she'd already jumped after him. Searching the alley, he didn't see anything but heard another gunshot in the commercial space next to the pizza restaurant. The back door had been kicked in. Windows still had stickers on them and a Dumpster full of debris indicated renovations were underway.

Easing into the darkened building, he didn't see or hear anything. Jocelyn covered him as he moved and searched.

She tapped his shoulder and pointed her gun to the far corner. The space was open with one wall extending out near the back door.

The shape ducked out of sight.

Trevor stepped to the end of the wall and peered around it. Stacks of plywood and hanging plastic blocked his view.

Where was Josie?

Jocelyn pointed two fingers from her to the far end of the plywood and then from him to the nearest side.

He shook his head and pointed from himself to the far end and from her to the nearest.

Pursing her lips, she shook her head.

He jabbed his fingers harder, repeating his order. She'd better do as he said. He was still her boss.

With a roll of her eyes, she headed for the nearest end.

Trevor took the far end, inching to the edge, glancing back to make sure Jocelyn took the same precaution. She had, meeting his look with a nod, a sign for him to make the first move. Her respect for his authority rushed in with adrenaline. He peered around the plywood—and saw Josie just as the shape of someone in an oversize hoodie appeared from around the other side.

Trevor grabbed his sister's arm and yanked her out of the way. She sprawled on the concrete floor with a grunt as Trevor fired his pistol.

The gunman jumped back behind the plywood. Trevor ran there, pausing to look around the corner. The gunman ran in Jocelyn's direction.

"Jocelyn!"

"I got it!"

Did she? He checked on Josie, who'd gotten up and leaned against the plywood next to him.

"Wait here," he said to Josie and retraced his steps to the other side of the plywood.

The gunman ran out from behind the plywood on Jocelyn's end, firing a gun. Jocelyn ducked for cover.

"FBI! Stop!" Jocelyn yelled at the same time as him.

They both ran after the person. Trevor didn't want to kill the shooter. He couldn't tell if it was a man or a woman. He needed to identify the person.

Out the back door, he and Jocelyn stopped, aiming weapons, covering each other as they searched the alley. The person in the hoodie was gone, vanished as though a ghost. The back door to the pizza restaurant was closed, the alley void of people. Everyone had taken shelter.

The sound of sirens assured the gunman would flee as fast and far as possible.

"You got here fast."

Trevor lowered his weapon and turned to his sister.

"We were on our way when you called." Jocelyn put her pistol into her holster, drawing Trevor's eye to what he knew to be a soft, smooth hip. "We talked to Erica Morgan's ex-boyfriend. Just came from there. He had some interesting things to say about you."

Josie drew her head back in surprise. "Me? Who's Erica Morgan?" Then dawning came to her. "Isn't she one of the Alphabet Killer's victims?"

Just as Trevor had suspected, Josie didn't know Erica, much less her boyfriend. "Yes. Hershel Stewart was her ex-boyfriend. He claims to have seen you with Erica before she was killed. Apparently you met her for lunch."

Josie screwed up her face to that news. "What? I didn't have lunch with Erica, and I don't even know anyone named Hershel Stewart. Who is he and what does he have to do with Regina?"

"We aren't sure yet. We thought he lied, so we came to talk to you about it." He glanced up and down the alley, hearing sirens stop in front of the pizza restaurant. They'd have to answer questions. The chief would need to know what happened.

"We think he's hiding something," Jocelyn said, starting to walk toward the back door of the pizza restaurant. "Or afraid of being accused of something he didn't do."

Trevor loved how she thought the same as him. They almost didn't need to talk out loud. Usually they were on the same track—except when she insisted on posing as bait. But even then, Trevor had to admit if she wasn't pregnant and he didn't want to get naked with her all the time, he'd agree it was a good idea.

"Do you think he could be the killer and not Regina?" Josie asked.

"He looks guilty, lying the way he did, but Regina wrote the letter with the bull's-eye to Matthew," Jocelyn said.

The killer had to be female. Trevor didn't think they were wrong about that. Regina was still their strongest suspect. But Hershel must know something about Erica's death, or he wouldn't have lied to cover his tracks.

"It's the kingpin," Josie said. "It has to be. One of them must still be on the loose."

"That makes no sense," Trevor countered. "How could the kingpin be related to Erica's murder?"

"Maybe this gunman isn't related," Jocelyn said.

"Right. Kingpin." Josie stopped at the pizza restaurant door.

"No." Trevor shook his head. "That's not possible. This is something different."

"Stalker." Jocelyn reached for the door handle, but it was locked.

"Stalkers don't kill their victims. That's the whole point in stalking. They savor the lurking and scaring." Trevor knocked on the door and then looked at his sister. "Erica had a red bull's-eye on her forehead and your ex-fiancé was seen with a woman with long dark hair. That's what had everyone thinking you were the Alphabet Killer."

Josie considered that a moment. "You really think this is connected to the murders?"

"I think it's possible."

"Hershel could be trying to put more suspicion on you," Jocelyn said. "He doesn't know about Regina Willard, or doesn't believe she's the killer."

Josie mulled that over, not resisting the plausibility. "A copycat of a copycat?"

The back door opened and an officer appeared. Trevor showed him his badge.

With Trevor worried about Josie, Jocelyn walked with him to the All Night Diner. He'd put an agent on Josie, but he'd gone to the bathroom when she left the house. A call to her confirmed she'd gone with Chris and Holly for lunch. Inside the entry, Jocelyn looked for the waitress she'd hurt but didn't see her. Probably, she'd taken some time off to recover...

Chris and his fiancée headed for them ahead of Josie. They'd just finished lunch.

"Hey, big brother." Chris leaned in for a hug. "You here for lunch?"

Chris's demeanor with Trevor had changed drastically since they'd talked. Trevor stepped back from the embrace. He finally had his little brother back.

"Josie's bodyguard lost track of her," Trevor said.

"And being the protector he is," Jocelyn said in her teasing tone, "he had to come see for himself that you were all right."

"Hi, Jocelyn." Josie said, and then to her brother, "I am capable to taking care of myself, you know."

"Don't even start that," he said.

"Jocelyn, it's good to see you again." Holly smiled and gave her hand a squeeze, which Jocelyn found peculiar. She'd never been this chummy with her before.

Beside Holly, Chris grinned in a similar way. Both

wore expressions as though they'd just been let in on a secret—that involved Jocelyn.

They made a striking couple; Chris, tall and muscular with bright blue eyes and dark blond hair that made them really stand out, and Holly, whose willowy figure and long blond hair would be the envy of lots of women. From what Jocelyn had heard, Chris had been her knight in shining armor, saving Holly from her malicious in-laws.

Through the course of the investigation, Jocelyn had run into Trevor's family this way, whenever she was with him and their paths crossed. Although, the encounters had always been professional. This felt… more personal.

Holly glanced down as she released Jocelyn's hand. Jocelyn saw her catch sight of her other hand. Chris followed Holly's gaze.

Jocelyn tucked her left hand behind her leg a bit, but it was too late.

"What's this?" Holly took Jocelyn's left hand to inspect the ring, looking over at Trevor with an open mouth.

Josie smiled. "He's got one, too."

Chris looked up at his brother. "What have you been holding back from us?"

He seemed almost injurious. What had caused that reaction? She checked Trevor and couldn't tell how he felt. Were he and his brother close?

"We were married earlier this week." He turned with a proud grin to Jocelyn. "Jocelyn is pregnant."

Was he acting? Jocelyn eyed him as she tried to decipher his expression.

Josie inhaled. Holly put her hand to her upper chest. And Chris took a second to recover.

"Why didn't you tell us?" Chris asked, his hurt obvious.

"It happened so fast. And with everything going on, this is the first chance I had."

Jocelyn had to agree there. "Shotgun."

Trevor sent her an unappreciative look.

"Of all the Colton boys, I'd have thought you'd be the last to get hitched," Josie said.

Why? Jocelyn wanted to ask but kept quiet.

"Congratulations, Trevor." Chris stepped forward to give him a brotherly pat, no longer injured.

"We have to have a party for you." Josie looked at Jocelyn. "You didn't have a shower, did you?"

Jocelyn shook her head. She didn't really need one.

"And a bachelorette party." Holly winked.

"Oh, you don't have to go to all that trouble."

"It's no trouble. You're part of the family now," Josie said.

An unmarked, dark sedan pulled to the curb in front of the restaurant. Josie's agent. He looked apologetically at Trevor when he got out and waited for her to get in.

"I'm only doing this for you." Josie rose up onto her toes to kiss Trevor's cheek. Then she headed for the car. There, she turned back. "I'll be in touch with the party details." She waved cheerily.

Jocelyn waved back with considerably less enthusiasm. She found little point in celebrating a fake marriage. The baby was a different matter.

"We should get going, too," Chris said. "We promised to meet Ethan this afternoon."

"Good seeing you." Trevor hugged him.

Again, Jocelyn noticed the stiffness between them. Watching them walk down the sidewalk as the car drove away, Jocelyn asked, "What's going on between the two of you?"

Trevor shot a glance her way, clearly surprised she'd picked up on the vibes between him and Chris. "Nothing." He started walking.

She walked beside him. "You seem like…" What was the word? "Strangers. And yet, you're not."

"Being sent to separate foster homes does that to family members."

He'd grown surly. The state had torn his family apart. Jocelyn could see how that would distance the siblings, but where had the tension come from? Chris was younger than Trevor.

"Did he feel abandoned?" she asked.

"You're too insightful, Jocelyn. Yes. He thought I didn't try to get custody of him. Now he knows I did try. We're getting close again."

His adolescence had such a profound impact on him. He sounded upset, or unsettled, at odds. Uncomfortable. As though the closeness bothered him. As a teenager, he'd learned to harden himself to his circumstances. Now, as an adult, he couldn't break the wall.

No wonder he'd rushed into marriage. Had he given it any further thought, he'd have surely backed out.

Chapter 8

Trevor enjoyed the art of interrogation. Picking out details subjects sometimes didn't realize they'd missed, and getting them to fall into his trap. Waiting until the last minute to show them what he knew about them, expose them for liars.

Why did the chase appeal to him so much? He never liked to go down that dark path. Because he liked the chase. He *liked* catching killers. He *liked* looking into their empty eyes with life in his, letting them know he'd beat their evil game. But he never liked facing *why*. The unquenchable thirst of beating, catching and punishing his father—over and over again—was what drove him. Would he ever escape the need to bury the ugliness of what his father had done?

Hershel Stewart sat with his dirty, jeans-clad legs open, leaning back, eyes unblinking and waiting for the questions to begin. He'd been through this before. Trevor had his sheet. He knew his rights. Knew the system. He'd play it until Trevor was forced to let him walk. Trevor knew he was innocent. And yet he'd lied. The guilty always lied, but sometimes the innocent lied.

Trevor had thought this through in detail. Hershel wasn't guilty. Not of murder. But he might reveal something significant. He'd asked Jocelyn to stay in the room behind one-way glass. This would be a man-to-man talk. Hershel might feel safer to talk that way.

Hershel lived by street code. No white picket fence childhood for this kid. Typical tragedy. Except his soul hadn't given up the fight, not completely.

"You were never a suspect in Erica Morgan's murder," Trevor said.

The straightforward announcement elicited a slow, comprehensive blink in Hershel.

"We're looking for a woman who works as a waitress," he said. "I can't discuss many details."

Trevor sat down across from him and folded his hands on the table.

Hershel leaned forward, hands flat on the table. "Then why am I here?"

"How do you know Josie Colton?" He treated her as a person involved in the investigation, not his sister. Making it too personal might lose him some ground. Keep it friendly, nonthreatening and never personal. Criminals talked when compelled.

"She's your sister."

"You…know her because she's my sister?"

"I didn't know that until after you came to see me. I heard she was a suspect in Erica's murder."

"Where did you hear that? Who told you?"

"I don't know, man." He sat up and leaned back in that slouching pose again. "Some friends talked at a party."

"Why did you lie about Josie meeting Erica?"

Hershel lowered his head. "I didn't lie."

"No?"

"No." After his defensive response, Hershel lifted his head. "Okay, maybe I did. But I didn't kill her. I was afraid of being pinned for Erica's murder."

"Why would you be afraid of that?"

He shrugged without looking at him. "I was her boyfriend. We split up."

Now that, Trevor believed. "Where were you the night she was killed?"

"Out drinking. A bunch of us went to Fort Worth that night."

"So, you had an alibi. Nothing to be afraid of." He kept his tone even.

"I left early."

"So, you could have gone to the crime scene in time?"

Hershel propped his elbow on the armchair and tapped his curled fingers against his chin, a nervous movement. "I thought you said you were looking for a woman."

"We are, but you lied to us. I'm trying to find out why."

"I told you." He lowered his hand.

"Tell me about Erica. You both still had feelings for each other. You wanted to get back together with her. That's not the MO of a killer."

As Trevor intended, Hershel visibly relaxed. "I love Erica. I loved her."

Trevor nodded his understanding, not saying anything to stop any inclination to keep talking.

"We just fought a lot."

He stuck with what he'd said previously.

"I wanted to talk it through, you know?" He looked imploringly at Trevor. "She liked to go to this burger place outside of town. I went there the day she was killed."

Trevor perked up to this news. Hershel had seen Erica the day of her murder, and she'd gone to a restaurant. "Where was this? What's the name of the burger restaurant?"

"Buckaroo Burgers."

"Did you see her there?"

"Yeah. She was having dinner with a man." He grew visibly hurt. "We had words. I just wanted to talk to her."

"Did you notice anything else? Did you go inside the restaurant?"

"Yeah. They were still eating. I went to their table and asked her to come outside with me to talk. She refused and said it was over. I didn't believe her."

"When you first arrived, did you notice anything about the waitstaff?"

Hershel drew his head back, not understanding the strange question. "They were ordering when I got there." He shrugged. "Erica was picky with her orders. She always took a long time."

"Did the waitress seem annoyed?"

"They all are annoyed." He breathed a laugh. "Yeah, the lady was annoyed."

"What did she look like?"

He thought a moment. "I don't really remember. I

was more into Erica. I guess she had dark hair, back in a ponytail. Average-type lady. Nothing special to look at. I don't remember much about her." He looked closer at Trevor. "You think the waitress killed her?"

"We're looking at every possibility. Why did you say you saw Josie with Erica?"

"Everybody said she was a suspect."

Trever wasn't sure if he picked up on some hesitation in Hershel's tone. Had he tried to put more suspicion on Josie and off himself? Possibly.

Deciding he had enough for now, Trevor said, "Thanks for talking to me today. You're free to go."

Trevor left the interrogation room, excited for this lead.

Jocelyn came striding with equal excitement out of the observation room. "Do you think she could still work there?"

"If Erica's waitress was our subject, maybe. She could work for more than one restaurant."

"She's been so hard to track, though."

"Let's go talk to the manager there."

Jocelyn stopped, putting her hand on his bicep to make him do the same.

The force of it did nothing to that end, but the contact made him aware of her physically and that had more to do with it. Call it heat. Heat stopped him, or the opportunity it presented his man instincts.

"No," she said adamantly. "You have to send another agent, and you have to do it quietly. We'll go there for dinner tonight."

"Why not go right now?"

"Dinner. I need time to get ready." With that, she

lowered her hand and walked away, glancing back with a sexy wink.

Great. He was in for some torture. Sweet torture.

Jocelyn dressed sexy for a very specific purpose. While her pregnancy still didn't show, she could get away with this figure-hugging black number. Tease Trevor. Make him admit the mistake in rushing into this marriage. She'd just have to ignore the other, nagging desire to also make him realize what a catch she was, family package and all. Entering the restaurant with burning heat that had ignited the moment he'd seen her come out of the bedroom, she felt emboldened.

He held the door for her and their gazes locked as she passed by, feeling his warm breath and then his hand on her lower back. At their table, he pulled out her chair and she sat down.

"See? It's not so tough being a gentleman," she said.

He sat across from her, his dark eyes never leaving her. "I'm a gentleman?"

"But we're supposed to be working, Agent Colton." She didn't even have to try to put the sultry tone in her voice. Is this how he behaved outside of work? "You're crossing your own line."

"We are working. We're a couple out for dinner. A married couple." He glanced around the restaurant.

Jocelyn did, too, looking for a waitress who might fit the description of Regina Willard. Not seeing anyone, she turned back to Trevor. "So, you're just acting?"

The left side of his mouth hitched up. "I don't have to act when I'm with you. Didn't you notice the night I got you pregnant?"

It wasn't like Trevor to be this blunt—especially

regarding intimacy. He hadn't pretended that night. Neither had she.

"I want what you want, Jocelyn."

What was that? A family? House, kids, dog and a cat? Everything? "You're saying…this is real." For him?

He reached across the table and put his hand over hers. "I'm saying I'd like to give it a real shot."

Tingles chased up from where he touched. Dare she believe him? Trust in this? She needed to be sure. "But…you never wanted a family. You might have thought you did, but you didn't."

He turned his head away as the truth of that sank in. For a moment she thought she'd be disappointed, that he'd withdraw and agree.

"What family I knew was taken from me." When his dark, sexy eyes met hers again, warmth hugged her. He wasn't going to give up. "Now I have a chance to make another of my own. I'll do all I can to keep us together."

Oh. Jocelyn would never have dreamed he'd say something like that. She entwined her fingers with his, falling deeper and deeper into an infatuated abyss. After her dad and brother were killed, she'd gotten lost in loneliness. Only the assurance that someday she'd have a family of her own pulled her through. Now that day seemed to have arrived. If she trusted it…trusted Trevor.

"What can I get you to drink?"

Jarred from the sweet exchange, she looked up at the waitress. Blond-haired, blue-eyed and much too young to be Regina, the woman looked at Jocelyn expectantly.

"Water is fine for me," she said.

"Iced tea," Trevor said.

"Are you ready to order?"

They hadn't even looked at their menus yet.

"Give us a minute." Trevor slid his menu toward him, leaning back and taking his hand with him.

Jocelyn lifted her menu, missing his hand already. Seeing a waitress across the restaurant around the right age to pass as Regina, Jocelyn watched her take the order from a woman dressed in a suit who sat next to a man, also in a suit. They appeared to be here on business, the man with a briefcase on the floor and the woman with a notepad and pen beside her plate.

She took a long time ordering and Jocelyn saw how the waitress's mouth tightened just before she forced a smile. Her hair was a medium chocolate color, but mousy-brown roots had begun to grow out.

"Hey. My three o'clock," Jocelyn said.

Trevor followed her direction.

"See the roots?"

The waitress turned from the table and walked back to the kitchen, complaining to a fellow waitress, who glanced at the table and said something back with a shake of her head.

"Too bad we weren't seated in her section," Jocelyn said.

"Keep a low profile. We'll come back."

They watched for the waitress to emerge from the kitchen. When she did, she carried a platter with three plates and took them to another table. She smiled genuinely at the family, who treated her nicely.

Back into the kitchen, then she emerged with two more plates, and this time headed for the long-order woman and her business companion. Setting the first plate in front of the man, she then placed the other in front of the blonde. The blonde looked down at her plate and then up in displeasure at the waitress. She pointed to the food and said something with a scowl marring her pretty face.

The waitress took the plate back to the kitchen.

When she reemerged with a new plate, her face was set in stone.

"That's got to be her," Jocelyn said.

"We have to be sure. I'll get an agent to come by and ask the manager about her."

"Let's not scare her away. She'll just get a new identity and go to work somewhere else."

She watched with Trevor as the blonde rudely accepted the new plate and then waved the waitress away. They ordered their own food and finished close to the same time as the business meeting wrapped up. The blonde paid.

Jocelyn saw the waitress watch the two leave. She left a check on one of her tables and then walked to the window, watching as the blonde got into one car and the man into another. But her gaze stayed on the woman as she drove out of the parking lot.

"Let's get out of here." Trevor put down some cash and stood.

Jocelyn stood with him. When the waitress went back to the kitchen, they headed for the door. Trevor passed the blonde's table and opened the black check holder and read the woman's name. Jocelyn kept her eye out for the waitress. No one other than the table next to them saw what he'd done.

Outside, he said to her, "Janice Tapp."

Her name started with a *J*.

Janice was the CEO of a local bank and lived in an upscale home west of town. Trevor and Jocelyn drove straight there after their dinner. On the front doorstep, Trevor rang the bell.

He heard footsteps on the other side of the door.

When no one answered, he said loudly. "FBI. We'd like a word with you. It's urgent."

Seconds later, the blonde cracked the door open. Her brow creased with her befuddlement.

Trevor showed her his badge. "You were just at the Buckaroo Burgers restaurant?"

"Yes. H-how did you—"

"We were just there." Jocelyn showed her badge. "Surveillance on a potential suspect. Your waitress."

"My…" She opened the door wider. "Please. Come inside."

He and Jocelyn stepped onto white marble floor, the ceiling high above. From beyond a partial wall, a television played at a low volume.

A midfifties woman in black slacks and a white long-sleeved blouse appeared from around the wall.

"Is everything all right, Ms. Tapp?"

"Yes." Janice turned to her. "You can go ahead and go now. Thank you for everything."

The woman nodded once and with a wary eye at Trevor and Jocelyn turned and vanished from view.

"My nanny. She takes care of my son while I work." She lifted her eyebrows. "Which is a lot."

"As CEO we can well imagine."

She stopped smiling and bestowed Trevor a direct look. "You're quick, Agent…"

"Colton. We looked you up on the way over."

"What's this about a waitress?"

"We're looking for a woman that fits your waitress's description in connection to some serial murders,"

Trevor said. "She's been working under false identities as a waitress in local restaurants. Are you familiar with the Alphabet Killer?"

Janice put her hand above her breasts with a gasp. "Yes. She goes after women with long dark hair and…" She put her hand up to her dark hair, which she'd clipped up into a bun. "What letter is she on?"

"*J,*" Jocelyn provided.

Janice gasped again.

"She seems to prey on rude women she serves," Jocelyn said.

"Oh my Lord." Janice covered her mouth with her hand and stepped in a stunned circle before going still facing them again. She lowered her hand. "Someone told me her fiancé ran off with another woman and she kills anyone who reminds her of the other woman."

"Yes. That's our theory," Trevor said. "That's why we came here today. Is there somewhere you can go and stay for a while? Maybe take some time off. Leave town for a week or two."

"You…you really think I'm in that much danger?"

"We'd rather not take any chances," Trevor said. "Any woman with a name that starts with *J* and has long dark hair is a risk as far as we're concerned." He looked at Jocelyn pointedly.

She gave a slight roll of her eyes and returned her attention to Janice. "And you may have had contact with the killer. We'd like to know you're safe."

"I'll… Yes… I'll take some time off. Work remotely for a week or two. Sure. Right. I've got a vacation home in the Bahamas. I'll go there."

"Good. Let us know if you notice anything in the

meantime. We'll get a tail on the waitress." Trevor guided Jocelyn to the door, opening it and ushering her outside.

"There you go again, being overly protective."

He took in her smooth gait, long, shapely legs stretching the snug skirt of the black dress, hips swaying just enough. Higher up, her breasts plumped where the bodice cupped her, firm, creamy skin tempting him. Finally moving on to her face, he caught her raised-brow look and grinned.

"It's not just you who makes me protective." It was their baby, too. "Maybe you should think about being more careful."

"I'm doing my job, Trevor. That hasn't changed. I was doing my job before I got pregnant. Jeez. I liked you better when you were being professional." Although her words leaned toward a bite, he heard flirtation, too, a sort of sultry purr. She didn't like his protectiveness from a professional standpoint, but she did from a personal one.

"You're more than one of my agents now. You're my wife."

The teasing light warmed in her beautiful eyes, and he felt a thrill over assessing her correctly.

He stopped. She faced him and a long, silent moment filled the energy between them. Lifting his hand, he caressed her cheek with his thumb.

"You're going to make a great mom."

Her slow blink told him she received his comment favorably, in opposition to her choice in profession. Maybe he overgeneralized. Moms could take on any type of career and be great moms. Jocelyn's case differed in how she'd come to her decision. It didn't matter. She fascinated him.

Without any thought over why he shouldn't, he leaned in and kissed her.

Chapter 9

Back in the apartment above the phony real estate office, Jocelyn changed into something more comfortable. The kiss had her hands reaching for a modest but alluring nightgown. The soft, stretchy sleepshirt with boyish button-up front, collar and pocket dipped low, and stopped midthigh. Ivory trim popped from black material, a boyish style, but designed to attract. How much of what the sleepshirt might bring could she take on in the morning? Or maybe a better question: How much could Trevor take?

She went with the warm wave the kiss still carried and put it on. No underwear. Might as well go all out.

Checking her hair, giving it a tousle, she went out into the open space of the living, dining and kitchen area. Soft light from the lamp beside an off-white couch touched upon teal and brown accents and the antiquated high, flat, textured ceiling. Off-white cabinets and a kitchen island topped with brown granite and more teal accents blended the room. The owner had just finished renovating and hadn't gotten to the office below when the FBI approached them to rent the space.

Not seeing Trevor, she endured a moment of regret just before she heard him emerge from the hall. Still in jeans, he'd removed his shirt. The apartment did feel a little warm, but she wondered if he had the same thing in mind as she did. His dark eyes roamed down her nightgown as he walked to the French doors, opening them to let air inside.

She went there, smelling the fresh air and following Trevor onto the deck. The building backed to rolling fields and cattle. A few other businesses dotted the road in front, growing busier closer to town. She suffered no hardship living here, away from her own home.

"Meow."

Sigmund appeared in the doorway, tail swishing leisurely. She bent to pick him up. The cat snuggled against her, going into a deep purr with sleepy eyes blinking.

Trevor reclined on one of two lounge chairs, a wood table between.

Jocelyn did the same on the vacant chair.

"I've never seen a cat seek attention like that," Trevor said.

Glad for the nonthreatening, nonsexual talk, she let Sigmund go when he'd had enough. "It's all about the owner."

Sigmund walked like a prince down the cushioned lounge chair and jumped down onto the deck. With all the time in the world, he went to Trevor's chair, jumped up and stepped onto his legs.

Trevor chuckled as Sigmund curled onto his six-pack stomach, Trevor folding his arms to create a cozy bed.

"I've never seen him warm up to anyone so quickly," Jocelyn said. "I'm a little jealous." Usually she had Sigmund's attention all to herself.

Sigmund leaned into Trevor's hand as he pet his head. "He's more like a dog than a cat."

"And you thought dogs were better."

"Maybe we should have both." Sigmund lifted his head when Trevor paused in his petting.

The way he said *we* burned into her heart. Maybe this could work. They had no shortage of desire for each other. Would it last?

"We'd have to buy a house. How attached are you to your condo?"

"What about your house?" She'd never been there, which amazed her at first, until she reminded herself that his exaggerated work ethic had kept him from inviting her.

"It's too small. Two bedroom. Not much of a yard. I went for low maintenance."

Like her with her condo. Because they were both workaholics? Each with a different reason, but both stemming from experiences with family.

"I've always imagined myself in a four-bedroom house," she said. "Maybe with a loft or an office with French doors." Or both. "Something with enough elbow room to raise kids."

He looked up from Sigmund, his hand stilling as he contemplated her. "How detailed did you imagine that?"

Detailed. Jocelyn relaxed back against the chair, gazing out into the calm night, smelling the air, feeling the warm, soft breeze, swept away on imagination.

"*Frozen*-themed bedroom for the firstborn girl. Cars or sports for the boy. Cartoon-painted walls. Vibrant colors. Toy chests. Lots of pillows and soft blankets. For me, I'd like an office where I can run a tutoring business. Teach slow-learning kids math and English, and maybe some unique history classes for others. *Lord of the Rings* style." She smiled over at him and noticed how deeply he absorbed what she said. Normally when she started talking babies and family, he changed the subject. She sighed and rested her head back against the chair, still dreaming. "I'd like to go to festivals with my husband and kids. Neighborhood barbecues. Movies. Trips to Disney World and Yellowstone and historic landmarks." When he said nothing, she rolled her head so she could see him. He watched her as though entranced by the picture she'd presented. "Haven't you ever thought of that?"

"Yes." His gruff voice held pent-up emotion. "I've thought of all I lost when Matthew killed my mother."

That doused her fantasy, but encouraged her, as well. She'd taken him down a path he hadn't taken, one filled with light and love. He followed a darker path. His imaginings centered on loss. Hers centered on abundance.

He sought a brighter future, but did he know how to obtain it? She didn't think so, and she wanted to show him the way.

Getting up from the chair, she went to him. Sigmund saw her looming and hopped down from Trevor's lap. She fully intended to take his place.

Trevor followed her movements with dark intensity. He put his hands on her hips, the soft material of her nightgown hiking up. She felt air on the underside of her buttocks. The fly of his jeans felt rough against her softness.

With her hands on each side of his stubbly face, she leaned in and kissed him, much as he'd done before. Swirling fire took her.

His hands moved up her sides to her breasts. Their joined mouths and his caressing hands made her pulse soar.

When his hands slid back down her sides and over her rear, she stopped kissing him. As he touched bare flesh, his eyes opened. Steaming passion flared there.

Breathing through her mouth, Jocelyn moved back to unbutton his jeans. He watched her with those smoldering eyes, lifting his hips so she could push down his pants and boxers out of the way just enough.

Rising up on her knees, she guided him while his hands tightened on her rear. Easing down on his thick circumference, she felt his iron-rod hardness stretch her. With her hands on his chest, she tipped her head back to sheer ecstasy as he kneaded her while she took him all the way inside of her.

Burning hot for him, she moved her hips back and forth, starting a mild grind. The friction, the open air, his dark eyes, all sent her senses flying.

He urged her for more, not moving his hips, letting her set the pace.

She gyrated her hips, circular grinding that grew wilder with raging passion. She came with a building climax that erupted into mindless beauty.

Trevor groaned and laid her back on the chair, with her head at the edge of the foot end. Her knees up and open, he reentered her with a hard shove. She leveraged herself with her heels on the arms of the chair. He thrust into her several times, mounting with urgency until he reached his peak, leaving nothing but awe when he finished.

The next day, Trevor took Jocelyn to lunch at Buckaroo Burgers. He'd just been briefed on the interview with the general manager, who'd sworn he wouldn't say anything to the waitress. Last night kept playing sweet reruns, tormenting him into heated fantasies and distracting him in a major way. Jocelyn's occasional bedroom-eyed glances weren't helping. He'd caught her looking at him more than once and could tell she had last night on her mind, too.

"She's worked here for months?" Jocelyn asked, bringing him back to the present. "How is it that we never caught on to her?"

"It's remote. And according to the manager, she worked other jobs."

He held the door for her. At least today she wasn't wearing a slinky black dress. Still, she'd put on tight jeans and a low-cut top that when stretched he could see the protrusion of her nipples. Did his presence do that to her? Memories of last night? It was a warm Texas day, so it couldn't be from cold.

He spotted the Regina look-alike. The manager had also told them what her shift was for today. She worked the lunch.

"We'd like a table over there," Jocelyn said to the hostess, who led them to the waitress's section.

Sitting down, Trevor watched Jocelyn get into her role, readying herself to annoy their possible suspect. Except every time she looked at him, sparks renewed.

They'd both been a little awkward with each other.

Jocelyn had noticed Trevor's wariness when they woke this morning. But as soon as she kissed him, he melted all over again. It felt so great. She couldn't believe this turn in their relationship. She felt lucky. Blessed. And on her way to a great love affair—with her new husband.

Even now she caught him looking at her with those dark, intense eyes.

She smiled and saw the effect on him. She loved that, how she turned him on so easily. He did the same for her. Did the newness do that, the excitement of being intimate with someone new? Someone she knew but not as deeply as a wife should. Naughty for making love after rushing into a marriage.

"Would you like anything to drink?"

Jocelyn looked with Trevor up at their waitress. Her name tag read Sally Reed.

"I'll have a glass of water with very little ice."

Sally's eyes rolled half-lidded to her as she wrote on her order book.

"Coke for me."

She caught Trevor's struggle not to grin over her acting.

"Do you know what you'd like to order yet?"

"How would we know that? We just sat down," Jocelyn said.

With impressive restraint, Sally said, "I'll give you a few minutes, then."

"Thanks," Trevor said.

The waitress smiled at him and left.

"She might not be Regina. Don't upset her too much."

Jocelyn didn't want to upset another innocent waitress, but they had to be sure. "I'll apologize if I'm wrong, but you saw her. She fits the description. Did you see her roots?"

"Yes, I saw her roots. She does fit the description. But I'm concerned word has spread that we're visiting restaurants."

Her last apology ran through her mind and she realized he'd allowed her to do so for personal reasons. "You want them to find out this is a sting op?"

"No. But I confess, I didn't stop you because if we are discovered, you're safer. Just the way I want you. Safe."

"Trevor…" He injured her with his lack of faith. "I'm good at my job."

"No argument there. You are good. But I think you'll make a much better mother." He reached across the table and she couldn't resist the warmth of his hand over hers.

He'd expressed his opinion before, but this time she heard his sincerity. And after last night, she trusted him. He didn't mean it as an insult.

The waitress returned with a plastered smile. "Have we decided yet or do you need more time?"

"Oh." Jocelyn made a show of picking up her menu, regretting she had to pull her hand away from Trevor's. "I've been so busy talking to my husband that I forgot to look." She beamed a haughty smile back at Sally.

"That's okay." Sally tucked her book away. "I'll come back momentarily."

Jocelyn dismissed her, saying directly to Trevor, "What do you like here? I love burgers."

He opened the menu with a curbed grin. "The mushroom burger is good."

Sally walked away.

"Is it?"

"You can stop acting now. No. The burgers aren't that good here. I'd get a salad or a club sandwich."

"I'll do a burger. Mushroom it is." She closed the menu and looked for Sally. She'd gone to another table.

When Sally finished taking the order from a trio of women, she glanced their way. Jocelyn did her best to be annoying as she waved her to come back.

Without a smile, Sally walked to their table. "All decided?"

"Yes. I'll have the mushroom hamburger, but please make sure you tell the chef to cook it medium-well."

"And for you, sir?" Sally said to Trevor.

"The club sandwich."

"And your side?"

"Fries."

"Oh. You didn't ask me about my side," Jocelyn said. "I want fries, but they have to be crispy."

"Of course." Sally plastered on another smile and left.

"I think it's her," Jocelyn said in a loud whisper.

"Easy," he calmed her.

"Don't you?"

She watched him hesitate, but in the end he couldn't contain his eagerness any more than she could. "Yes. But let's not give ourselves away."

He was right, of course. Jocelyn sobered. "We should focus on our roles." Deliberately goading, she extended her arm across the table and curled her fingers over his. "Husband."

"Stop it."

"Stop what? You *are* my husband."

"Yeah, but you don't believe it yet."

"Maybe I'm starting to." After last night, the things

he said over dinner, and the way they'd made love, how could she resist? But did she imagine his slight reticence? He likely didn't trust her, with her mockery of their wedding.

Sally returned with their meals, placing Jocelyn's down first and then Trevor's. Jocelyn checked her burger, and although it looked delicious and cooked to perfection, she had to complain.

"I don't like any pink in my beef." She looked up at Sally. "I asked for medium-well. That's more of a dull pink."

"It was cooked medium-well."

"You're going to argue with a customer?" She pushed the plate toward her. "Take this back and bring me something cooked more."

Sally took the plate and, with a caustic look, left the table.

"You'd be dead if that look had blades," Trevor said. "Don't goad her anymore."

A few minutes later, Sally returned with tight lips and deposited the plate down. Jocelyn wondered if she'd spat in it. Checking the fries—done crispy—she nodded at Sally. "Thank you. This looks much better. The hamburger was charred, but she had to draw the line somewhere.

Without a word Sally left again and didn't return for several minutes.

"Should we go in for dessert?" Jocelyn asked.

"No. I think you've done enough."

"Stop being overprotective, Trevor. This could work if she's Regina. Let's get her good and mad so she exposes herself. Then we can arrest her and the sting will be a success." When his look of unease and disagreement remained, she added, "I'll take a leave of absence after this. Maybe I'll quit. Have our baby and stay home after he or she is born." As she spoke, she fell back into a dreamworld and saw Trevor's demeanor soften with her.

"You would do that?" he asked. "Really?"

She reached over and put her hand on his. "Yes. I promise." The uncertainty of their relationship set aside, nothing would bring her more joy than raising her baby.

He took her hand in his and gave her a thankful squeeze.

Just as another warm moment began to sizzle, Sally returned, glancing at their hands.

Jocelyn slipped her hand from Trevor's and sat back. "I was beginning to think you forgot about us," Jocelyn said, hoping she didn't sound too subdued. "You've been attending everyone else but us."

Sally's eyes narrowed briefly before she recovered. "Is there anything else you'd like?"

"Yes. Apple pie. But it has to be the right temperature. Do you think you can manage that?" If Sally was Regina, a dangerous serial killer, then Jocelyn would have no mercy on her. She'd torment her and push every button she could to make her come out.

And then she could begin her life with Trevor and their baby.

"Warm apple pie. Coming right up."

Sally returned less than five minutes later with the pie. She set the plate down hard in front of Jocelyn.

Jocelyn cut into the pie and took a bite. It was delicious. And cold. She looked up at the waitress, who watched with pleasure. She'd deliberately served her cold pie.

Of all the…

Jocelyn had to force back laughter. She dropped her fork with a loud clank onto the plate. "This pie is cold."

"Is it? Oh, my. I told them you wanted it warm. Shall I get you another piece?"

"No. You can take it out of your tip." Jocelyn ate another bite.

Fuming mad, Sally left the table, clearly no longer caring about satisfying the customer.

"Let's go. Leave her a card."

Jocelyn ate the rest of her pie, savoring every bite, and then put a real estate card on the table, writing a nasty note for Sally. Then they left the table, leaving no tip at all. The card contained the fake real estate office number.

As Jocelyn made her way through the restaurant, she spotted Sally standing at the expo window waiting for her next order of food. Mouth no longer tight, her eyes bore a lethal message to Jocelyn.

Jocelyn flipped her long dark hair and walked haughtily out of the restaurant.

Chapter 10

Everyone but Ridge and Darcy made it to the barbecue. Ridge had been called on a search and rescue mission unrelated to the Alphabet Killer, and Darcy had gone to visit a friend.

Trevor went over to Chris and gave him a manly pat on the back.

"Hey, big brother."

Trevor liked hearing him talk that way, with brotherly love in his tone.

Chris stood next to his twin sister, Annabel, and Sam. Ethan manned the grill, sending smoke billowing around his sandy-brown hair, the scent of cooking hamburgers wafting through the warm late-afternoon air. At least Jocelyn hadn't eaten her charred hamburger at Buckaroo Burgers earlier today. Josie had whipped up this family get-together as though making up for lost time, since none of the family had been invited to the wedding. Ethan had volunteered his house for the bash.

Holly swung next to Josie and the two talked with occasional smiles or laughter. The whole atmosphere touched Trevor. He'd wished for this so many times. Them. Together.

Sam strode up with a beer. "How's the investigation going?"

"You're not seriously going to talk about that today, are you?" Ethan glanced back after flipping a burger.

"It's going fine," Trevor said. Ethan didn't like talking about the case because it resembled Matthew's crimes and their mother's murder. He had been the one to find their mother dead—just before Matthew disposed of the body. No one could blame him for not liking the subject. He'd gotten better at handling it, but how could he not be affected at least to some degree? Something like that never left a person.

"Let's go inside to talk." Sam led the way.

Trevor winked at Jocelyn as he passed her talking to Lizzie and Zoe. She smiled back with intimate secrets in her eyes. He liked her reaction to him, liked even more how she'd come around to taking this marriage seriously despite the speedy rush to the altar.

Inside the office across from the bathroom, Sam pushed the door in a slow swing. It touched the door-jamb and didn't latch.

"I don't want to ruin Ethan's party," Sam said, explaining why he'd brought Trevor here.

"He is enjoying himself with any excuse to celebrate."

Sam chuckled. "As a family. It does feel good. And he's a good host."

"It's Josie's party. Ethan couldn't whip something like this together as fast." Josie had been the one to put all the balloons in the living room and dining area and corral everyone to bring presents. And Holly had brought the hors d'oeuvres and put them out on the patio table. Never mind they'd attracted a couple of flies.

"It's good to have her back."

"Yes." All of his brothers and sisters shared that sentiment, to be together again.

Sam fingered a pen sticking out of a pen holder, lapsing into thought on the past, foster homes, loneliness, everything Trevor and the others had experienced. Then he shook himself of it and turned back to Trevor.

"Anyway, the case. Has Matthew handed over any more letters?"

"Are you kidding? No. But I've been in touch with the prison. Regina hasn't written any new letters."

"So, you're still stalled?"

"Jocelyn and I made some promising headway this week. We think we may have found Regina."

Sam's eyes grew rounder with eager anticipation. "Where?"

He explained about Buckaroo Burgers and Jocelyn's fine—maybe too fine—acting job.

His brother laughed knowingly. "You have your hands full. I know the feeling."

"She's a good agent, but I wish she'd be more careful."

"Being married to her makes a big difference. She's capable, but you love the softer side of her."

Trevor tried to subdue the flinch that went through him. Love?

Sam noticed, scrutinizing him closer. "Are you and Jocelyn all right?"

"Of course. Well, as fine as we can be after rushing into this."

"Yeah. You did rush."

Trevor couldn't say he'd been consumed with joy. His reaction and resulting decision had come from more of a sense of obligation to do the right thing.

Sam's smile showed brotherly pride and joy over another Colton baby on the way. He patted Trevor's shoulder. "Don't worry. The shock will wear off."

Trevor didn't respond. Maybe Sam had a good point. Maybe he just needed time for the reality to hit, the reality of the miracle.

"Hey, I heard about the task force meeting," Sam said. "The chief told me. I bet you wanted to fight Jocelyn posing as bait, after marrying her and what with her pregnancy. We Coltons can be rather protective."

Trevor grunted. "Don't get in a room with Jocelyn. I don't need both of you against me."

"I'm not against you. I'd have reacted the same way."

"I wish she would take a leave."

"She will. Motherhood will take care of her misguided ambitions."

Misguided in that she didn't need to prove anything by being an FBI agent. Josie must have done some talking. Word spread around his siblings like a brush fire now that they were back in contact with each other. Which might not be a good thing for Trevor. Not when an uncertain future dragged him down—when he felt it shouldn't.

"Ethan and Trevor are a lot alike," Lizzie Colton said.

"All the boys have something in common," Zoe Robison said.

Jocelyn had been standing here in Ethan and Lizzie's living room engaged in refreshing girl talk with these two: Zoe, in love with Trevor's brother Sam, and Lizzie, now married to another brother, Ethan. She'd enjoyed listening to their stories, mostly about how they'd worked through some hurdles to grow into a family unit. Some of the stories were funny. Some touching. All inspiring. Jocelyn didn't feel alone. She felt connected to people who shared similar tragedies. Loss. She'd had to fend for herself, too, after her father and brother were killed.

"Ethan didn't want kids, either, until he found out our baby was his." Lizzie laughed fondly, in love with her new husband, glowing.

At first Jocelyn glowed herself as she realized she'd begun to bask in that blossoming love, with Trevor's softening toward her, and not in his role-playing as husband to a real estate agent who talked nastily to waitresses. But then Lizzie's analogy registered.

"Trevor didn't want kids?" she asked.

Lizzie's bubble of maternal joy faded. "Well…it just seemed that way. But don't worry. All the Colton kids had to overcome their separation when they were sent to foster care. They just have to…readjust. I mean… Ethan found his mother dead. Before police could get there, Matthew moved the body. That's serious baggage, right? And Trevor's had the most contact with that monster out of all of the kids. Think about it. Matthew is their dad and he's a monster."

"Yeah, but…he didn't want kids?" She supposed she shouldn't be surprised. She'd picked up on some anxiousness over having a serial killer for a father. That was bound to inject a certain amount of insecurities. But she expected fear of having kids, not unwelcome.

"He didn't want to end up failing as a father. You know, since he had such a bad role model in Matthew."

"Stop going off, Lizzie," Zoe said, a petite, beautiful woman with shoulder-length blond hair. "I know you're in the clouds with your new baby, but Jocelyn and Trevor were coworkers until he got her pregnant. Give them some time before you corner her like that."

"I didn't mean to corner her." She turned to Jocelyn. "Was I cornering you?" Lizzie put her hand on Jocelyn's arm. "I'm babbling. Trevor's in love with you. He just doesn't know it yet. That's all I was trying to say. And yes, maybe newborn baby magic has me a bit scattered right now. I'm so happy!"

"She does have a point about miracles," Zoe said, her tortoiseshell glasses showcasing her stunning blue eyes and bringing out the librarian in her. "When I met Sam, I never dreamed I'd fall for someone like Sam. And Lizzie and Ethan were both in foster care. They both know what it's like to lose parents, and not have them at critical times growing up."

"You and Sam are meant for each other," Lizzie said to Zoe, short, swooping light brown hair swinging as she moved her head with green eyes flashing energetically. "It makes perfect sense. He's a cop and your sister was murdered." She put her hand over her mouth. "Oops. Sorry. More newborn baby magic making me say things without thinking."

Zoe laughed, but her loss dimmed the sound and kept full lightness from her eyes. "Don't worry. It's true her murder did play into bringing us closer."

"That's all good." Jocelyn had to get away from them. "I have to go to the bathroom."

"See?" Zoe turned on Lizzie. "You're freaking her out."

"I didn't mean—"

Jocelyn held her hand up. "It's okay. Really. I have to go to the bathroom."

She walked toward the hallway. She liked everyone in Trevor's family, but she must not be ready to talk frankly about her and Trevor's arrangement.

"You seem regretful, Trevor. What's going on? Do you regret marrying Jocelyn?"

Hearing Sam say that, Jocelyn stopped short. There was an office across from the bathroom and the door was ajar just a little bit.

"No."

Jocelyn heard Trevor sigh. His anxiety radiated through the space separating them.

"No?"

"No, of course not. We're going to be parents."

"So…you're thinking of the child."

"Yes. First and foremost. But…marriage. Family. Kids. Dogs. Cats. It's such a huge leap."

Jocelyn heard shuffling as though Sam had moved. "Why did you marry her if you aren't sure?"

"I am sure."

"That's not what I'm hearing, Trevor."

"It's not that I'm unsure. I did the right thing. *We* did the right thing. It's just…"

After a few seconds, Sam asked outright, "Do you love her?"

Trevor hesitated, a telling reaction for Jocelyn. Her

chest tightened with this shocking change in the way she'd perceived them.

"You've known her long enough," Sam said. "You work with her."

"Yeah." Another stressed sigh. "I think that's the problem."

Jocelyn heard the truth in what he said. She'd known that about him—his adamancy to keep things professional. Was he having trouble making the transition? She could deal with that.

"Jocelyn is great," Trevor went on. "She's genuine and smart and beautiful. The physical attraction is… wow. Fantastic. No problem there. It's just… I don't think I'm ready for marriage, Sam. She wants a family. The real deal. A house in town. Babies—you should hear her when she talks about that."

"You're having a baby."

"Yeah, but maybe Jocelyn is right. Maybe we shouldn't have rushed into marriage."

He still didn't want to have kids. Blood left her face, leaving her chilled with this revelation. He'd pretended that intimacy, hidden what lay beneath—dread—regret. He said he didn't regret marrying her but he did. When she'd talked about her dream of being a family, she thought she felt warmth from him, not doubt. She couldn't believe he'd faked his reaction.

"You need love," Sam said.

"I think so. I think Jocelyn would agree, too."

No, Jocelyn did not agree. Jocelyn thought they'd already fallen in love.

"That's heavy, Trevor. What are you going to do?"

"I don't know. The only thing I know is this marriage doesn't feel right."

Jocelyn covered her mouth before emotion betrayed her with an audible breath. She pivoted and considered leaving through the living room. But then she'd have to face his family. His lovely, love-abundant family.

Just as she turned to find a window to slip through, she remembered Trevor had driven and his keys were on the table by the front door, where he'd set them as though he'd done so many times before. While she contemplated the consequences of taking his SUV, her need to be gone from here overshadowed her moral compass. She walked as nonchalantly as she could into the living room.

Zoe and Lizzie had moved to the kitchen and were on their way out onto the back patio, where it appeared Ethan had finished grilling the hamburgers and the patio table was ready for gathering. Jocelyn glanced back as she reached the table by the door. No one noticed as she snatched up the keys. She left without another look back.

Jocelyn entered the apartment she shared with Trevor. Fake apartment. Fake marriage. She fumbled with the door and shut it, unable to believe what she'd heard. Still. The shock clung. Just when she'd let go of her doubt, let her guard down, Trevor broke her. Nothing had changed. He'd married her only for the baby. To do the right thing for the baby, not her. The baby did have priority, but what about her? Should she sacrifice herself for a man who would never love her?

This marriage doesn't feel right.

The guttural truth in his voice haunted her. He meant what he'd said. He'd confided in his brother something he'd kept to himself, something he must have buried when he talked with Jocelyn, when he'd told her all those things.

I want what you want... I want a family. I want us to work. For real.

Liar. He'd put on quite a show for her, acting his part as her husband to draw out Regina. Maybe he did want a family, but not for the same reasons she did. Obligation compelled him, not any burning desire to fall in love and share every intimacy with a woman. Her.

The fresh sting of tears threatened.

Jocelyn flung open her suitcase and began throwing clothes inside. Her cell phone rang. She didn't even look to see who called. Trevor's obligation would bring him here, make him go after her, to convince her to go along with his plan. Heartless plan. For a man who tried so very hard to be the polar opposite from his father, he failed miserably. Not the killer part, but the family part. He'd never have what he wanted if he continued to shut himself off to close relationships.

He had formed close relationships with his siblings. Why did he have so much trouble with women?

Maybe it wasn't all women. Maybe it was just her.

This marriage doesn't feel right...

Sigmund hopped up onto the bed with a meow, a deep growl. He sensed her distress. Jocelyn picked him up and held him, scratching the back of his neck behind his ears.

"It's just you and me again, Siggie." She kissed the top of his head and then looked into his soft eyes. "But we don't have much time." She did not want to be around when Trevor found a way here.

She put Sigmund down and finished tossing clothes

into the suitcase. After gathering her toiletries, she put the cat into his carrier and then left the building.

Tucking the cat carrier onto the passenger seat, she sat behind the wheel and started off, on her way to a new life. Where should she go? If she went to her condo, Trevor would find her. She needed time to think. To figure out what she'd do.

Maybe Trevor would stay away. As torn as he'd sounded, he might be glad she left.

No. He'd find her. For the baby, not her. The more that gnawed at her, the angrier she became. Didn't he care how she felt about all of this? So far he'd only expressed his concern for the baby. Again, the baby did take priority, but she mattered in this situation, too.

As she drove down Main Street, she noticed a car behind her. At first she didn't think anything of it, but when she turned to head for the highway, the car followed.

She couldn't see the driver.

Testing, Jocelyn turned off the road onto a side street. When the car turned with her, she fought a rush of apprehension. Sigmund meowed, reminding her she had to be careful not to injure him with a high-speed getaway attempt. She'd have to be careful losing this tail. She had more than a cat to worry about. Her baby. She had to protect the tiny, helpless life inside her.

"Great," she muttered. "Great timing. Get me while I'm low." Well, she'd give all she had getting away. If she played this right, she might be able to make an arrest. She was an FBI agent. Trained for situations like this. Trevor and his false leading to the prospect of living as a wife and mother had gotten to her, made her soft.

Jocelyn dug into her purse and removed her pistol, flicking off the safety. Placing the gun on her lap, she turned onto another street that would take her to the police station—if she needed the backup.

A mile from the turn to the station, the driver behind her sped up and rammed into the back of the SUV. The impact jolted Jocelyn, her seat belt tightening. Sigmund meowed, a more urgent growl than earlier.

Gunfire and shattering glass added to the chaos. The driver shot at her! Regina.

"Okay." Jocelyn sped up and rolled down her window. "Hang on, Sigmund!" When she gained some distance from Regina, she turned the SUV into a hard one-eighty, picking up her gun as the SUV spun in front of Regina's car.

Jocelyn fired. Regina ducked and swerved her car as Jocelyn screeched full circle so that she now faced Regina's front bumper.

"You want to play bumper cars?" Jocelyn sped forward, ramming Regina's car and holding the pistol outside the window, firing again.

Regina reversed and veered out of the bigger SUV's way, then floored her vehicle and raced away. Jocelyn turned around and chased after her. Continuing to fire. The rear window of the car shattered with the fourth strike. Jocelyn's aim was off, but she came close to her mark when the next bullet broke the rearview mirror.

"I bet you didn't think you were coming after an armed woman!" Jocelyn yelled. "That's right. I'm FBI!" Regina didn't know that yet. Jocelyn firing at her might get her wondering, but she wouldn't guess the truth. Not yet.

Reaching speeds beyond ninety and the lights of

town fading as she chased Regina on the highway, Jocelyn slowed. She'd let Regina go for now. She had other issues to deal with tonight.

Chapter 11

"Where the hell is she?" Trevor had searched every inch of Ethan's house. Jocelyn was nowhere to be found. No one had seen her leave.

Sick with worry, Trevor ran his fingers through his hair.

"Your SUV is gone." Ethan closed the front door after searching outside. He hadn't been out there long.

She'd taken his SUV? Trevor stared at Ethan, unable to fathom what would make her do such a thing.

"She seemed fine," Lizzie said. "Except I did say you were like Ethan in that you didn't want kids."

"What?"

"She had diarrhea of the mouth," Zoe said. "But she's right. Jocelyn did seem fine. She didn't seem bothered much by that comment. Lizzie was only explaining how Ethan used to be like that, and Trevor is going down a similar path."

Lizzie folded her arm and put her fingers beneath her lower lip, thinking. "She did rush off to the bathroom. I think it did bother her." She looked regretfully at Ethan, who went to her.

"You didn't say anything to make her run off." He looked over at Trevor. "Something else must have done that."

Josie and Holly exchanged baffled looks.

Sam entered from the patio. "She's not out back."

"Not in the basement, either." Chris came to a stop in the living room, where the rest had gathered.

"The bathroom is across from the room where Sam and I talked," Trevor spoke the dawning thought aloud. "The door was open."

"I shut it," Sam said.

"It didn't close all the way." Apprehension crowded Trevor. She'd heard him tell Sam how uncertain he felt over their marriage.

After the progress they'd made, after the incredible lovemaking and intimate talks, she'd likely assumed the worst. She must think he'd lied. He hadn't, but he also hadn't lied about their marriage.

"I need a car." Trevor headed for the door.

"Take my truck," Ethan said, going to the entry table and handing him the keys.

"Thanks, brother."

As he left, an ominous premonition weighed down. Jocelyn was alone, upset. She might not pay attention when she needed to most. And Trevor wasn't there to protect her and their baby.

The premonition only grew worse when his phone rang and he saw Chief Murray's name.

"We received a call reporting gunshots fired approaching the highway north of town," the chief said. "Witnesses said a female driver with dark hair was shooting at a woman in an SUV."

Trevor cursed. "Jocelyn." Where was she now?

"The shooter left and the SUV turned around and drove away. No one's seen it since."

At least he knew she was alive. But if Regina found her, what then?

He had to find her first.

By the time Trevor tracked Jocelyn to a pet-friendly hotel, she'd already checked out. Relief tempered his worry. She hadn't answered any of his calls, but she'd spent a safe night at an out-of-the-way hotel. With Sigmund, who'd probably curl up and cuddle with Regina herself.

After going to her condo and waiting there, Trevor left and returned to the apartment. Jocelyn wouldn't go anywhere Regina would think to look, but she might come back to the apartment to finish the job. One thing he knew about Jocelyn; she did not quit.

How much did Regina now know about Jocelyn? That she was armed, for sure. But would she suspect the police were onto her? She might vanish again. Or she may want Jocelyn dead now more than ever. Who dared go against a woman shunned? One who lived in a demented fantasy, believing her fiancé would marry her even though he'd left her for another long ago.

Trevor paced to the front window and checked the time. It had been hours since Jocelyn had checked out of the hotel. He had every police officer in the county on the lookout for her or his SUV.

Just when he began to fear for her life with renewed

urgency, he heard her come up the stairs to the apartment. Facing the door, he turned from the window and watched her enter. She had Sigmund in her arms and a duffel bag slung over her shoulder. She put the cat down and then the bag. Sigmund meowed and ran to his favorite spot on the couch. Jocelyn stood at the door. Trevor didn't know what to say. She'd come back. That was all that mattered.

She seemed at a loss, like him.

"I see you stayed at a hotel," he finally said. "Where've you been all morning?"

She walked into the apartment, going to the window and standing beside him, looking down at the street.

"She isn't here," he said.

Jocelyn eyed him intuitively. "You know about the chase?"

"Witnesses reported the gunshots and described you and my SUV."

Nodding, she broke their eye contact and went to the other side of the white kitchen table. "We need to talk."

Trevor recalled himself saying something similar to her after they'd first slept together. Now he felt what she must have felt.

"Jocelyn, about what I said—"

Holding up her hand, she interrupted. "Don't try to explain that. I heard you. I understood you. I came back to tell you I'm going to finish this case, and then I'm going to ask for a transfer. I won't go far. You'll be able to see our child. I'll be fair with the visitation."

"No. We can make this work."

"On your terms?" Curbed anger clipped her tone. "No, we can't. I'm going to be a single mom."

Her certainty punched him in the stomach, pulling

and sinking with dread. "You didn't hear the rest of what I said to Sam."

"And I don't want to, Trevor. I've listened to your empty words too much. You made me believe this was real, when you must have had serious doubts all along. You should have been honest with me."

"I was honest. The truth is, I'm confused over the way I feel."

"Any man who grew up in your family environment, might be. I'm not blaming you. There's nothing either of us can do about the way we feel. We'll just have to make the best of it."

"We're still married, Jocelyn. I don't want a divorce."

"We don't need one. I filed for an annulment this morning. That's where I went after I checked out of the hotel."

An…annulment? Trevor went cold inside. "You can't get an annulment. I didn't coerce you and there was no fraud involved."

"No, but you didn't wait seventy-two hours after getting the marriage license to marry me." She stepped over to him and touched him with her pointed finger. "That made it easy."

He could kick himself just then. He'd thought of that at the time, but he'd been in such an almighty hurry to get her to an altar that he'd dismissed the possible repercussions. He supposed he'd thought once he made her his wife, he could keep her. But now this.

Taking her finger, he held her hand and lowered it to their sides. "I want more than visitation."

"Yes, you've made that abundantly clear. I have one question for you."

"Okay."

"What about me?"

What about her? What was she talking about? Their child would be raised by two parents together, not each of them taking a part-time role. And they'd have lots of great sex. Love. Jocelyn wanted it all. Well, so did he, but they'd been rushed into this. Didn't she understand that? Couldn't she just go with it?

"I'll take care of you," he said.

"You don't want this marriage."

"I don't want to rush into it like this. You must agree about that much."

She blinked a few times, averted her head and didn't respond.

"I think we share the same feelings in that regard," he said.

"We don't share the same feelings about staying married for the baby."

The baby wasn't enough for her. She needed more from him and he wasn't sure he could give that to her. He had so many doubts, about himself, about his adolescence, about the future.

"Don't get an annulment." He all but pleaded.

"It's too late. I already filed. The only way you're going to have me is if you give me a real wedding. And I'll know if it's real or not, Trevor. You won't be telling your brother how much you regret the one we had in Vegas."

"I don't regret it."

"Yes, you do."

He didn't, but she wouldn't believe him, not after hearing him talk frankly to Sam. She didn't understand that he hoped it would work between them. He'd be a fool not to hope for that. Anyone, any normal person, would want that. True love. Happiness. Only one problem stood in his way—his uncertainty that he was normal with a serial killer for a father.

Following her into the bedroom, he watched her put her wedding ring into a jewelry box. He didn't stop her. How could he? All he could do was work on getting her to put it back on.

Chapter 12

*B*lue. Pretty blue. Josie fell into the part as painter, with flamboyant brushstrokes back and forth, arching and shooting straight along the wood, sending splats of paint over her cheeks and probably her shirt. More paint dotted the white daisies and grass at the base of the picket fence. Delightful. Her mother had allowed her this freedom today, to let her creativity take flight with blue paint.

"You missed a spot."

Josie looked up at her beautiful mother, smiling with light in her eyes, trim and youthful even though she was a lot older than her. She pointed at the spot of peeling white. Giggling, Josie sank her brush into the pan and brought it dripping up to a wood plank. The fence needed a fresh coat. Time to get serious. Paint the fence a solid color rather than the Picasso she'd imagined.

Her mother stood straighter and looked out across the farmland. Sunlight splashed the sky into a gem-like blue. A warm breeze lifted her hair. Perfect weather made the day more fun. No rain today. That and being with her mother had a strangely nostalgic feel, as though she'd been deprived of her, as though she missed her. But yet her mother acted different. Her smile seemed pasted on and didn't seem to reach her eyes, which looked...well, kind of dead.

Even that smile faded as the light changed. Josie followed her mother's gaze, seeing a cloud moving over the horizon, dark and ominous. Closer and closer it came, casting the landscape and her mother's face into something that could be out of an Alice in Wonderland movie.

The landscape changed, too. The ground moved where it shouldn't, escalators going in different directions. She sometimes experienced that when she got migraines. She hadn't gotten them when she was a kid, but she wasn't a kid anymore. She was just stuck in a time when she had been, when she'd spent a day with her mother, painting this fence.

The wind kicked up. Overhead, clouds began to circle. And in the distance, darkness began to swallow the land, escalators and all.

The fence blurred and melted away. The magic vanished.

"Run, Josie!" her mother shouted.

Josie stumbled to her feet, kicking the pan of cheery blue paint over. It turned black as her foot sank into it. As she took her first step, the paint became glue. She couldn't run. Frantically, she searched for her mother. She'd gone. Vanished. Had the blackness taken her?

Where was she? She looked all around and saw only blackness.

Yanking her foot, she freed it from the muck and ran. But something else took hold of her. This had happened before. Her feet were stuck in the middle of the daisies, which had begun to wilt.

A cold wind picked up, blowing hard. If the ground didn't keep her in place, she'd be taken in the wind. She coughed and tried to protect her face.

The shape of a man emerged from flying debris and blackness. He held a sword covered in blue paint. He raised the weapon high over his head, striding toward her, growing more identifiable as he neared. His steps hastened, as though eager to quench his deathly thirst.

The paint changed to blood, dripping to the ground. The face of a man grew visible just before the rest of his body. He raised the sword for a swing...

Matthew. Her father.

The image dissipated with the sound of smashing glass.

Josie woke with a jolt, a scream locked in her throat as she struggled to organize reality from terrible dream. An instant later, she realized the smashing glass had actually happened. And now she heard someone moving through her house, feet on the hardwood floor in her living room and rapidly approaching her bedroom. She sprang off the bed just as a woman appeared in her doorway with a gun.

Josie choked back another scream and ducked at the side of the bed.

"There's no one to protect you now!" the woman hissed.

She hadn't shot at her yet, but she moved slowly, stalking what she must view as caught prey.

"You think you got away with it, don't you?" the woman said, clearly overly confident she'd at last accomplished what she'd set out to accomplish.

"Sneaking around, dodging me. You must think you're real good at what you do. You're a *sicko*."

Josie begged to differ. She wasn't the one going after an innocent woman with the intent of killing her. For what reason?

"I don't know what you're talking about."

"Don't play dumb with me. I've caught you, and now you're going to pay!"

Biding her time just right, Josie waited until the woman had almost reached the side of the bed. Then she stood and lunged for her, grabbing a hold of her wrist as the gun went off. She landed on top of the woman, someone she'd never seen before. The woman bared her teeth as she struggled for control of the weapon. She wrapped her leg around Josie's and arched upward, rolling so she now loomed over her. Josie didn't let go of the bigger woman's wrists and struggled to keep her from aiming down at her.

"I won't let you get away with it!" the crazed woman hissed some more.

As the woman pushed hard against Josie's resistance, her head lowered just enough. Josie rammed her forehead against her head.

Disoriented, caught off guard, the woman loosened her grip and Josie shoved her off, kicking with her knee. The woman sprawled onto the floor at the foot of Josie's bed.

Still holding the gun, the woman recovered from

the hit that still stung Josie's forehead. She was going to shoot her!

Josie dived to the other side of the bed as the gun went off. She scrambled to the nightstand, where she picked up a ceramic-based lamp. The woman appeared at the foot of the bed and Josie threw the lamp, hitting the woman in the head. Both woman and lamp fell down, the lamp breaking.

Josie didn't waste any time. She ran from the bedroom and into the living room, grabbing another lamp in there, this one made of metal.

When the woman appeared in the doorway, dazed but unrelenting in her determination to kill Josie, Josie put all her strength in the next throw. She missed the woman's head but caught her arm. The gun sailed upward, hitting a bookshelf and somersaulting to the floor near Josie's feet.

Josie leaped for it, colliding with the woman. Josie grasped the handle, but the woman dug her nails into Josie's hands. Josie put all her weight into a shove and felt a powerful surge of relief and triumph when the woman fell onto her hip.

Hands on the floor, knees bent, the woman stared up at Josie in shock. Her crazed look vanished as she realized she'd lost the fight.

"Who are you? Start talking or I'll let the police take you out of here in a body bag."

In the next instant, the agent watching over her busted open her door with his gun drawn.

Jocelyn went with Trevor to Buckaroo Burgers. Right now they waited for the general manager to come out and talk to them. Her entire body went rigid from being so close to Trevor and hyperaware of each time his forearm or even a piece of his clothes touched her, the lapel of his leather jacket, the bump of his leg in dark slacks. G-man. She wished he didn't do that to her, attract her to his masculinity, fill her with so much feeling.

The general manager appeared, a tall, dark-haired, dapper man in slacks, dress shirt and tie. "Let's have a seat over here. I've instructed my staff to keep customers out of this section."

He'd protect the restaurant's reputation along with giving them privacy.

They sat at a booth in one corner of the establishment.

"You're here because of Sally?" the GM asked.

"Do you know where we can find her?" Trevor asked.

The GM didn't blanch at all. "No. She didn't show up for her shift yesterday. I think I always expected that from her. Some people you can just…tell." He contemplated them both curiously. "Did something happen to her?"

"We believe she worked for you under a false name," Trevor said.

"What's her real name?" His head darted back and forth. "I checked her out. Her ID was legitimate."

"Legitimately stolen," Jocelyn said.

"Who is she?"

Jocelyn glanced at Trevor. His call.

He nodded once.

She turned to the GM. "We believe she's the Alphabet Killer."

"Really." The GM moved his head back in surprise.

"Don't feel bad about not recognizing any signs. Criminals like this are known for their cunning."

Jocelyn felt Trevor's look of approval and glowed. He often did that, made her feel good about doing her job.

Working together, they'd come to know each other as friends and coworkers. They made a good team. The chemistry had always been there. Right from the start.

She recalled their first meeting.

He in his suit and tie, silky material floating over yum. Dark, tall, impossibly gorgeous. And then the assistant who'd led her to him had informed her he was her boss. He was the lead on the case she'd been assigned. The Alphabet Killer case. She'd been so excited. The honor of being awarded that. Her training and her intelligence had earned her the spot. Her desire to honor her father and brother had earned her that spot.

"A—a serial killer? *Sally?*" The GM, still recovering from the news, briefly turned bewildered eyes away. "She did seem a bit…off, but a *killer*?"

"Some serial killers are good at disguises," Trevor said. "Most of the time they seem smart, professional, even normal. They're masters at fooling others, living dual lives."

"How can I help? Employment records? Associates? Anything. It's at your disposal. And I'll make sure you talk to all of my staff."

"We have a team on the way to do just that," Trevor said as his phone rang.

"Agent Colton," a man breathlessly said. "I'm inside Josie's house. I need backup."

Prepared for this call, but not the worry for Josie, Trevor turned to Jocelyn. She searched his face, seeing his reaction.

"Is anything wrong?" the GM asked.

"Thank you," Trevor said to him and then took Jocelyn's hand to take her after him, saying to the agent on the phone, "We're on our way."

"What's happening?" Jocelyn asked as she ran after him.

"It's Josie. She's in trouble."

By the time Jocelyn followed Trevor into Josie's town house, the police had arrived. The agent who had been assigned for her protection stood in the living room near a woman with her hands cuffed behind her back and head bowed in defeat.

"I held them off until you got here," the agent said, indicating the police, who waited to take the woman away.

"Thank you."

Jocelyn watched the woman lift her head and drew in a sharp breath as she immediately recognized Caressa Franklin.

"She broke in and attacked me." Josie went over to the kitchen table and sat, as though the arrival of her brother signaled the point at which she could relax.

"Caressa?" Jocelyn stepped closer to the couch. "Why?"

Caressa lifted sad eyes. "Because I had to."

"No one has to kill people. Why did you feel you had to?" It seemed such an absurd question, but to someone like Caressa, who'd lost normal rationale due to some personal trauma, the answer had become the center of her universe.

"She killed Erica."

"No." Jocelyn shook her head. "Josie didn't kill anyone." Hadn't she listened to them when they'd gone to question her?

The woman's sad desperation morphed into irritation. "You of all people should understand."

"Me? What should I understand? Help me, Caressa. Tell me."

"You cared about Erica. I could see it in your eyes when you came to see me," Caressa said, her most lucid words since Jocelyn and Trevor had arrived. "You made me see what I lost. Because of her!" She roared the last at Josie, who scoffed and looked away, disgusted.

"Josie didn't kill Erica," Jocelyn said again.

"Yes, she did. She ran off and hid like she did something wrong. She takes after her murdering father. Copies him. She uses red markers on her victims, victims who all have long dark hair. She's the Alphabet Killer! Arrest her, not me!"

How had she come to that crazy conclusion?

"Why do you think she killed all those women? Why Erica?" Trevor asked.

At first Caressa appeared baffled, confused, and then she said simply, "She dated Hershel."

Josie scoffed again. "I've never met him before."

Caressa looked from Josie up to Trevor. "She had to have known him. She had to! A-and even if she didn't, Erica had long dark hair. She must have fit the profile of a woman who wronged her. Just like her father. She's the killer! She is!"

Jocelyn marveled for a moment on how this woman had conjured up a motive for Josie, regardless of the lack of truth or facts backing up her theory. She must have stewed for hours and days, convincing herself that Josie had killed Erica, and therefore the rest of the women. She'd heard Josie could be a suspect by virtue of her relationship to Matthew Colton. Like father, like daughter.

"Caressa," Jocelyn said gently, trying to calm the woman, bring her back to rational thought. If that was possible. "We told you the truth when we came to see you that day. Josie couldn't have killed any of the women. She wasn't in Granite Gulch when some of the murders took place. She was in witness protection. That's been verified. She isn't our suspect. Regina Willard is. She works as a waitress under false names and targets women with long dark hair. She's written to Matthew Colton and copies his method of killing. We have her letters in evidence."

Caressa turned drooping eyes to her as she spoke, the reality that she'd been wrong sinking in. "It can't be."

"It is. Josie isn't a killer."

Shifting on the couch, Caressa twisted her wrists. Now that she realized what she'd done, she tried to erase the fact, wish she could be free and take everything back.

"No." Caressa shook her head and stared off, beyond Jocelyn. "Hershel treated Erica badly. He had an affair. He admitted he did."

"You spoke with Hershel?" Trevor asked.

Caressa came out of her stare. "Of course I did. After I found out Erica was murdered, I thought he might have done it. When Erica and I were still friends, she told me he'd had affairs. I could never understand why she kept going back to him."

"Didn't you know about the Alphabet Killer?" Trevor asked.

With flashing, indignant eyes, Caressa turned on him. "The media said her murder appeared to be the work of a copycat killer, but they didn't know her history with Hershel. He could have made it look like the copycat killer."

"You had it out for Hershel, then?" Trevor said more than asked.

Her emotion cooled. "I thought he killed her. I wanted to make sure police caught him."

Nothing like the ignorant trying to help out law enforcement. "But he didn't kill Erica."

"No. I realized that after talking to him and learning about Josie."

"Then why blackmail him into claiming he knew Josie?" Jocelyn asked.

"Erica would still be alive if not for him. If they were still together, she would not have captured Josie's attention."

"Josie is not the killer, either," Jocelyn said again. "We told you Regina Willard is our prime suspect."

"Hershel was afraid of being accused of her murder. I eased off him after I realized it was Josie."

Did she not hear her? "Caressa, I'll only say this once more. Josie Colton is not a suspect in the Alphabet Killer case. Regina Willard is."

Trevor held up his hand, a silent direction to give up trying to get through to Caressa.

Jocelyn backed away from the woman. Caressa was a lost, demented soul who'd convinced herself first Hershel and then Josie killed her friend. Unfortunately, her logic had been quite unsound and she'd acted on it.

Jocelyn stood next to Trevor, who turned to the policeman standing nearby. He gave the man a nod.

The police officer went to Caressa, taking her arm. "Let's go."

"No!" Caressa struggled. "I made a mistake! You can't arrest me. I didn't kill anyone! I'm not the Alphabet Killer!"

All the way out the door, Caressa protested. The desperate sound tugged at Jocelyn's sympathy. She may have acted without facts backing her decisions, but she carried deep guilt over shutting Erica out of her life. Erica had gone to reconcile and still Caressa had shut her out. That had pushed her over the edge. She acted on her remorse, seeking revenge for Erica's death. Only, she'd blamed the wrong people and had dreamed up weak motives.

Josie came to stand with them, watching Caressa being guided away and her last look back, bewilderment over the turn of events in her widened eyes. The reality of what she'd done—the magnitude of her mistake—crashed upon her now. She faced prison time for what she'd done. She'd attempted to kill an innocent person.

"I can't believe it," Josie said. "It's so crazy."

The investigation had initially suspected Josie for the same reason Caressa had latched on to. If Matthew had killed because of the betrayal of a man, had his daughter done the same because of the betrayal of a woman? Her disappearance had been the only fact giving that theory any credence. But as soon as she'd reappeared, the theory lost hold.

"Now do you feel safe?" Trevor asked.

Josie's face softened in relief and gratitude. "Yes. I think I can finally put the kingpin behind me."

"They're all gone," Trevor said. "In prison or dead. You are safe. You can live your life without looking over your shoulder."

"That's something new." She smiled. "But what about you? This isn't helping you solve the Alphabet Killer case."

No, it led them off course, took their attention away from it.

"We'll keep working until we catch her," Jocelyn said, seeing Trevor look over with concern. His thoughts had already gone back to the investigation. Caressa's arrest didn't get them any closer to catching Regina. But where did his concern come from? An instant later she shouldn't have had to wonder at all.

He felt obligated to protect her. Maybe the case warranted that. She put herself in grave danger every time she posed as a mean customer.

She did appreciate having Trevor there, but she wished he'd appreciate *her* as a qualified agent. And then she wondered why he even bothered. He should have no trouble treating her like any other agent, after what he'd said to his brother. She couldn't get past that and didn't like how hurt she felt. This kind of hurt came from strong feelings for someone. If she didn't feel strongly for Trevor, what he'd said wouldn't bother her this much, right?

She didn't want to have feelings for him.

A nagging voice inside contradicted her. *Yes, you do.*

"Are you okay, Jocelyn?" Josie asked.

"Yes. Fine," she answered stiffly.

Josie exchanged a look with Trevor, who volunteered no information.

"You left awfully fast from the barbecue. No one knew where you were."

"Something came up."

Josie looked from her to Trevor again and then back at Jocelyn. "You didn't even say goodbye. Trevor was out of his mind with worry. Did you two have a fight?"

"No." Jocelyn headed for the door. "We have to get going."

"She filed for an annulment because of what she heard me say to Sam," Trevor finally admitted.

"What did you say?"

Jocelyn stopped, annoyed that she cared. "That he wishes he never married me."

Josie's jaw dropped. "You didn't."

"Not like that, but I did express my doubts…because of Matthew."

He didn't have to say much to his sister for her to know exactly what he meant.

"Someday we'll look back on all of this and not feel poisoned by that man. Just because our father was evil doesn't mean we are. And you should never have doubts about the kind of man you are, Trevor." She put her hand on his arm. "You're a good, strong, honorable one. That's going to flow into your family."

Jocelyn saw Trevor blink with warmth. Josie had reached him. Too bad Jocelyn didn't have that magic touch. She left the building without another look back. If only she could keep walking right out of his life. Instead, she had to endure more role-playing. And the impending birth of their child.

Chapter 13

Jocelyn wasn't talking to him much. Trevor entered the apartment after checking the surrounding area for signs of Regina. They'd just gotten back from the fourth restaurant they'd been to in the past several hours, trying to track her down.

The restaurant they'd staked out was located a few miles from town in the opposite direction from Buckaroo Burgers. It had ended up being another dead end. If Regina had sought work somewhere else, she hadn't done so at any of the establishments outside town. She may have gone back to previous restaurants she'd haunted, or she may not have sought a job at all.

While Jocelyn went into the kitchen, he went over to the window and looked down at a quiet street.

"I hope we haven't scared her away," Jocelyn said.

She may have caught wind of the sting operation,

but Trevor didn't think Regina would give up on going after Jocelyn—or any other woman who reminded her of the one who stole her fiancé.

He moved to the kitchen island. "You're finally talking to me."

She paused in the act of putting dishes away from the dishwasher. "I haven't been talking to you?"

He gave her a moment to answer her own question.

"I guess I haven't. A lot on my mind."

"You don't have to worry. I'm not going anywhere."

She ignored him and put away a glass.

"You didn't hear everything I told my brother. You heard my doubt. Who wouldn't have doubt after getting married the way we did?"

"We've gone over this already."

"After I voiced my doubt, I told him how good it was between us."

"You mean sex?"

"That's part of it, but there's also something about you. I haven't figured it out yet. But strangely, I think it's your desire to have a family, and that you wanted to be a teacher before your dad and brother died."

That made her stop working on the dishes. She put her hands down on the counter, her back to him, listening.

"While it terrifies me, it also warms my heart. It makes me believe there's a chance for me. Like I might really have a shot at this."

Jocelyn turned to face him, moving to the other side of the island, sunlight fading with the day. In the darkening apartment, cottage charm set the mood, or enhanced it. He didn't fancy himself much of a romantic, but he sure felt it now.

"You've told me something similar before, and I believed you."

"You still can." As he spoke the words, something clashed inside. Fear? Yes, he couldn't shed his father's poison, the fear that his DNA contained the same darkness, the inevitable failure as a family man. That was what had him confessing to Sam. Torn between the sparks flying with Jocelyn and the stark reality of his lineage, the latter had gotten the best of him.

Watching him, she shook her head. "You convinced me you wanted what I want."

"I do." Despite his worry and doubt.

Her mouth opened and she let out a disgruntled breath. "How can you say that? You also think our marriage was a mistake."

"It was. We deserve a real wedding, Jocelyn."

He saw her stiffen and heard her indrawn breath. He'd reached her. Abruptly she pivoted. "Stop doing that." Dishes banged and clanked as she put them away with jerkier motions. "You say you want this—*us*—but I don't believe…" She stopped putting dishes away and faced him again, hands gripping the counter behind her. "I don't *feel* it, Trevor. I did before, but you had me fooled. Now I see you. I see what your father's crimes have done to you. And I don't trust you. I need you to be with me all the way, not halfway. You have to know in your heart that this is for you, that *I'm* for you. This isn't just about our baby. This is about love."

Damn. She nailed him with that accurate assessment. He didn't know. He didn't trust himself. He'd always thought he had everything figured out. Someday he'd make a family. He made a good living as a successful FBI agent. It had meaning. But it also gave him an excuse to delay the family.

"You would make a great profiler," he said, trying to keep things light.

"I mean it, Trevor."

He couldn't persuade her, and the uncertainty of their future left him empty. But he understood. She needed the real thing. And until he could give her that, they'd move nowhere as a couple—a married couple with a baby on the way.

A pinging sound accompanied something skimming Trevor's neck. A bullet. Someone had fired through the window.

"Get down!" Trevor dived over the island and tackled Jocelyn. She grunted from the impact of his body on top of hers.

Rolling off her, he drew his gun and crouched on his way to the wall beside the window. Jocelyn drew her own gun. He held his hand up for her to stop.

"Stay there, Jocelyn." He spoke low as though the shooter would hear him.

Jocelyn ran to the other side of the window, pistol aimed upward.

When she met his look, he admonished her without saying a word.

She admonished him back with a defiant frown and shake of her head.

Inching closer to the window, he peered outside. Not many buildings lined the road in this part of town. A gas station on the same side of the street closed at ten. An elderly couple, a family of three and a single man lived in the three houses in the opposite direction and across the street. The shots had to have come from the nearest one.

He popped his head farther out from the protection of the wall and caught a glimpse of the house, dark except for a streetlight in front of the middle house. He amended his assumption when he saw a figure jump down from a tree almost directly across from the real estate office and run into the shadows.

"I'm going down." He ran to the door.

"I've got your back." Jocelyn ran behind him.

While he wished she'd let him take care of the dangerous situations, he had no time to argue. The gunman had a pretty good head start and had run toward a neighborhood on the other side of the open space behind the three houses.

At the front door of the real estate office, he paused to check the street. Seeing no movement near the tree, he left the building, ever aware of Jocelyn's proximity. A car approached on the road, leaving the well-lit street where the town center began and entering the shadows closer to the real estate office, where none of the lights were on inside or outside.

Trevor held his hand out to stop Jocelyn. She paused in the doorway. The car passed, the driver not noticing them in the darkness.

Staying in line with the tree, Trevor crossed the street, holding his gun aimed down for now. Jocelyn followed behind him. He could see lights from the houses across the open space. They'd have to be careful if they had to use their weapons.

At the tree, he stopped and searched the darkness, moving so that Jocelyn stood closer to the tree. If the shooter took fire, the trunk would block the bullets.

Had the shooter gone into the open space or toward the three houses? He had no way of knowing and saw nothing through the darkness.

"She got away," Jocelyn said.

"Maybe." He didn't like the idea of going back to the apartment without finding the shooter. But neither did he want to take Jocelyn into the dark open space, where the shooter might be waiting to pluck them down one at a time—or him. The shooter had to be Regina, who wouldn't give up a chance to use her red marker on Jocelyn. But first she had to get rid of him.

Just then, a car emerged over the hill past the three houses. Where the hill flattened, a side street led to the open space, skirting around that to the neighborhood in the distance. The car slowed as it neared them.

Trevor grabbed Jocelyn and moved her to the other side of the trunk. The driver aimed a gun through the open passenger window and began firing.

Trevor fired back, pinning Jocelyn to the trunk. One of the shooter's bullets struck the bark. Trevor's hit the rear taillight of the car, an old Honda. He ran after it, reading the plate number and firing twice more.

Jocelyn appeared at his side, gun raised although she hadn't taken a shot, watching Regina get away. Trevor dialed the chief and followed Jocelyn back toward the real estate office.

When the chief answered, Trevor said, "Jocelyn and I were just shot at. Suspect is Regina Willard. I have a plate number."

After the chief swore a few times, he said, "All right, give it to me. We have to catch this woman. Maybe the plate number will give us a much needed break."

Trevor could not agree more. As he followed Jocelyn

through the office and up the stairs to the apartment, he gave him the number, not having much faith it would lead them to the killer. Regina likely had stolen the car. He went on to explain what happened during the shooting. Jocelyn went into the bathroom and came back out with a damp cloth.

When she began dabbing his neck, he remembered the bullet fired through the apartment window had grazed him.

After disconnecting the call, he saw Jocelyn spoiling for a fight.

"You have to stop looking out for me when you should be paying attention to the subject," she said.

He had made sure to keep her out of the line of fire and now he would get an earful. He had to make her understand.

"One of these times, you might slip up, Jocelyn. What if you put yourself in one too many dangerous situations and get yourself into trouble? What if I can't save you?"

"That's your biggest fear? That you won't be able to save me? I'm an agent, just like you." She dabbed his wound again.

He slipped his hand around her wrist and gently took the cloth from her, tossing it across the living room to the kitchen, where it landed in the sink. He wasn't hurt that badly. "Yeah, but you don't belong here. You belong at home." Imagining her at home with their baby tantalized him and he pushed aside his usual reaction to recoil with worry. Instead, he let the fantasy take shape.

"In a bed," he said. Vivid picture now. "With me next to you." He held her around her waist and pulled her to him, pressing his mouth to hers.

* * *

Flattened against Trevor's tall, hard-muscled form, Jocelyn kept her eyes open, having to recover from surprise. She had not expected him to do this. Kiss her. Haul her against him and plant his mouth on hers as though stamping her. He must have thought this would get her to shut up, to stop disagreeing with him and reprimanding him for treating her as though she weren't trained to handle a gun.

But as always, the kiss caught fire and mindless passion took over. She didn't see much point in fighting it. They'd done this before. Except how would she feel if she kept allowing this? Would she fall more in love with him?

More in love?

Jocelyn pulled away and stared up at Trevor's dark, passionate eyes. Did she love him?

The first day they'd met popped into her head. Her first day on the job, the administrative assistant had taken her to division and introduced her to Trevor. She'd taken her to his office, a glassed-in square with a window view of the city.

Seated behind his desk, head bent over an open file, he'd struck her as a typical FBI agent. And then he'd looked up.

Those dark, intense eyes had found her and stayed. He wore his thick black hair short. He'd captured all of her attention. When he rose to stand, she couldn't breathe. Tall and strapping, physically fit in a silky black suit and dashing tie, he stirred her senses like no other. She hadn't sought any particular type of man, hadn't been looking at all. For this one to attract her so incredibly had perplexed her. The only explanation could be the mystery in his eyes and his utter manly yum factor. No woman would be immune to his good looks.

Agent Jocelyn Locke, this is Agent Trevor Colton, lead profiler and in charge of your division, the assistant had said.

Jocelyn had felt him stare at her a moment and the assistant had taken notice.

Thank you, Trevor had said. *Come in, Agent Locke.*

Would you like me to close the door? the assistant had asked as she began to leave the office.

Jocelyn turned away from Trevor as the memory played on in detail, taking her back to a time she hadn't thought significant until now.

"Uh," Trevor stammered, his voice deeper, or had she imagined that? "No. Leave it open."

Jocelyn moved farther into the office, unable to look away from his interesting eyes. He seemed afflicted with the same enchantment, this instant attraction, a powerful, buzzing energy that tickled her insides.

"Welcome," he said. Yeah, definitely deeper. "Have a seat."

"Thank you." *Her own voice had gone a little sultry. She caught him giving her a telling up-and-down before she sat and he sat back down with her.*

"So you're the new rookie," he said.

"Top of my class. You won't even notice I just started."

"Oh, I'll notice."

Warmth flushed her, not mistaking his real meaning. Just when she would have turned up the heat, he cleared his throat and began fidgeting.

Closing the file, stacking it on top of some others,

he said, "I—I'd notice you're a rookie. Rookies need to be trained. Looked after."

He hadn't meant that. Why the sudden change in him?

He put his hands on the desk as though willing them to keep still. "You report to me."

"Oh." He worried about propriety. Ethics in the workplace. She could understand that.

"I take professionalism very seriously. I assure you, you'll be treated fairly and with respect. We have an outstanding new-hire program. People around here consider me the best to train the new rookies. I agreed to take on that role. Hence, the reason you'll be working for me. I'm your boss."

"Yes. I...got that when your assistant told me." Boy, this man really kept things on the straight and narrow.

While disappointment cooled her smoking desire to get to know him better—and not just on the job—she could see he'd made the right decision. Getting involved with her boss wouldn't be smart. She needed this job. She had personal reasons for needing it, too. She had something to prove. Romance in the office would only interfere.

"Jocelyn?"

Trevor's voice broke her drifting.

"Are you all right?" He put his hand on her shoulder.

She faced him, more to get his hand off her and stop the renewed tingles. "Yes."

"What's wrong?" He seemed genuinely concerned. "I'm sorry. I shouldn't have… You need more time."

More time? He didn't get it. "Do you remember when we met the first time?"

Her question confused him a moment. She saw it in his eyes and the slight flinch of his head.

"Yes."

"You were attracted to me."

He half grinned. "I'd have had to be blind not to be."

"But then you stopped it. You turned all professional and shut out whatever passed between us." The more she thought it through, the angrier she got.

"Of course, Jocelyn—"

"No." She put her hands on his chest and shoved. "You're not a weak man, Trevor Colton. You were attracted to me. You didn't have to cool the sparks. But you did. Because you're afraid every time a woman threatens to get too close. You used that other agent as an excuse. She started to get too close, but she got back together with her ex-boyfriend." She shoved him again. "I bet you were relieved!"

"No, I wasn't. She slept with him and still saw me."

So, add distrust to the list of reasons why Trevor would protect himself and avoid true love. "Deep down, I bet you were. If you're really honest with yourself, I bet you were relieved. She probably knew she didn't have a chance with you and hung on to you in case she was wrong." She eyed him sarcastically, his powerful chest, arms and shoulders. "You're pretty hot, Agent Colton."

"Okay, stop. You and I are much different than that. You're different than her."

Really? While that filled her with warm satisfaction, she couldn't trust her reaction to him.

"Do you love me?" she asked bluntly.

As expected, the question made him freeze.

"Right." Jocelyn thought she'd fallen in love with

him the minute she'd met him. And the more they talked, the more she'd felt a real possibility. He must have felt something similar. But he had been so adamant about keeping it professional she'd let go of any hope for them.

"I forgot what it was like when we met," she said. "Until now."

His eyes must have been what made her love him from the very instant she'd seen him. No immaturity in them. Just a life story that held something big, possibly something dramatic, definitely something interesting. A hero on the edge of darkness. In a way, she'd felt a connection to him on a deep level, as though the universe had let her know this man would fit her well, both physically and in experiences and personality.

"I never forgot that," he said.

"Yeah, well, you have a terrible way of showing me."

"I was right for keeping it professional," he said. "What do you think would have happened if I had acted on my urges? And you yours?"

Jocelyn tipped her head back. She had to agree. They worked together. He was her boss. "But you used it as an excuse."

"Maybe. But I knew how explosive we'd be together."

She lowered her head, hearing the truth. They'd both sensed how good they'd be together, and they'd found out when neither of them could hold back temptation. That night after Jane McDonald's murder proved they'd been right.

He met her eyes a moment and that same heat overcame her. And then he stepped toward her.

"You want me to show you why I never forgot the first time I saw you?"

Yes.

"No." Her voice, and what had to be in her eyes, must have convinced him she didn't mean it.

He moved toward her. Taking her hand, he pulled her to him again. Once more pressed to his body, Jocelyn couldn't find it in her to resist.

"Let me show you how much you mean to me."

"Trevor…" This could end up hurting them both in the long run—her more than him based on what he'd told his brother, something completely different than he'd led her to believe.

But his body…

His eyes, dark and flaring with passion…

She tipped her head back, unable to fight the rush of desire.

He took the action as consent and kissed her, this time much slower. She moved her mouth in sync with his, felt the heat build to the point when she knew there'd be no turning back.

When he lifted her, she wrapped her arms around him and kept kissing him as he carried her to the bedroom— her bedroom—now their bedroom.

Their fake bedroom in their fake apartment…

Trevor put her down on the bed and she almost got up and told him to leave. But he'd begun to remove his clothes and she couldn't stop watching. His bare chest. Strong arms that would soon be holding himself over her.

He unfastened his pants, slid them down along with his boxers. Naked before her, he stood for her viewing pleasure.

"Your turn," he rasped.

His jutting penis held most of her attention. She

loved how he filled her, stretched her and touched her in places no other man had managed, and not in the physical sense. He set her on fire. The male anatomy varied slightly, skewed from the average, but delivered the same reward. Only, with Trevor, what made him different was him. Trevor making love to her differed in leaps and bounds from others she'd been with.

That terrified her. But also awed her.

The awe had her removing her clothes, piece at a time. When she reached her bra and underwear, she left them on with a smile up at him and invitation to join her. She put her arms above her head and waited.

"You like to tease me."

"I do."

Those words reminded her of the mock wedding they'd had, when her *I do* had felt too real for the circumstances.

He crawled over her. Straddling her hips, he unfastened her bra, freeing her breasts. She slipped out of the contraption and tossed it to the floor while his hands paid homage to her flesh, tickling her as they roamed over nipples and down over her ribs. His fingers hooked her underwear. She lifted her hips to help him slide them all the way off.

Naked with him, she made room for him between her legs. He pushed them a bit wider and leaned down for a kiss.

Taking her hands, he put them above her head. She held on to a bar of the headboard as he rose up and probed for entry.

"Look at me."

Realizing she'd closed her eyes, she looked up at him. He held her gaze in the building firestorm created with their joining. Riveting and powerful, his repeated thrust and withdrawal took her away from this world, from the world she had with Trevor, to one of fantasy. Without any troubles, this was what they had. Something incredible.

When they both reached their grand finale, Jocelyn covered herself and lay on her back, thinking. Trevor lay beside her, head on one folded arm, staring up at the ceiling in a similar state.

They'd done this before, so she couldn't say it mattered that they continued. She loved him. She could no longer deny it. Loving him wouldn't change. But as long as she understood him and the obstacles in their way, she could remain strong. She might be hurt in the end, but she'd be hurt no matter what, loving him as she did.

"This doesn't change anything." He had to know that. Her terms remained in place. She would not marry for their baby. She would not mislead her child in a marriage where she didn't feel an equal part.

She rose from the bed, drawing Trevor's attention. He said nothing. He knew what she meant and didn't have to ask or talk further on the matter. He knew what she needed. He just had to be sure he could do so. Would that day ever come? And how long would Jocelyn wait?

Chapter 14

The next morning, Trevor stood with a steaming cup of coffee, keeping watch at the front window. Confident Regina wouldn't try anything foolish in the light of day, his thoughts wandered back to Jocelyn. Making love with her had taken on a new dimension, one where he no longer placed his obligation on raising their child. She had become a part of that equation. And in its wake, something loosened in him, a barrier. While he'd known he had reservations because of Matthew, he had no idea they ran this deep.

Every so often, a wave of terror gripped him. What he had with Jocelyn could be the real thing. Wife. Children. House in suburbia. Dog...and one cat. Sigmund would be a nice addition to the family. For the first time in his life, he'd be a cat person.

He heard her come out of the bedroom.

"Thinking about last night?"

The question packed enough punch, but the sight of her smile and self-confident, sexy, hip-hitching strides toward him finished the bomb. Detonated. She had on another black number that hugged her figure and show-cased her chest.

She sauntered over to him, slid an arm over his shoulder and smiled. "What's the matter? Scared?"

Something had reinvigorated her. She hadn't teased him like this since before she heard him talking to Sam. And never this boldly. He welcomed the lightening air. Or was she only putting on a show? Hiding her true feelings?

"You're the one who filed for an annulment." He couldn't help it. He had to know her strength had truly returned, because that would mean she had begun to forgive him—or believe him.

When her other arm slipped over his other shoulder, he grinned.

"Only because I deserve a real wedding."

Things heated up between them. He'd never get tired of the natural ease. "I can give you that. No costumes this time."

"Even costumes can't mask the real thing."

They could wear their costumes for a real wedding, and if real, the costumes wouldn't matter. She needed to know he could wear a costume and she'd see genuine love. She asked a lot. Everything happened so fast. The first night they'd had sex. Her pregnancy announcement. The wedding—the *Vegas* wedding. Which he'd actually loved, but how could she expect him to keep up with her? And how could she be so sure about a real marriage? That had him at a loss.

"Don't freak out." She rose up and pressed her soft, warm lips to his, her sweet breath going into him.

What she'd surely intended to be a fun, quick kiss turned into an instant boiling cauldron of some mysterious spell. He pulled her to him, feeling her with his palms on her firm, trim back, pressing her breasts against him.

She moved into a deeper kiss right along with him, in sync. That was how they did this. They synced. Just as he reached for the hem of her dress, his cell chimed.

Easing away, he put his hands on each side of her head, fingers in her soft hair, debating whether to answer or not.

The cell chimed again.

"You better get that." Jocelyn stepped back, hazel eyes a smoldering green.

As he connected the call from Chief Murray, she put her hand to her mouth. Nothing could convey she felt the kiss more.

"Colton?" Chief Murray jarred him to the call.

"Yeah. I'm here."

"We got a call from Janice Tapp. She called 911, frantic that someone was in her house. Police arrived less than ten minutes later. She's gone."

Looking at Jocelyn, Trevor went still. "She was supposed to leave town."

"Well, apparently she didn't listen."

"We're on our way."

"What happened?" Jocelyn asked.

Then the landline rang. Another phone on the lower level rang with it. Trevor could hear it through the air vents. In the otherwise eerie silence, he turned to the phone the same time she did. Jocelyn's business card contained that number. Only one person would call.

"Colton?" Chief Murray said.

"The phone is ringing," he said. "The Operation Apple Pie phone," he clarified.

He needed to say no more.

"I'll be…she's going to use Janice to draw us in."

Or just Jocelyn.

Jocelyn pressed the speaker button on the telephone. "Hometown Real Estate."

"Well, if it isn't Miss Well Done, I Want My Pie Hot," a woman's voice said, low with menace. Regina.

"Who is this?" Jocelyn asked, playing ignorant.

"I'm the waitress you didn't tip at Buckaroo Burgers. A haughty one like you wouldn't remember someone like me. But I'm going to make sure you never forget me as long as you live."

"Waitress… Oh." Jocelyn feigned dawning. "You're that incompetent woman who served us lunch the other day." Trevor made a slicing motion across his neck, signaling her not to incite the woman too much.

"Are you calling to harass me? If so, I'll report you to police."

Of course, Jocelyn wouldn't do what he told her. For once, he wished she'd listen to him. He sliced with a harder, jerkier motion.

"I have something for you."

Through the speaker, a woman whimpered and then half screamed.

"Come on, tell the bitch on the phone how much you'd like to live. This is Janice Tapp. She's another rude patron such as yourself. I waited on her table and she had not one nice thing to say to me. Isn't that right, *Janice?*"

Trevor caught Jocelyn's instant change. From tough cop playing a role, she went right into the woman who'd rushed out of the house from a gory crime scene.

"Please," the woman begged, crying. "Please don't kill me."

"You people are all alike. When you're in control and giving orders, you feel safe treating those you view as less important poorly. But when the control is stripped away, this is what's left." The woman whimpered over the phone again.

"Tell her what I have in my hand," Regina said.

"A—a...knife. She cut me with it. Please. She's going to kill me. I need hel—" The sound of flesh hitting flesh preceded a thump, Janice falling to the floor after being struck.

"You heard her. I'm going to kill her."

"Why are you calling me? What can I do?"

"You can join the party. We can call it my bachelorette party, one you all tried to take away from me. But I'm here to tell you—and so is Janice here—I'm not about to let that happen. You go to the South Street bus stop and wait for my call. Be there in two hours. And come alone. If I find out you're with that boyfriend of yours, or if you don't show up for my call, I will kill this woman. It will give me great pleasure to do so, too. She's just like you, man stealer."

Keep her talking, Trevor mouthed to Jocelyn. He'd put his cell on speaker so the chief could listen. The chief must be trying to trace the call.

"Man stealer? Why are you saying that?"

"South Street. Two hours. Or the lady dies."

"You want me to meet you at a bus stop?" Jocelyn asked.

"You heard me. Be there. Alone. Or I mean it, the woman dies." The line went dead.

Jocelyn looked at Trevor.

Through the cell speaker, the chief humphed in frustration. "We lost it."

"Get a task force meeting put together," Trevor said. "Jocelyn and I will be there in ten minutes."

When he disconnected, he didn't move. He just stared at Jocelyn, knowing what would come next.

"I'm going, Trevor."

After a long hesitation, going over every other option first, he said in resignation, "I know." If they'd ever catch Regina and stop her murderous rampage, they'd have to take some risks. *He'd* have to take some risks, one big one in particular.

The crowd of officers and detectives gathered in the meeting room, a murmur of voices combining to create a uniform sound. An occasional laugh or loud exclamation rose above the quiet din. Even though Facilities didn't allow smoking, a hint of the scent drifted in with the smokers, which pretty much included everyone. Except Trevor. She glanced at him standing next to her, chatting with the chief about the exceptionally warm weather they'd been having in Texas, a small piece of normalcy that might keep the gravity of the situation from overtaking the job ahead of everyone.

Finally, the chief glanced around. "Looks like we have everyone." Then he gave Trevor a single pat on his shoulder. "It's all yours. You know our perp better than anyone."

Jocelyn watched proudly as Trevor passed with a glance her way, worry mixing with intimacy before his cop hat went on and he took the podium.

"Thank you everyone for meeting on such short notice." He made eye contact with each person in the room as he began. Dressed in a black suit and tie, Trevor's aura of vitality and power would intimidate some. For Jocelyn, his presence radiated sex appeal.

"We have a serious break in the Alphabet Killer case and I need you all to be on the top of your game." He turned to Jocelyn, touching her with a look. "Regina Willard called our real estate office demanding Jocelyn meet her at a bus stop. Once again, we need to put one of our own in a very dangerous situation." He turned back to the group. "I'm not in favor of this tactic, but I believe it's the best one we have to work with. Before we put our plan in motion, let's go over the details."

He turned with a laser pointer at the projector screen. "This is the location of the bus stop." The red dot aimed at the bus stop. "Jocelyn will go there and see what Regina will do next." Lowering the laser pointer, he faced the team. "Given her profile, I'm pretty certain Regina will have next steps. She's copied a serial killer's methods and escaped capture up until now. She's smart. But she's also unstable. She isn't aware of Operation Apple Pie, or that Jocelyn is an FBI agent. If she were, she wouldn't have called and used another woman's life as leverage. She wouldn't risk exposure that way. We need to keep it that way. At most, she suspects Jocelyn will bring me along for protection. She'll try to throw me off, possibly by telling Jocelyn to meet in one of the nearby buildings, possibly by telling her to take a bus ride to another location."

Trevor moved out from behind the podium, brushing the lapels of his silky suit aside to place his hands on his hips. Stopping, he faced the room. "We have to be prepared for every scenario."

"There are a lot of vacant warehouses in that area," one of the officers said.

"That bus line goes into a rough part of Fort Worth. Next stop up is close to East Lancaster Avenue," another team member said.

Trevor nodded, glad they'd done some checking before they'd arrived. "Yes, which is why we need to prepare. We don't have much time. Regina is getting desperate. She's tried unsuccessfully to capture and kill Jocelyn. She's got her next victim. Janice has been kidnapped. That's two women with names that begin with *J*. She's getting sloppy. Overconfident. Now is our best chance to move in. If she knew about this task force, she'd feel how close we are to catching her and she'd back off. We just cannot allow her to discover who we are. She has to continue to be overconfident."

Now Jocelyn understood why Trevor had gone along with this plan—to allow Jocelyn into a dangerous situation. He'd give away the sting operation if he sent in backup or sent someone else in Jocelyn's place. The only way forward was to send Jocelyn, to make Regina believe she'd drawn a real estate agent with long dark hair and a name that began with a *J* into her clutches. She'd try to live out her warped plan, picking out women who reminded her of the one who'd damaged her.

"We need surveillance vans near each bus stop on the line. A sniper up high. Boots on the ground and wheels on the street." Trevor began assigning tasks to the members.

SWAT would cover the street; the surveillance teams were already in place. Two snipers left the room to go to their locations.

"Any questions?"

An officer raised his hand, pointer finger up.

Trevor nodded.

"Will Jocelyn be wired?"

"She'll wear a tracking device. No radio. We'll have the ability to listen to everything said within two hundred yards."

"At what point do we go in for the package?" a burly man standing in the back of the room with his arms folded over his beefy chest asked.

By *package*, he meant Jocelyn. At what point would the team move in to rescue her? She turned to Trevor, who met her look grimly.

"At any point when her safety is compromised. Regina pulls a weapon. We lose sight of Jocelyn. Take no chances."

"I'll give you a sign," Jocelyn said, and when Trevor's gaze grew impatient, she added, "If I'm in a position to hand her over to authorities, or can keep her from getting away, give me the opportunity. I'll know when I need help."

Trevor thought that through and said, "Fine. The code is *Time for some pie*. You say that, the team goes in."

"Agreed," she said.

"But if I think you're in too much danger, I can say the same." He scanned the entire team, meeting each man's and woman's eyes. "Each and every one of you is authorized to use the code. If you see Jocelyn in danger, if you think she needs help, use the code."

A chorus of "Yes, sir" passed through the crowd.

"Roger that," the burly man said, giving Jocelyn a nod.

Reassuring, to know she had a team of confident commandos backing her. But Trevor might be taking his protectiveness too far. And then again, maybe not. She trusted him to keep her safe.

When no one else asked any more questions, Trevor said, "All right. Let's catch this killer."

Chapter 15

Jocelyn drove to the bus stop in a car the bureau gave her. The plates would trace to Jocelyn the real estate agent, not Jocelyn of the FBI. She parked and climbed out, walking down the sidewalk with soundless steps. She'd dressed in slacks and a business jacket and tactical shoes that would pass as business. She'd clipped her hair up in a prudish bun and donned her stylish sunglasses. She and Trevor had had just enough time to go back to the apartment to change and arm up.

With a gun in her purse and a knife strapped to her calf, she arrived at the bus stop and searched the area. A man waited for the bus, sitting on the bench absorbed with his cell phone. Cars passed on the four-lane road, one-story strip malls on each side, dated and run-down. She took out the cell phone they used for the sting operation and waited.

As the bus approached, the phone rang.

"Looks like I'll be getting on the bus," she said, knowing the team would hear. She answered the call. "Yes?"

"Get on the bus."

"And then what?"

"Just get on the bus." Regina disconnected.

With a look around, Jocelyn boarded and sat in the middle, checking each face. None looked like the waitress from Buckaroo Burgers. The man who'd sat on the bench passed her and sat a few rows down.

The bus rolled out and Jocelyn looked down at the phone. It didn't ring until the bus reached the next stop.

"Yes?"

"Get off here."

Jocelyn looked back and checked all the faces again. How had Regina known exactly when she'd arrive? She checked the street through the windows. Traffic passed as the bus stopped along the curb.

She followed the man from the other stop off the bus. He walked down the street, seeming oblivious.

Jocelyn searched for signs of Regina. The last stop had been located in a rough area, but this one far surpassed that. A topless bar across the street wouldn't be open for several more hours, but the hole-in-the-wall a couple of doors down had already drawn a bawdy crowd. A drunk man stumbled outside and two more leather-clad, tattooed men with greasy hair entered.

The bus pulled back out into the street and Jocelyn felt a moment of aloneness that had her questioning the wisdom of doing this.

Trevor had the team in place. He had everything under control…except his overprotectiveness.

A car drove up and parked. The passenger window rolled down.

"You're the lady who's meeting the waitress?" the driver asked. A middle-aged man with an untrimmed mustache and tired, bloodshot brown eyes, he seemed ignorant of the purpose of the meeting.

"Who are you?" Jocelyn stepped closer to the car as the cell rang again.

"I'm your driver. I'll take you where you need to go."

"You're a cab driver?"

"A private one. I don't work for any company. I do this on the side."

The cell rang twice more. She answered.

"Get in the car."

"Why? Where will it take me?"

"Get in the car or the woman dies."

Jocelyn began to have a bad feeling. She looked for Trevor's team and didn't see anyone. She didn't see the man who'd left the bus in front of her, either.

"Who is the driver?"

"You ask too many questions. He doesn't know anything. Get in the car." Regina hung up.

Jocelyn debated going into the car a few seconds and then opened the back door. She checked the interior for anything suspicious. No litter cluttered the floor or seats. The driver had no identification.

"Your fare has already been paid," the driver said.

Jocelyn sat in the back and reluctantly closed the door. "How do you know Regina Willard?"

"Who?" The driver pulled out into the street, glancing in the rearview mirror.

"Regina Willard. Isn't that who paid you?"

"I don't know no Regina Willard."

"Who paid you, then?"

"She didn't give me her name. It's the kind of business I do. I don't ask. I just get paid well for what I do."

"Driving people to suspicious places?"

"Driving, errands. I'm a multitasker."

For criminals? Maybe he'd be arrested when this was over.

"How did she know to call you?"

"Don't know how she got my name. Word travels on the street. I have a reputation for discretion."

"Even when crimes are committed."

"I don't get involved in anyone's business, ma'am. I'll drop you off at the address given to me, and then I'll leave. Whatever business you have with the lady who paid me is none of mine."

"What did the woman look like?" Jocelyn removed her wallet from her purse and took out a photo of Regina. "Did she look like this?"

The driver took the photo she handed to him and looked from that to the road a few times.

"Yeah. 'Cept with red hair." He handed the photo back.

The driver looked into the rearview mirror, clearly curious as to why she carried a picture of the woman who'd paid him to drive her somewhere.

Regina had kidnapped Janice and decided to use her to draw Jocelyn. A real two-for-one. This time Regina planned to kill two women who had names that began with *J*.

"She paid you in advance?" Jocelyn asked.

"Yes. That's one of my requirements. The other is not to tell me your business." His gaze stayed in the mirror longer than the other times.

"Where did you meet her?"

"I mean no disrespect, ma'am. You don't discuss your business and I don't discuss mine."

When he drove out of the city and onto a country road, Jocelyn had to quell rising apprehension.

Trevor did not like this. "She's moving her too many times."

"Easy," Chief Murray said. He'd driven the unmarked police car behind the bus. They'd parked down the street to wait. When the strange car had appeared and Regina instructed Jocelyn to get in, Trevor felt an ulcer developing in his stomach. Now the car left the city.

"We're going to be made," one of the teammates said into the radio. "It's too open out here."

"Stay back," Trevor said. The best way to protect Jocelyn right now would be to avoid detection.

Murray slowed and let the other car gain distance.

"Don't let us get farther than two hundred yards from her." As long as they could hear her, they could find her. He hoped.

"This must have cost her a fortune." How could a waitress afford to pay for an expensive taxi fee? Janice was a successful woman. Maybe she'd taken the money from her.

A ranch came into view. When the driver slowed to make the turn onto the driveway, Jocelyn knew she'd reached her destination.

"An abandoned ranch?" She spoke aloud so the team could hear.

The house had boarded-up windows and missing trim. The roof must surely leak. Weeds grew into the driveway. The barn appeared the least weathered, metal roof still intact, red paint fading but still passable. Whoever owned the place, or used to, must have cared more for their livestock than their home.

"What is this place?" she asked.

"Don't know." The driver stopped at the end of the driveway, where a carport had fallen over and broken into several pieces.

Jocelyn studied the buildings, looking for signs of Regina. She could be hiding somewhere with a gun aimed at her, red marker ready.

"You going to meet this woman or not?" the driver asked.

At least he wouldn't leave her here. Balancing his clientele must get challenging in situations like this. Had he ever been threatened by anyone for not dropping off his riders?

"Won't you be in trouble if you drive me back to the city?"

"I have my terms, and I have security—also part of my reputation. Discretion comes with a price. People respect mine, I respect theirs. It's simple."

"Right. Simple." Jocelyn took out her pistol. She had a big purse to carry this beauty. Seeing the driver twist to see better what she had in her hand, Jocelyn opened the back door. "Thanks for the ride."

He said nothing as she left the vehicle. Regina had to be his most dangerous client to date.

With no trees to cover her approach she had to assume Regina already saw her. She walked with her hand on the gun inside her purse, the purse securely strapped from shoulder to hip.

When the sound of the unmarked taxi driving away

faded, the doors to the barn opened and Regina appeared. She went back into the barn and got into a car. Driving out, she stopped in front of Jocelyn, the passenger window down.

"Get in."

"I think I'll pass. Where's your friend Janice?" Jocelyn saw no sign of her.

Clever.

"Don't try anything or you will never find her. Get in."

It didn't matter if Regina thought Jocelyn had come armed and would consider trying to overtake her. Jocelyn wouldn't try anything until she knew Janice was safe.

Wherever she kept Janice, she'd arranged for Jocelyn to be dropped off here. Even the discreet driver wouldn't be able to say where Jocelyn had been taken.

"I'll just drive away and no one will be able to save Janice. Do you want that on your conscience? You let an innocent woman die because you wouldn't get into the car?"

"Why should I care about some woman I've never met?"

Regina smiled wickedly. "You obviously do, or you wouldn't have come this far. You passed your first test."

So, she had tested Jocelyn to see how much she cared? If she hadn't been able to draw her out, what then? Just be satisfied with killing one woman whose name began with a *J*?

"Why are you doing this?" Jocelyn asked.

"All you cheating women are the same. You'll take any man from a woman who's better suited for him.

You control them and warp their thinking. You poison them. Well, no more. Get in."

"I'd be stupid to get in this car with you."

"Then Janice dies." She began to slide up the window.

"Wait." Jocelyn had pushed all she could. She had to get into the car. She did.

Sitting in a killer's vehicle unnerved her. She struggled to get back on track. Be the agent. She'd trained for this.

Regina drove her back in the direction of the city, all the way to the first bus stop, turning on a street not far from there and driving into the parking lot of an abandoned warehouse.

Jocelyn recalled that Janice's pleading voice had echoed. She was inside this building.

"You took Janice to this warehouse?" she said for the team.

"Shut up and go inside."

Jocelyn got out of the car and walked toward a metal door. Regina used a key to unlock it, looking around to make sure no one saw, not knowing that she had an audience of police and FBI personnel.

Inside, the warehouse gaped open and empty.

"Help me!" a woman screamed. "I'm in here!"

Jocelyn had to decide her next action. Should she wait or take her chance now to overpower Regina.

The crazed woman had her back to her, overconfident as Trevor had accurately assessed, more concerned with the noise Janice made than anything Jocelyn might do. Now would be an opportune time.

Not wasting another second, Jocelyn took out her pistol and pressed it to Regina's head. "Hands up, Regina." For the team, she said, "Time for some pie."

Regina stopped and her head whipped to see her. "What did you say?"

"Time for some pie. Hands up where I can see them. Now."

"Who the—"

"Get your hands up now!" Jocelyn shouted.

Regina lifted her hands. She had made a mistake not keeping her attention on Jocelyn. "You're under arrest for the murders of several women." She began to name off the victims one by one. Her backup would be here anytime. Regina was captured.

"Who are you?" Regina asked when Jocelyn finished reading her rights.

"Jocelyn Locke, FBI." She patted Regina down and quickly found her weapon. Sliding it out from the back waist of her jeans, she held it up in front of Regina's face before tucking it in her own pants.

When all she got was a glare, Jocelyn finished patting her down. "We've had you under surveillance for a while now." She reached for her handcuffs and then remembered she'd left them behind because too much gear would be too noticeable.

Regina eyed her with mounting hatred. "You've been watching me?"

"Yes. The restaurant? The hamburger complaints?" She put both hands on the pistol as she aimed. "The *pie*?" She breathed a short laugh. "Delicious, by the way."

"You faked all that." Disbelief rang in Regina's tone.

Enough chatter. "Walk," Jocelyn ordered. "Take me to Janice." Jocelyn jabbed Regina's ribs with her gun. "Keep your hands up."

Regina obeyed and headed for an enclosed office

near the front, using a key for the padlock holding the door secure and inescapable. As she pushed the door open, Jocelyn spotted a frightened, tear-streaked Janice cowering on the floor, knees bent and shaking, hands tied behind her back and to the exposed plumbing of what had once been a bathroom. On the ledge and out of reach, Regina had left a big knife.

"Untie her." Jocelyn gave Regina another jab. "Now." She glanced back at the warehouse entrance. Where the hell was the team? They should be swarming this place by now.

Regina untied Janice, who scurried over to Jocelyn.

"You're safe now. Help is on the way."

Wasn't it?

"Damn it!" Trevor slapped the dashboard. "I told you not to fall more than two hundred yards away!"

"Regina would have made us. It was too open by the abandoned ranch. We had to wait until she started driving down the highway."

Regina had driven fast back into town. They'd reached the city with no signal from Jocelyn.

"Unit 1, any sign?" Trevor asked into the radio.

"Negative."

"Negative for Unit 2."

"Unit 3, as well."

"Drive a grid." He ordered the units to spread out and work their way deeper into the city. They had enough vehicles to cover the ground fairly quickly, but would it be fast enough?

"What are we waiting for?" Janice asked.

Jocelyn would like to know the answer to that, as

well. That gnawing apprehension had mushroomed in the past few minutes. Had the team lost contact with her?

"My team will be here any moment." Although Jocelyn sounded confident, Regina didn't look convinced.

Maybe she should move them somewhere more public.

"Let's go for a walk." Jocelyn motioned with her pistol. "Come on. Outside."

Regina stood from the floor, where Jocelyn had made her sit.

"Janice, you go on ahead. Go find help."

"I'd be happy to." Frightened and dirty and disheveled, Janice hurried from the room. She kept going until she reached the outer door, going through without a backward glance.

Regina turned her head to glance back at Jocelyn.

"Don't even think about it," Jocelyn said. The woman would try to escape. Jocelyn stayed on high alert, but her worry that something had happened to the team distracted her.

At the door, Jocelyn gave Regina room—in case she decided to fight. But the woman calmly went through the door.

Bright sunlight blinded her a moment. She shaded her eyes and spotted Janice running toward the street. Once she made it there, she'd head toward the highway and the strip mall. Hopefully she wouldn't run into any more trouble in this part of the city.

The brief seconds she spent checking on Janice cost her. Regina paid attention now. She used that moment to swing her fist back and knock Jocelyn's gun. Jocelyn managed to hang on to it, but Regina swung around and kicked her. She flew backward, landing on her backside.

Regina got into her car and started it up as Jocelyn pushed back onto her feet. She aimed her weapon and fired as Regina fishtailed toward the opposite exit of the parking lot from where Janice had fled. Her bullets shattered the rear window, but she missed Regina.

Jocelyn flashed back to the crime scene she'd seen with Trevor. The blood and gore. The lifeless body. The lifelessness was what had gotten to her most. Vacant eyes. No more energy left, just flesh and bone. She felt almost relieved she'd missed Regina. But then she thought of the victims and kept firing.

When she kept missing, she aimed for the rear tires and fired. If she couldn't stop Regina by killing her, maybe she could stop her another way. But Regina had gained too much distance and she missed those shots, too.

Lowering her gun to her side, Jocelyn turned and started walking the way Janice had gone. A minute later, she heard vehicles approach.

The SUV swerved into the parking lot. Behind them, the first surveillance van appeared.

The SUV stopped, stirring up dust with the abruptness.

Jocelyn rushed toward Trevor as he alighted from the passenger side. "She went that way!" Jocelyn pointed.

Trevor strode toward her, man on a mission. He took hold of her wrists and lifted, examining her up and down.

"Are you all right?" He touched her face and turned it from side to side and then ran his hands down her ribs, leaning to see behind her, all with acutely alert eyes.

"I'm fine. Regina is getting away."

"Get in!" the chief shouted.

Jocelyn climbed into the back and Trevor the front as the chief drove through the parking lot, radioing to the surveillance team to stay behind.

"She went that way." Jocelyn pointed.

The chief turned right onto a street. As they sped along, it became readily obvious that Regina had vanished yet again.

The chief drove down several streets and made it to the highway before giving up.

He drove them back to the warehouse parking lot, where the surveillance team waited.

Getting out of the vehicle, Jocelyn went to stand near the van. They'd gather evidence and continue their search for Regina.

Trevor moved in front of her. "Are you sure you're okay?" He slid his hands down her ribs to her thighs.

She smiled and put her hands on his chest. "Yes. You can stop feeling me up."

He relaxed, a slight grin creasing the corners of his mouth. "You must be fine. You're teasing again."

"I handled myself well all alone, Agent Colton. You should have seen me." But she began to see the mistakes she'd made, a lone agent without guaranteed backup.

Chief Murray came to stand beside them, taking notice of their personal exchange and acting a bit awkward about it.

Jocelyn removed her hands from Trevor. "I managed to get a plate number."

"Good work," the chief said. "We got out of range after you left the ranch."

She returned her attention to him. He seemed apologetic.

"We didn't want to be seen," Trevor added, looking around. "Where's Janice?"

"She went to get help. Since help wasn't coming." She only half teased. What must Janice think of their task force? Jocelyn had saved her, yes, but her would-be killer still ran free.

Trevor ran his fingers through his hair. They kept failing to catch Regina. That had to get to him. But had his concern for Jocelyn cost them?

"You have no idea what that did to him," Chief Murray said. "Not knowing what was going on with you made him a little crazy." The chief turned to the officers who'd gotten out of the surveillance van. "The vic went to find help. Go find her."

"Yes, sir." The men hopped back in the van.

"What happened?" Trevor asked as the van drove off.

"I drew my gun and held her at gunpoint, thinking you were all hearing everything. I expected you to be here moments after I subdued her."

"Damn it, Jocelyn. You should have waited."

That sparked her ire. "How can you say that? If I'd waited, she would have overpowered me. She was armed."

He sighed and looked away, unable to refute that. He was being unreasonable because he'd been so scared. She appreciated his concern. It said he cared more than he felt comfortable.

"Did you arrest her?"

"Of course, without cuffs."

The chief shared a look with Trevor. "So now she knows who we are."

Jocelyn hadn't thought of that.

"She might go into hiding." Trevor ran his fingers through his hair again. "We're back to square one."

Jocelyn felt like the rookie Trevor always said she was as he paced in a frustrated circle.

"What else should I have done?" she asked.

He stopped, looked at her and then stepped over to her, brushing his curled fingers down her cheek, sending tingles spreading. "Nothing. You did the right thing. We lost contact with you. The plan failed. You didn't. I went out of my mind with worry, but you did what you were supposed to do. Your dad and your brother would both be proud of you, of the way you handled yourself."

Oh. An inner wave of truth swept her. She felt as though she'd reached a milestone, as though she'd achieved what she'd set out to achieve ever since losing her dad and brother. This was why she'd joined the FBI. She'd joined to honor them, to do what they'd have done. And they'd have done exactly what she had.

So the perp had gotten away. They wouldn't stop chasing Regina. They wouldn't stop until she was captured and put behind bars. Then Jocelyn could say she was finished. That she was ready for the next chapter in her life. The chapter on family.

Would Trevor be with her? Really with her?

She still wasn't sure, but his saying this proved he was closer than ever before.

"Thank you." She rose up and pecked his cheek with a kiss.

By the time she stopped gushing over his sweetness, the chief had wandered away. But he'd stopped in the area where Regina's car had been parked.

Bending, he picked up a twice-folded piece of paper. Unraveling it, he read and then lifted his head.

"It's a pay stub under one of Regina's aliases." He looked down again.

Jocelyn moved closer with Trevor.

"It's from a restaurant in Fort Worth," the chief said. "One we haven't staked out."

When Trevor's head turned toward her, Jocelyn met his look. They didn't have to speak. Regina had dropped the stub on purpose. She'd gotten another job at a new restaurant and seemed to be trying to lure them there.

Chapter 16

Chief Murray said he'd gather intel on the restaurant and contact Trevor and Jocelyn when he had something to report. That left Trevor with some alone time with Jocelyn. Losing contact with her had tortured him, and also slapped the importance of getting over having a serial killer for a dad in his face. Why couldn't people just decide to shut out the negativity from their pasts? Decide, and make it be so. Shed the ugliness like snake skin. Choose to only be happy, to only focus on what made them happy.

Easier said than done. Unfortunately, experiences shaped lives.

After picking up a very upset Sigmund from the apartment, Trevor took Jocelyn to her condo. Now that Regina knew who they were, they had no reason to pretend anymore. They'd risk her attempting to come after them, but then, she'd also risk capture.

Jocelyn sat on her couch with a laptop open on the coffee table, tracking down Regina's various aliases, how she'd stolen them and from whom, putting together their evidence in preparation for a trial. He did adore her optimism.

Going over to her, he sat next to her and picked up the laptop, placing it on his lap.

She turned to him, startled.

Grinning, he leaned back. "There's something I want to show you."

As he began navigating to an internet browser, she leaned back with him.

"I've been thinking," he said. "When this investigation is over, we're going to need a place to live." He opened a real estate page. "As I have told you, my house is too small and I'm tired of it anyway. You live in a condo with no yard."

"Trevor," she said, hesitant.

"If we're going to have a dog…" He opened the page where he'd found a house.

"Trevor, what—"

"Just look, Jocelyn."

She did, leaning closer to see the page. When she saw the three-car, two-story with a basement, she took the laptop and angled it for a better view.

The smoky-green-with-white-trim house had a covered porch and a flower bed along the front.

"It's four bedrooms. The basement is unfinished, so there's plenty of growing room," he said.

She clicked on the next picture.

Trevor watched her absorption. She intently studied each photo. The living room open to the kitchen. The dining area. Formal living room. Den with double

French doors. The master bedroom with five-piece bath and spacious walk-in closet. A loft. Everything a family needed to make years of memories. He had the concept down, just not the practice.

At last she moved back and looked up at him, speechless.

"Yeah." He smiled. "I like it, too."

"Have you gone there?" she asked.

"No. I wanted to show you first. I'll call and set up a showing."

She looked away. Her uncertainty bothered him.

"Jocelyn, I want to make this work."

She nodded. "You've said that before." Standing, she walked across the living room to the window. Dark outside, lights twinkled.

He stood and went to her. "I have some work to do." On himself. On separating his identity from his father's. "I can do that."

Slowly she faced him. "I know you want to, Trevor. But wanting and it being a reality are very different."

"Give me a chance, Jocelyn. Just give me that."

Her eyes softened and for a moment he thought she'd come around. But then his phone chimed. And she closed her mouth, stopping whatever she'd have said.

Seeing the chief called, Trevor didn't push her. Answering, he turned away from Jocelyn, the sight of her almost painful. Her doubt, her lack of faith in him, dug deep.

"We checked out the Fort Worth restaurant," Chief Murray said.

Jocelyn reached around him and snatched his cell phone. Pressing the speaker button, she put it down on the table.

"Colton?"

"Yeah. Just put the phone on speaker." He met Jocelyn's mock reproach. "You were saying?"

"Checked out the restaurant and discovered the damnedest thing. It was just closed down by the health department yesterday."

"You don't say."

"Why was it closed down?" Jocelyn asked.

"Contaminated meat and the presence of rats. A real live *Ratatouille*. We spoke to the owner, who said he reported the incident to the police. We verified and, sure enough, he reported that he suspected the meat and rats were planted. His food order records were wiped. Someone hacked in and deleted them. So he has no proof he ordered the meat. The usual vendor he uses to deliver his orders didn't show an order, but said they don't sell the kind of meat found in the restaurant. Two other companies do. There was an order placed for meat, but the person who ordered wasn't identified. Furthermore, the delivery address didn't match the restaurant. It matched the address to the warehouse."

Trevor connected with Jocelyn's sharp glance.

"Did you ask him about Regina?" Jocelyn asked.

"Oh, yes. We had a lengthy conversation about her. He didn't suspect anything about her. Not until we explained who she is. He said she's shown up to work on time and the customers and coworkers all had no complaints about her."

Not until one of them pissed her off.

"The owner was shocked to learn she's our prime suspect in the Alphabet Killer case."

"Does he know where to find her?"

He gave us an address. We checked it out. It's an

address of a house that's been on the market for weeks. Vacant. No sign of her staying there, but we did find the car she drove in the garage. Stolen, of course. She's moved on."

Regina always moved on. She quickly did so. She stayed a step ahead of them, always knowing the right time to flee.

But why would she lead them to a restaurant? Why stage a health department violation and close it down? An elaborate scheme like that took time. But maybe that was what Regina craved. She needed the challenge, the requirement for brainpower, the feeling that she could outsmart everyone. But why the restaurant? She'd lured Jocelyn to the warehouse, an equally elaborate plan with the anonymous taxi driver and the multiple stops. Why had she thought that plan wouldn't work? The risk that Jocelyn would bring her man? Or a step higher. Maybe she'd anticipated Jocelyn would call the police.

"She must have had this planned ahead of time," Jocelyn said as the very same thought came to him.

Regina had clearly intended to draw them to the restaurant so she could capture Jocelyn. She wouldn't have dropped the pay stub otherwise. She'd planned for the restaurant to be closed. No one would be there. A brilliant backup plan. And she intended to go through with it, even though she now knew the feds were onto her. She'd caused the health department violation, determined to lure Jocelyn.

Jocelyn had done a great job acting her part. She'd angered the serial killer, turned herself into a top target. Regina had gone full out to get her. Now she would take on the FBI. Bold.

Overconfident.

"We're setting up the team now," the chief said.

"She'll be expecting a party," Trevor said.

From all Trevor knew about Regina, she'd love to outsmart the FBI. She may even be planning something else to fool them. If she could come up with two clever plans to lure her prey, why not a third? Plan A. Plan B. Plan C, D and E. She would do anything not to lose. And the closer she came to that, the more daring her actions, the more risk she'd be willing to take. She'd thrive on the excitement.

He began to have serious reservations about this. Looking over at Jocelyn, he saw her thinking along with him, eyes down on the phone and then lifting to meet his.

Instantly, she read him and her mouth pinched in slight frustration.

He held up his hand. "Hey, just looking at the facts."

"She's desperate."

"That makes her dangerous." He stepped closer to her.

She put her hand on her hip. "She's already dangerous."

While he noticed the hitch of her hip as she bent one leg, he stopped an escalating retort with a grunt and a long exhale. "Jocelyn…"

"She's going to extremes to get me. I know. So let's get her instead."

"I'd…" Should he say it? "Jocelyn, I—I don't mean to sound overprotective. I just… I wish you'd stay here. I want our family life to start now." He wanted her out of this line of work.

Whether his stuttering softened her or his reasoning, she lowered her hand and looked less confrontational. "How do we know that's not part of her plan?

She could anticipate us doing something like that. I'm not safe anywhere right now."

Except right next to him.

"She has a good point," the chief said. "And, yes, I'm still here."

He'd listened to their personal exchange, which held plenty of emotion.

What was worse, Trevor had to agree with him.

"So, we're a go," the chief said. "I'm sending over the meeting place and time. We'll surround the restaurant and clear it. If Regina is there, we'll catch her."

That all sounded fantastic in theory, but Trevor had been trained to look through the eyes of a killer, and what he saw filled him with dread.

Jocelyn refrained from going over to Trevor and touching him. The way he directed the task force, in charge but a team player. Everyone respected him. He had such finesse. Such an authoritative, sophisticated, and yet physically strong presence. Trevor saw her suiting up, putting on a bulletproof vest, and she felt his approval.

"Some might say you're the one who'll protect him tonight."

Jocelyn pulled herself together. Had Chief Murray noticed her ogling Trevor? "Excuse me? *Trevor?*"

The chief chuckled. "Brush it off all you want. I can recognize young people in love, especially young people who either don't believe it or refuse to." He finished securing her earpiece in place. "Give him a shot."

"What?"

Chief Murray chuckled again, this time deeper. "I've known Trevor awhile. He takes everything so seriously.

But he's come a long way despite what he's been through. Catching this Alphabet Killer—this copycat—will help him put to bed all the demons Matthew Colton brought into his life."

Jocelyn could only stare.

"You'll see."

Would she?

"If you give him a chance."

He humbled her by zeroing in on exactly what she and Trevor had discussed—and saying what Trevor had. "Did he talk to you?"

Only an understanding smile, soft and expressing the wisdom in his eyes, answered her.

"Listen to Trevor. Work as a team. We'll have this wrapped up in no time," he said.

She watched him walk away, going over to some other agents to have some final words.

Then she turned her head and caught Trevor looking at her, taking in her vest and seeing more than its protective layer. God, she loved the way he looked at her.

He pointed and mouthed, *You.* He moved his point to himself. *Are mine.*

Oh, really? His playfulness touched her. Playful, but then, not. Their banter had always come easy.

She pointed at him and mouthed, *You.* She pointed to her stomach. *Are hers.*

Intense passion, satisfaction, masculine power lowered his head and put a hooded shadow over his eyes. He pointed to her stomach. *His.*

"Okay, people," the chief called. "Time to go to work." He recapped their strategy.

They'd arrived at the meet—a few blocks away. The backup would stay concealed and the task force SWAT team would accompany her and Trevor to the restaurant. They didn't want to alert Regina and send her running, so after they secured the perimeter, the SWAT team would go in after them.

Whereas before Jocelyn felt the buzz of purpose every time she faced a situation, she didn't now. And she realized she hadn't felt it when she'd caught Regina at the warehouse. She'd had a sense of duty—what needed to be done to apprehend the woman, but not that inner need to fill an empty space, the space her father and brother once filled.

Getting out of Trevor's SUV and looking over the hood at him as he looked at her, she felt him filling that space instead.

How had that happened? How had she gone from missing her dad and brother—her family—to yearning for Trevor at her side?

And even more perplexing, how had he wormed his way into her heart enough to make her really see that she could be happy in that house he showed her? With kids and pets, no longer working for the FBI, no longer working dangerous cases, no longer needing to.

She checked her pistol. Trevor doing the same as they met in front of the SUV, waiting for the lead SWAT officer to give them the go-ahead. They stayed out of sight. Jocelyn hadn't seen them when they'd arrived. If anyone inside the restaurant had seen them, they would not see the team. Surveillance had parked down the street, out of sight. The SWAT team stealthily surrounded the building, prepared to rush in as soon as she and Trevor entered.

Trevor stepped to her. "I go in first." He leaned down and kissed her, then hovered there until she opened her eyes and met his. "Wife."

Warmth lit her up inside, humming in her chest and tickling her with pleasure. "Okay, *husband.*"

His crooked grin kept her high until he moved back and readied a second gun he had tucked in the back waist of his jeans.

Back to the task at hand.

"Let's do this." Holding her gun up, she walked with him to the back door.

The restaurant owner had given them a key. Trevor inserted it, on constant vigil for movement that wasn't SWAT. He opened the door and slowly pushed it wider, gun aimed, scanning the darkness.

No one was here.

Had Regina fled after discovering the FBI had zeroed in on her? No. Why leave the pay stub after she had discovered Jocelyn's true identity?

Jocelyn moved into the dim kitchen, commercial-grade stainless steel appliances gleaming. Counters and floors were immaculate. Neat and tidy. Light above one section shone on corners that hadn't been neglected. This restaurant was clean. Although dim, Jocelyn could see that. The owner could have ordered his staff to do a thorough cleaning, but Jocelyn didn't think this much cleaning could have been done in such a short period of time, not when the health department would have taken up a big chunk of it. The cleanliness only supported the theory that the meat had been planted.

Trevor checked the office off the kitchen, a small square space cluttered with papers, shelves with binders and a computer on a corner desk.

He gave a nod of all clear.

Jocelyn went to the dining room entrance. The owner had shown them floor plans and photos. Partial walls divided the dining room and bar area, some only half walls. She crouched for protection near one.

Trevor turned toward the private dining room to the right. He'd clear that before going through the rest of the building. He paused, turning to hold up his hand.

She nodded, lifting her eyes to let him know how annoying that was.

He went to the edge of the wall and she caught sight of the first SWAT officer in the kitchen. He moved out of sight as the next officer appeared.

Assured of their presence, she moved to the end of the wall, peering around and seeing only empty booths bathed in dim light. Moving through that area, she approached the front door and hostess area, meaning to take cover at another dividing wall there and let Trevor clear the entrance.

As she made it to the wall, an explosion erupted. She didn't know which direction it came from. The pressure knocked her backward. She flew through the air, losing her grip on her pistol. She hit one of the booths, her head smacking the edge of a table.

Vaguely she had images of Trevor flying through the air, too, opposite direction from her. He disappeared in a billow of flames and smoke, falling backward.

"Trevor," she barely got out as another explosion came from the kitchen, tearing down the wall where she'd fallen, the force throwing her several feet and debris hitting her. A board or something hard hit her head and she lost consciousness.

Coughing, Trevor rose up onto one elbow, wiping his burning eyes of dust. Two SWAT officers rushed to him. He pushed away their assistance.

"Jocelyn!" Pain sliced through his shoulder as he tried to stand. He'd taken a good hit when the explosion threw him back. He'd fallen back onto a table, his weight breaking the square slab in half. But Jocelyn had been closer to the explosions. The one from the kitchen might have killed her. It might have killed a few officers.

The SWAT member put his hand on his chest. "We have people searching for her. We have to get you out of here."

"Searching? Where is she? She was right next to me. She has to be here." He looked through the smoke and flames. Firefighters had arrived. Roaring flames engulfed the wall between the kitchen and dining area and the corner where Jocelyn had been standing. Intense heat went against the logic of staying inside the building.

He'd been out long enough for the emergency vehicle to arrive. Long enough for Regina to take Jocelyn. She had to be responsible for this.

Another man in black approached, the SWAT lead. "She's not here. Let's get him out of here."

Trevor moved to stand, coughing.

The officer who'd been with him when he'd regained consciousness provided support. "You need a paramedic."

Trevor swatted his hands away and stood, bracing his hand on the rubble, getting scratched and not caring. He staggered to his feet, dizzy, urgently needing to find Jocelyn.

The SWAT lead took the other officer's arm to keep him from getting in Trevor's way.

"Let him look."

Through smoke and avoiding the flames, Trevor moved so he could see the charred dining area where he'd last seen Jocelyn. She was not there. Smoke thickened and thinned as it billowed and moved with the flames.

He went to the next partitioned dining area. Not there. He faced the officers, who waited anxiously. To his right, he saw an ambulance through the open back door, the explosion having ripped a bigger hole, lights flashing and paramedics loading an injured officer.

They were in the firefighters' way.

Reluctantly, Trevor went outside with the lead and the officer.

"We're searching the perimeter," the lead said as they left through the open front door.

Outside, coughing along with Trevor and the officer, the lead said, "If you want to help, we need you to think, Trevor."

They needed his analysis experience. To find Jocelyn. Precious time slipped by. Every second wasted put her life in more danger.

Flames rose up over the vicinity of the kitchen, not so much over the dining area. A lesser charge had been used there. To preserve life? Regina needed Jocelyn alive so she could stage the death.

Trevor swallowed his fear. "Regina has her." There could be no other explanation.

Trevor moved in a circle, his head pounding and feeling thick, blood trickling down from a cut. None of that mattered.

Think.

Pedestrians gathered to watch the emergency unfolding before their eyes. But other than that, nothing moved near the restaurant. No cars. No people.

"Where's the owner?" Trevor asked.

"In the back, upset over the damage," the lead said.

"I need to talk to him." Trevor started walking toward the side of the building.

The lead stopped him and raised his hand, snapping at an officer standing next to them.

The officer nodded and spoke into his radio. The owner would be summoned.

Trevor paced, not liking the time that passed.

Jocelyn.

He could not lose her. Not now.

"This is Andy, the owner," the lead said.

Trevor faced the average-height man—if not on the short side—whose bald head accented his big, round blue eyes. Uncle Fester with blue eyes.

"My restaurant," the man complained, stressed and turning that look toward his building. "I'll never recover from this."

"The bureau will help as much as possible," Trevor said, putting on his political face. Jocelyn's life depended on him—on this entire team—finding her.

"Really?"

"I'll do my best to see it's so. Andy, is there anything you can tell us about your building? Are there any other exits than the front and back doors? A crawl space?" Something.

Andy's eyebrows popped wider. "There's a secret tunnel underneath the dining room."

A…secret tunnel?

"What?" the SWAT lead said, as shocked as Trevor.

Why hadn't he brought that up sooner? Like…*before* the team arrived. Trevor willed his anger into submission. Andy didn't know the tunnel would have been

significant. He explained he associated it with histori-
cal importance.

"What do you know about the tunnel?"

"It was dug during prohibition. Texas had a different take on the laws, but they still had bootleggers."

"Where does the tunnel go?"

"A couple of miles to what used to be open space but
is now a warehouse."

The sting of realization froze inside Trevor. "The
Fenton Street warehouse?"

"Yes."

Trevor bit back a curse. Regina had known about
the tunnel.

"That's quite a jog," the lead said.

Trevor marched back toward the building, not caring if the firefighters weren't finished yet. He reached
the front door and pushed aside a firefighter.

"Sir! You can't go in there."

He kept going. The fire had already been doused in
the dining area and firefighters worked mainly in the
kitchen now. Smoke choked him. He lifted his jacket
lapel up to cover his mouth and nose. The tunnel connected to the dining room where Jocelyn had fallen.
He searched the walls and floor. There were no secret
passageways in the walls. With the fireman watching,
and the SWAT lead going to stand beside him, Trevor
searched the floor. Most of the wood planks connected
in solid lines, but a small gap about three feet squared
indicated that section came free.

Kneeling, he felt along the crease. His finger slid into
a notch in the wood and he came against a small lever.
Pressing harder, it snapped free and the floor began to
swing downward.

"You better let us check this out first," the fire-fighter said.

"We've got it." The lead tossed Trevor a flashlight, which he caught, and then Trevor lowered himself into the hole.

"Nick. Harry," the lead called.

Two more SWAT officers followed the lead down. Trevor walked along the rough-walled dirt corridor, having to bend his head in places. Seeing tracks in the dirt ground, he stopped and crouched.

"Tire marks," he said. "She drove a 4-wheeler." He studied the tracks a bit longer. "Hauling a small trailer. The tracks are deep enough to have hauled a person."

Jocelyn.

Hanging his head with the terrifying images of her fighting for her life, he blew air out and stood, beginning to walk down the corridor.

The lead stopped him. "It will take us too long on foot. Let's drive to the warehouse."

Trevor nodded and with one last frustrated look down the dark tunnel, he climbed out and back into the smoky restaurant.

Five minutes later, he realized his worst nightmare.

They found the 4-wheeler, but no sign of Jocelyn whatsoever.

"She could have had a vehicle waiting here," the lead said, having just listened to his earpiece. "And the plate Jocelyn got is also a stolen car."

Regina could have taken her in any vehicle. She'd abandoned cars the way she abandoned her identities. A chameleon.

Where had she taken Jocelyn?

It could be anywhere.

He got out his phone and called the chief. "Regina got away with her. I need you to look for any reported stolen vehicles."

"I'm on it."

"And check the warehouse." Even though Trevor was certain Regina would not keep Jocelyn there.

"We're on it."

He disconnected and fought rising anxiety as he tried to think of what to do next. Only one thing came to him. One, last, desperate reach.

Chapter 17

Trevor headed for the prison entrance and almost didn't see his sister hurrying toward the parking lot. She'd gone to the prison. Had she spoken with Matthew? She looked frazzled. Upset.

"Josie," he called.

Stopping, she searched around and found him, standing still for a second or two, as shocked as him that they had run into each other here. Then she smiled and started toward him. He met her halfway.

"What are you doing here?" she asked. She must know she didn't need to tell him why she'd come.

The gravity of Jocelyn couldn't be calmed. He saw her notice his state.

"Trevor?" She touched his arm.

"Regina kidnapped Jocelyn. I don't know where she is." He looked toward the prison. "Matthew may have received more letters, or there may be something in them with clues he hasn't mentioned yet."

When he faced her again, he saw her doubt.

"Oh, Trevor. I'll go in with you." She hooked her arm with his and would have propelled him in that direction.

He resisted. "No."

She let go, confused. "Why not?"

"Have you talked to him?"

Her head bowed. "Not yet." She raised her eyes to him. "I—I just couldn't. I know I might be able to get a clue that might lead us to where he left Mom, and I had myself all ready to face him, but I entered the prison and it—it wasn't what I expected. It… I don't know. It was too much."

"It's okay, Josie. When the time is right, you'll know."

"I thought I knew now." She looked toward the prison again, the weight of facing their serial killer dad too sobering.

"We can talk later." He had to get moving.

"Jocelyn. How can I be so selfish? I'll go with you." She started walking back toward the prison. "Seeing me may make him help you."

Maybe divine intervention had arranged for them to run into each other. Matthew had complained Josie hadn't come back to see him. She of all the siblings had a certain sentimental effect on him. The youngest of them, maybe he had a soft spot for her. If that were possible.

"How can he help you anyway?" Josie asked.

"He's eluded to having information about Regina that he's kept to himself. That's why I keep coming to see him. I need him to give us more clues."

Josie didn't respond. She didn't believe Matthew

would divulge anything related to Regina or their mother. But she'd come to the prison, so she must have some hope.

Inside, the prison personnel made special arrangements for Trevor to see Matthew, a perk of being an agent. He requested a quiet place this time, and after waiting several agonizing minutes, the prison guard took him and Josie to a windowless room.

Sitting in chains at the rectangular table, Matthew looked pale, if a little grayish green. He slowly turned to see them, recognition lighting his tired eyes when he saw Josie.

"Josie," he said.

He almost sounded human, as though he truly had missed her.

Josie said nothing, folding her arms, not comfortable being here.

"Regina has taken Jocelyn," Trevor said. He didn't have much time anyway. Might as well dive right in and give Josie time to acclimate to seeing her murderous father again.

"Jocelyn, you say?" The left side of his mouth hitched up with the news until phlegmy, weak coughing overtook him. He bent forward, hands trembling as he struggled to breathe.

Trevor felt no pity for the man, especially not when he seemed proud of his copycat killer. Or did he just relish seeing people suffer at the hands of a killer? He related to Regina, to her plight. Maybe he supported her in some way. But he had to have some kind of feelings for his own flesh and blood. If not actual feelings, then some sort of connection. He wouldn't have insisted on visitation otherwise. And as a dying man, he faced oblivion. He must have last wishes he'd like to see done before he went.

But then, Trevor had been wrong about his father before. He was an unpredictable man.

"Your partner?" Matthew scrutinized him closer. "Or more?"

"She's pregnant," Trevor said. "We're married."

"You're married?" Matthew's brow shot down. "When did this happen? Why haven't you come to tell me?"

Trevor didn't understand why he felt he needed to be honest. "We rushed the wedding for the baby. I don't want the child born without both parents."

"That's important to him," Josie said. "Is that something you can understand?"

Matthew looked at her as though her rude interruption insulted his superior position in his warped world. "I had you kids with your mother."

"You mean the woman you murdered?"

"Josie." Trevor put his hand on her shoulder. She could ruin any chance he had of finding Jocelyn.

She seemed to see that and kept quiet after a low "Sorry."

Trevor knew curbing one's tongue could be a challenge with Matthew.

"I'm to be a grandfather, then." Matthew took on an unusual, uncharacteristic softness with the thought.

Trevor had not mentioned that Ethan and Lizzie had already given him a grandchild. Nor would he mention he had more than one.

He cringed with the idea of having to explain to his children about Matthew. Would he say their grandfather died? Would he say their grandmother had been murdered? He couldn't imagine poisoning his children's mind's with such horrors. Maybe when they were older...

"Matthew, I need you to tell me where Regina took Jocelyn."

Matthew's dreamy drift into thought ended. "What makes you think I know?"

"You know something about her. You've been keeping it from me on purpose. I need you to tell me now, before Regina kills her. She has long dark hair and her name starts with a *J.*"

"Regina has her next victim, huh?" Matthew smiled. "She's a busy girl." He laughed low and briefly. "I'm flattered she chose me to emulate."

"You'll let an innocent woman die?" Josie asked caustically. "Trevor's wife? *Your grandchild?*"

His delight waned and he contemplated Josie. Then turned to Trevor.

"There is something I know. Something we exchanged in letters early on."

Trevor gripped the edge of the table, hoping his desperation didn't show.

"I'll tell you." He lowered his head and then passed his gaze around the small room. "I don't have much time left. Days. Weeks. It's difficult to know. Fact is, I'm going to die, and I need certain affairs taken care of."

"What affairs?"

"First, you both have to promise me something."

That would depend on the request. Trevor would not appease the dying wishes of a mass murderer. But he said, "Name it."

Matthew looked at Josie. "You deserve it after all you witnessed. It's the reason I wanted you to come and visit me more often, why I didn't give you the clue when you came to see me that first time."

What was he talking about? Trevor saw Josie's confusion and wondered if Matthew would waste their time on another one of his lunatic exaggerations.

"You're going to tell me the clue, too?" Josie asked.

Was that what Matthew had meant by she *deserved it after all she'd witnessed*?

Trevor wanted to ask what she'd witnessed, but Jocelyn's life depended on him getting information as quickly as possible. He'd have to ask Josie later.

"Jocelyn," Trevor said. "Please. She doesn't have much time."

"Just like me." Matthew smiled again. And then he nodded and put up his hand, seeing Trevor's urgency. "I had a watch, a very valuable old watch that I buried on a distant cousin's property some twenty years ago."

This had taken an odd turn. Twenty years ago, Matthew had aligned with other criminals to carry out a series of heists. Trevor had forgotten about that in his search for the Alphabet Killer. Had the watch been part of the booty? Why hide it if not. And Matthew said the watch had value. What kind of value? Monetary? Or something more sinister?

Knowing his father, Trevor had to go with the latter.

"I want to be buried with the watch on," Matthew said, one of his strange, perverted grins creasing his cancer-sickened face.

"The watch is that important to you?" Trevor had to ask.

"Oh. Very." After overcoming another bout of coughing and wiping his mouth with a tissue, he went off into his thoughts again.

More likely the watch contained a chip with a map showing the location of the fortune he and his cohorts had stolen, or information that would lead to the location. Trevor could see Matthew taking that to his grave, could see him in his coffin, arms folded, wearing the watch, a sick smile formed on his face for all eternity. No one would find the fortune as long as he had the watch. His last hurrah. His last triumph over law enforcement and victims, which, in this case, would be his own children. Again.

Over his dead body would Trevor allow him that gluttony, but, for now, he had to think of Jocelyn.

"You have to promise someone will find the watch and bury me with it."

"Where is the distant cousin's property?" Josie asked.

"Texas." Matthew told them the name of the town. "Promise me you'll find it."

"I promise," Josie said. "I'll find the watch."

And Trevor would decode whatever the watch contained, even if he had to exhume Matthew's body.

He didn't question Josie's motive for wanting to go look for the watch. He worried too much about Jocelyn. Quite possibly, she guessed the same as him.

"Jocelyn," Trevor said, bringing Matthew back to him.

"You haven't made your promise yet," Matthew said. "And I know what a man of your word you are. FBI agent. Lawman. You stick to the straight and narrow. So promise me now. You'll bury me with the watch after Josie finds it."

"I promise." Trevor said the words, but he didn't mean them. Matthew didn't deserve promises. "I speak for all of us when I say that." His thoughts, that was.

A smile curved up Matthew's pale mouth, his eyes taking on a crazed gleam. He must have looked like that when he killed all those people, picturing Big J Colton beaten, bloody and lifeless.

Matthew leaned forward as though he had something juicy to say, something that thrilled him. "In one of Regina's earlier letters, I told her about a bunker I built in the first town I moved to when I left Oklahoma." He told them the name of the town. "I told Regina about it. She seemed keen on the idea of a bunker, especially after I mentioned if she ever needed a place to hide, no one would find her there. You're onto her. She's feeling the pressure. She'll be afraid of capture. If she intends to kill your woman, she'll do it there, where she would feel safe from capture."

"Where is the bunker?"

Matthew touched the oxygen tube beneath his nostrils as though doing so would give him more air. "In the backyard of the house where I lived. Wouldn't surprise me if Regina bought that old place under a false name."

Trevor had all he needed. He turned to go, Josie turning with him.

"Wait." Matthew struggled to catch his breath as Trevor and Josie paused.

"What about your clue, Josie?"

Throbbing pain in her head woke Jocelyn. She came to consciousness groggily, disoriented. Where was she? At the apartment with Trevor? Home? Wincing as she lifted her head, she blinked her eyes open.

A low ceiling roughly framed without drywall registered first. The bare lightbulb hurting her eyes with a chain hanging down for a switch next. Pushing up onto her elbow, she realized her wrists were tied and so were her ankles. Regina. The fire.

Trevor.

Was he all right?

She lay on a mattress with a dark green wool blanket. Her head had rested on a rusty-orange throw pillow. Regina had removed her bulletproof vest.

Hearing movement to her left, she turned.

Regina stood before a wall mirror, wearing a wedding dress and a veil, swaying before her image, admiring herself. Humming.

The dress must be old and had grown brittle. Some of the hem had torn, along with pieces here and there on the bodice. The gown had a gray hue, no longer the pristine white it must have once been.

Regina smiled at some thought—some demented thought. And then her eyes shifted and she saw Jocelyn. The smile slipped away and she turned.

"For a while I thought I hit you on the head too hard." She sashayed over to her, obviously thinking she made quite a fetching picture in the dress. The material swished and the hem swayed.

Jocelyn sat up, twisting her wrists to find the rope secure.

Regina stopped before her. "You won't get away."

"I'm not the woman who took your fiancé from you." Jocelyn had to talk her way out of this. Maybe the more they talked, the more time she'd give Trevor and the team to find her.

If Trevor hadn't been killed in the explosion…

Jocelyn thought to the last time they'd been together at the condo—how she'd doubted him. The prospect of losing him changed the way she thought. She'd rather be with him not knowing if he'd ever fall in love with her than never see him again. She'd take him as the father of their baby than not having him at all.

Regina backhanded her so hard she fell onto the mattress. Her head spun and for a moment she thought she'd go unconscious again.

"You're all the same," Regina hissed. "You deny any responsibility—as if you're these innocent waifs blithely going through life, without a single moment spared in thought for the other woman. You don't care what your actions do to others. You only care about your own selfish gratification!"

"I'm married to my partner. You saw him. Trevor Colton. Not your man. I've never even met your man. Who is he? Where is he? Where can we find him?"

"Find him?" Regina laughed coarsely. "I don't have to find him. As soon as I get rid of all of you, he'll come to me." She smoothed the torn, old skirt of the wedding gown. "And I'll be ready." Her face took on that weird dreamy look again. "I've waited so long. I'll finally have my day."

Yeah…her day in hell. But not before a few in prison.

Jocelyn had to find a way out of here.

"Normally I kill you women by now," Regina said. "But you…" She propped her elbow on her folded arm and curled her fingers under her chin. "You were especially rude to me at the restaurant. I wondered why. I thought it bizarre, and a bit out of place, almost as though you'd done it on purpose. And then you surprised me when you tried to arrest me." She dropped her arms and raised her eyes incredulously. "FBI agents. I had no idea you were that close to catching me." She leaned down and pointed her finger. "That made things a lot more interesting for me."

"Killing a federal agent will make it worse for you. You'll go to prison for the rest of your life. You might even get the death penalty. You're in Texas, after all."

"How do you know we are still in Texas?" Regina laughed, low and cynical. "And you talk as if I'm going to get caught."

Would she take Jocelyn outside Texas? Jocelyn subdued her rising apprehension. "You will. Trevor is going to find you. He won't stop until he does."

"No one is going to find us here. I have all the time in the world to spend with you before I put a bullet in you."

And mark her with a red permanent marker…

Jocelyn looked around. "Where are we?"

Regina straightened. "In an underground bunker, far away from Granite Gulch and your FBI friends. They will never find you." She turned and went back to the mirror. "Not until after you're dead." She swished the skirt of the wedding dress back and forth, admiring herself again. "And then my love will come for me… at last."

Jocelyn looked for something to cut her binds. The room didn't appear to have been prepared to hold a prisoner. Regina hadn't been here before taking her here. That suggested she'd changed her plans. She hadn't anticipated the FBI on her so soon.

A mini refrigerator and small counter with a sink took up the space at the far end, a dresser next to the mirror where Regina remained mesmerized by her reflection. There must be knives in the kitchenette.

Checking Regina, who'd begun to hum, Jocelyn

moved her legs over the edge of the mattress. Regina looked at her through the mirror.

Jocelyn pushed up onto her bound feet and hopped for the kitchenette. She reached the counter and yanked open the first drawer. Forks and other utensils. No knives.

"What do you think you're doing?" Regina grabbed her arm.

Jocelyn had the next drawer open and found the knives. She had her fingers on the handle of one when Regina jerked her away and sent her sprawling to the floor. She scraped her hand and forearm on the hard dirt. Rolling over, she blocked Regina swinging a frying pan.

"You want to play in the kitchen?" Regina hollered.

The pan struck her arm with sharp pain. Jocelyn yelled as it shot up her arm.

Regina swung again, this time hitting Jocelyn's head. She blacked out for a few seconds. When she came to, Regina dragged her by her bound hands back to the mattress.

"I suppose I'll have no time to savor this one," Regina said. She pulled Jocelyn onto the mattress and went to the dresser.

To Jocelyn's horror, she picked up a red permanent marker and snapped the lid off. Then she turned and opened a dresser drawer, bringing out a pistol.

Jocelyn crawled off the mattress. She had to do something. Had to get to the knives. Or wrestle the gun away from this crazy woman.

She got halfway when Regina approached her. Jocelyn got up onto her feet and plowed unsteadily into the woman, sending them both falling. She grabbed Regina's hand that held the pistol with both of her bound ones. Regina punched her head.

Dizzy, Jocelyn bashed Regina with her own gun.

"Ah!" Regina cried like a witch.

Jocelyn hit her again and banged the gun onto the hard ground. Dust billowed up and made them both cough. The gun loosened from Regina's hand, falling to the dirt. Jocelyn tried to reach for it, but Regina batted the gun away, having the advantage of two unbound hands. The gun hit the bottom post of the stairs leading to the door above.

Jocelyn beat Regina on her head with the base of her hands. Regina's head jerked backward. Joclyn pushed to her feet and hopped back to the kitchen. Opening the knife drawer, she took one out. As she turned, Regina had the frying pan again. Jocelyn had no time to block the blow. Her head couldn't take many more hits.

She fell, going unconscious for the third time. When she came to, all she could think of was her baby. What would happen to the baby?

Unaware of how much time had passed, she discovered she'd been tied to the stairs, sitting upright. Lifting her head, her neck aching from her head being bent over, she frantically looked for Regina.

She found her drawing with the red marker. Faded red lines marked white printer paper. She'd changed back into street clothes, jeans and a gray T-shirt that matched the grayish tint to her dishwater-brown hair.

"Damn it!" Regina exclaimed.

Then she saw Jocelyn had awakened. She held up the marker.

"This is out of ink."

Jocelyn said nothing. Her head pounded and her

vision blurred. She felt nauseous. She needed to get to a hospital. What if her brain started hemorrhaging or something? She wished she'd listened to Trevor and quit as soon as she found out she was pregnant.

Regina came over to her. "Looks like you get a few extra minutes before I send you off with all the other lucky ladies, *Jocelyn*." She smirked. "What luck that your name starts with a *J*. It almost doesn't bother me that Janice got away."

"I think I'm going to be sick." Jocelyn's stomach churned. She very likely had a concussion.

"You're going to be a lot more than that when I get back."

She was leaving?

"I have to go get a new red marker. My sign has to be fresh and clear."

Regina went to pick up her purse next to the mirror. She'd hung her wedding dress on a hanger, inside a garment bag, from a hook next to the mirror.

Going to the stairs, she bent and gripped Jocelyn's face, pinching her until she winced. "Don't go anywhere."

Laughing, she climbed the stairs, unhurried, confident she'd have her fun with Jocelyn when she returned.

As soon as the door slammed closed, Jocelyn began struggling to be free of her bindings. But Regina had tied her firmly to the staircase. And the post wouldn't budge.

She would not be able to free herself. She'd sit here, helpless prey, until Regina came back with her brand-new marker, ready to shoot her and give her the mark. Jocelyn would become another victim.

"Trevor," she whispered. "Help me."

Chapter 18

Josie felt ill, alone in the small room with her father. She kept glancing toward the door where Trevor had rushed through to go and rescue Jocelyn. She'd much rather have gone with him. Knowing the guards would not let anything happen to her didn't help.

"What did you mean when you said I deserve it?" she asked the horrible man seated at the table.

"Sit with me, Josie."

She didn't like his domineering look. Even near death he could intimidate her. He could intimidate anyone. He suffered through periodic coughing spells, and once recovered, the old Matthew found a way to shine even in the grip of cancer.

Telling herself she did this for her brothers and sisters, Josie sat.

"You were always my little girl," Matthew said.

Josie endured his rambling.

"I remember when you first started talking. The day I first heard you say *daddy* turned me to mush."

That hadn't lasted long. She wouldn't call him mushy when he'd begun killing people. She did remember times when he'd acted like a real father to her, though. Weird, how a person could be so different underneath the shell.

"You used to adore me. Followed me everywhere, you did. You loved when I held you. Those are some of my fondest memories, Josie. Of you."

Was he only saying this? Like Trevor, she didn't trust a word he said.

"That's what got you into trouble when your mother died."

What was he talking about? "You mean when you *killed* her?"

"Yes," he said simply. "That's exactly what I mean. You were so young. You may not have any memory of it. And if you do, they are likely patchy and unclear. Thankfully. I'd have had to kill you, too, otherwise."

Why would he have had to kill her, too? How disgusting.

Josie pushed back her chair. "I'm leaving. I knew you'd string me along again."

She started for the door, ready to knock for the guards to let her out. Matthew coughed some more. He wouldn't be able to move until they came in and unlocked his chain from the metal hooks keeping him in the chair, which she'd seen was bolted to the cement floor.

"I intend to give you your clue."

She stopped. The guard opened the door. She shook her head and went back to the table.

"Then tell me what it is."

"I only wished to spend some time with you," he said. "I'm dying, and I mean it when I say I have such fond memories of you."

Good for him, but she didn't care. "Tell me the clue."

He hesitated, then at last relented. "Blue."

Josie stared at him. "Blue?" Dripping blue paint from her dream chilled her.

"Yes." He smiled. "Blue. Don't you remember? It's one of my favorite memories of you."

Her recurring dream swarmed her. The significance of the fence sank in. She'd painted it blue. It must be from a memory when she was very young, before she could retain solid memories, a piece of something she'd done.

She'd painted the fence.

She remembered the fence now.

"Is that where you buried Mother?" she asked, feeling light-headed with shock.

Matthew smiled again, in that creepy way. "My smart girl. I'm so glad you came to see me today."

Josie fought nausea that threatened to have her throwing up. She banged on the door as Matthew fell into another coughing episode, this one sounding as though it would be his last. She hoped so.

"Wait." Matthew coughed some more, unable to speak any more, unable to stop her.

Good. This was the last she would see of him. She had done her duty. She had the clue.

The guard let her out and she ran from the prison.

After a long drive, Trevor drove fast on the way to the bunker. He'd already notified the rest of the team, so they wouldn't be far behind him. *Be alive, Jocelyn.*

Finding the right address on the mailbox, he drove up the long driveway to the house with white chipping paint and shutters over the windows. The house looked condemned; it had been vacant for so long.

Parking, he got out and searched for the bunker, not seeing any sign of it. Matthew might have given him the wrong address. He could be sitting in his cell, weak from cancer, laughing over his cleverness and Trevor's gullibility.

The house sat on a large parcel of land. He peered into the garage through a window that had been broken. No vehicle there. No vehicle in the driveway, either. No one appeared to be here, including Jocelyn. He experienced extreme apprehension wondering if Regina hadn't brought her here. What if she hadn't?

Looking closer at the driveway, going to where the concrete ended and gravel began, he found evidence of recent tracks. A wave of relief and renewed hope surged through him.

After searching the front for signs of a bunker entrance and finding none, he went around to the back. Weeds had taken over, some popping up through cracks in the concrete slab. An old grill sat weathered and falling apart, vines of weeds winding their way up to the side shelves and around the handle.

Trees blocked the neighbor's view of the backyard. He walked the perimeter. Halfway along one side, he stopped when he saw a wood-framed square door, parallel with the ground.

The underground structure had been built with secrecy in mind. Trees and shrubs concealed the entrance. Footprints indicated someone had recently been here.

Jocelyn was here. He felt her presence.

Had he made it in time?

Drawing his gun, he stood aside and turned the latch. Pulling up the door, he let it swing over onto the ground, falling with a soundless thud onto some low-growing bushes.

Peering inside, he heard Jocelyn scream before he saw her tied to the staircase post. She struggled with all her might.

"Jocelyn!"

She craned her neck to look up at him, her eyes closing in relief. "Trevor. Hurry. She left to get a new red marker."

He jumped down the stairs three at a time. Crouching before her, cupping her face and kissing her.

"The thought of losing you nearly killed me."

"Knife. Kitchen drawer. Hurry!"

He stood and went to the open drawer and lifted a knife. Going back to her, he sliced through the rope tying her ankles and then her wrists tied to the post.

She threw her arms around him. "Oh, Trevor. I thought she was going to kill me."

"I've got you now." He helped her to her feet, noticing how she swayed and blinked as though she had trouble seeing.

"Are you all right?"

"I think I have a concussion. She hit me hard on the head a few times."

Her speech sounded a little slurred.

He felt her head, finding a lump and a cut, her hair sticky with blood. He had to get her to a hospital. Not wanting to frighten her, he lifted her into the cradle of his arms and carried her to the surface. Kicking the door shut so Regina wouldn't be alerted that someone had been here, he knelt and turned the latch.

Standing, he felt a rush of protective warmth surge through him as Jocelyn looped her arm over his shoulder and rested her head on him. Taking her to the passenger side of the SUV, he went around to the driver's side and drove down the driveway. On the way to the hospital, he called the chief.

"We're almost there. We'll stay out of sight until she returns."

Regina Willard would be captured. It was over, the investigation closed. All but the trail and sentencing left.

Trevor could put Matthew behind him now. At last.

He just had one more thing he needed to do.

Jocelyn woke in the hospital. She had a concussion and the doctors wanted her to stay the night for observation. Dark at around nine at night, she saw what had awakened her.

Trevor entered with a huge bouquet of flowers. He'd cleaned up, too, wearing a fresh suit and tie, cleanly shaven. He'd said he was going to grab a bite to eat and for her to get some rest. That had been hours ago.

"Where have you been?"

"I met with the chief. Regina is in custody."

Jocelyn sighed. "That's one menace to society I'm very happy is behind bars where she belongs."

"Yes. Now we can get on with our lives." Trevor put the flowers down on the table beside the bed.

"They're beautiful." She smelled them from where she rested.

"Not as beautiful as you."

Jocelyn laughed. "I'm usually the one who teases."

"I'm not teasing. I'm as serious as always."

She smiled her love at him. He took a seat on the chair by the bed and reached into his pocket.

"Jocelyn, I have been a confused fool."

She sucked in a breath of air when she saw he held a familiar ring box. She'd removed the ring he'd gotten for her for the Vegas wedding. He must have found it in her jewelry box.

"I let the investigation get to me too much. Matthew. The copycat killer."

It had reminded him too much of his adolescence, being ripped from his family, his mother's murder and his father the killer.

"It's okay. When Regina captured me, I knew I'd been equally foolish. I—"

"Shh. Let me finish." He took out the ring, lifted her hand and slipped it on. Holding her hand, he said, "I love you, Jocelyn. I think I've loved you since the day we met."

She smiled and tears stung her eyes. "Really? Me, too. I love you, Trevor."

He leaned over her for a kiss. "I'll never disappoint you again. I'll spend the rest of my life making you happy."

"I couldn't possibly be any happier than I am now." She kissed him again. "Oh, Trevor."

He moved away, still holding her hand. "Will you marry me?"

"Trevor," she said breathlessly.

"For real this time. Marry me, Jocelyn. Let's buy that house and have kids and get a dog."

"Okay." She pulled her hand free to take his face and bring his mouth back to hers.

"Marry me."

"Yes. Yes. Yes, I'll marry you, Trevor Colton!"

"Looks like we came at a bad time."

Moving back from Trevor as he straightened, she saw Josie enter and then the rest of the Coltons follow. Sam and Zoe, Ethan and Lizzie with their baby in her arms, Ridge and Darcy, Jesse and Annabel, and Chris and Holly.

"Trevor asked me to marry him—for real." Jocelyn smiled.

"That's great news!" Annabel said.

"We'll have to get her out of this hospital first," Sam said. "Unless you'd like to get a minister in here now."

"Looked like they could use one when we came in." Zoe laughed lightly.

A few of the others laughed with her while everyone else wore happy smiles.

"I didn't ask you all to meet here to make wedding plans," Josie said. "There's something I need to tell you."

After everyone sobered, recalling that she had asked them to meet and obviously hadn't given a reason yet, Josie said, "Matthew gave me a clue."

Now a pin could be heard dropping in the room.

"I've been having nightmares where I'm painting a white fence. There are flowers and clear blue skies at first, but then that changes to darkness and wilting flowers and wind and I'm always trapped by the fence, trying to get away from a monster that chases me. In the last dream I had, the monster's face became clear. It was Dad."

"Matthew?" Trevor said.

Like Jocelyn, he didn't follow where she led.

"I didn't know what it meant, but now I do. My clue was the word *blue*." Josie looked at each of her siblings before saying. "In my dream, I'm painting the fence blue."

Several seconds went by.

"What does that mean?" Sam finally asked.

"I remember painting that fence when I was a toddler. It's not a clear memory, but I do remember painting it. Guess what color I used?"

"Blue." Annabel shrugged. "So?"

"You must have seen him bury Mom," Trevor said. "That's what he meant when he said you deserved it after all you'd witnessed."

Everyone fell silent with that awful revelation. Josie had been too young to remember.

"I know where the fence is," Sam said. "It's on our maternal grandmother's property, where all of the other clues have led us."

"I remember that fence, too," Ridge said. "Mom is buried there!"

Chapter 19

Everyone gathered around the area of ground slightly raised more than other areas, near the fence that Josie had painted as a toddler. Trevor held Jocelyn's hand, grappling with various emotions. He wasn't sure how he felt. Glad to have finally found their mother's body and burial spot, angry that she'd been killed. Empty.

"What are we going to do with her body?" Josie asked.

Matthew hadn't put her in a coffin. She'd likely long since decomposed. They might find some bones to bury.

"I think we should leave her here," Chris said.

"This is where a murderer dumped her," Annabel said, appalled.

"Where else would Mom want to be buried other than on her mother's property?" Sam asked. "She loved this place."

"She did love this place." Ethan looked back at the house. He and his wife had left their baby with a nanny for this trip.

Each of them fell silent, staring down at the ground.

"We could exhume her and give her a proper burial," Trevor said. "Put what's left of her in a nice coffin."

"Ugh." Annabel nearly gagged. "That is so morbid."

"We could plant a flower garden here," Josie said.

She'd dreamed of a flower garden before the darkness came.

"Do we disturb her? She's dead. She doesn't care anymore that she's buried where her husband put her after he killed her."

"If I was the one in that ground right now, I'd want my kids to put me in a coffin or cremate me and put my ashes on my property," Jocelyn said. "Maybe not where I was murdered, though." She looked at Josie. "Will it bother you that your mother is buried where you dreamed in your nightmares?"

Josie shook her head. "I think she was sending me messages. And I remember what a beautiful day that was, and how happy she looked. She loved this part of the yard."

"Dad knew that," Ethan said.

"That's probably why he buried her here," Sam added. "He cared enough about her and their life together to do that."

A chorus of agreement spread.

"Let's vote." Trevor looked at each of his siblings. "All in favor of leaving Mom here and possibly exhuming her to give her a proper burial, raise their hands."

Everyone but Annabel raised their hands.

"You'd rather move her?" Trevor asked.

"I don't know. I just think it's rotten that Dad murdered her and he put her here."

"She did love it here. She planned to make a big flower garden here," Ethan said.

Annabel nodded. "Yes, she did love this area. And I remember her talking about it, about what kind of flowers she wanted to plant, what kind of stone for the path."

"She wanted to put a bench here," Chris said.

"I say we leave her be," Josie said. "She's been here all this time anyway. Sorry to sound morbid, but there probably isn't much left of her body. We can plant a flower garden exactly the way she wished, and we can come visit her here."

"Annabel?" Trevor said. They all had to be in agreement.

She met his gaze. "I do like the idea of making her flower garden for her."

"None of us like it that she was murdered, much less that Dad killed her and buried her afterward, but he did at least honor her by putting her in a place he knew she loved," Ridge said.

"It will take time to get over how she got here," Trevor said. "But we will. Together."

Annabel softened and then nodded. "Yes. We will." She went to him and they hugged.

"We can leave her here, then," she said.

Trevor rubbed her back before she drew away. The show of affection compelled the rest of them to exchange hugs. Pretty soon they all laughed, hugging because they could, now that they were back together.

"Let's get out of here," Sam said. "We have a wedding to attend."

"There's a lot to celebrate." Chris put his arm around his wife and looked at her with love.

"Yes," Trevor said, taking Jocelyn's hand. "Let's have a wedding. A real wedding."

Trevor had found the old church, looking more like a castle with its spires and intricate stone trim work. Flowers out front, wide stairs leading into the chapel.

They'd kept it small—only immediate family. But the chief had spread the word through the department at the FBI field office, where Jocelyn had resigned just the day before.

She let the gossamer drapes go and turned from the view through the window. Josie entered the dressing room and stopped short.

"Oh. You look so beautiful."

Smiling, Jocelyn looked down at the V neckline and fit-and-flare skirt with Venice lace over tulle.

"Thank you." She'd put her hair up with a few tendrils hanging free, not wanting any correlation to the case—Regina and her aversion to long dark hair.

"You ready? I was sent to get you."

"Yes." She'd never been more ready for anything in her life.

Going with Josie downstairs, she saw Chris waiting there. He'd insisted on giving her away, since she and Trevor decided not to have attendants in the ceremony. She'd joked that she could have Sigmund stand beside them, though.

"See you out there." Josie left them and entered the chapel.

Chris offered his arm, dapper in his black tux, with

his blond hair and blue eyes. She slipped hers through the space beneath his bent arm.

"It's my pleasure to give you away, Jocelyn. I've always looked up to my big brother."

"He loves all of you more than you can imagine." She knew that would be important for him to hear.

He smiled. "I know that now."

"Good."

They walked to the chapel entrance. "Allow me to be the first to welcome you to the family."

She caught sight of Trevor, standing tall, dark and proud at the altar, hands clasped in front, dark gaze on her.

She had to breathe faster as she walked down the aisle. Officers in uniform, agents in suits and the rest of Trevor's family stood in the pews, watching.

Reaching the altar, the minister—the same who'd married them in Vegas; Trevor had flown him here—said, "Who gives this bride to this man?"

"I do." Chris smiled at his brother.

Jocelyn stepped up next to Trevor, unable to stop herself from smiling, either. He grinned in a sexy way, all the secrets they had speaking to her. Secrets in love.

"This is much different than the *Mr. and Mrs. Smith* outfits in Las Vegas," the minister said.

A wave of curbed laughter spread over the crowd.

"You look lovely, Jocelyn," the minister said.

"Thank you."

Trevor took Jocelyn's hands and held them in his palms, then hooked her arm with his. "Lovely indeed."

"Ladies and gentlemen, we are gathered here today to witness the joining of this man and woman. If there's anyone who objects, speak now or forever hold your peace." He scanned the crowd.

No one objected.

"I might have objected in Las Vegas," the minister said.

More brief chuckles spread.

"Let us begin." The minister turned to Trevor. "Trevor Colton, will you have this woman to be your wedded wife, to love her, comfort her, honor and keep her, and forsaking all others, keep you only unto her, for so long as you both shall live?"

"I do." He sounded much different than in Vegas. A lot more certain.

Smiling his approval, the minister turned to Jocelyn. "Jocelyn Locke, will you have this man to be your wedded husband, to love him, comfort him, honor and keep him, and forsaking all others, keep you only unto him, so long as you both shall live?"

"I do," she said.

"Very good. Hold hands and repeat after me."

Jocelyn removed her arm from the hook of his and he took her hands.

"I see I don't have to tell you to face each other and hold hands this time," the minister said to a few more chuckles.

"I, Trevor Colton..." the minister said.

Trevor looked deep into Jocelyn's eyes. She felt his sincerity and his love.

"I, Trevor Colton, take you, Jocelyn Locke, to be my wedded wife, to have and to hold, for better or for worse, for richer or for poorer, to love and to cherish, from this day forward."

"Now for the lady," the minister said. "I, Jocelyn Locke…"

"I, Jocelyn Locke, take you, Trevor Colton, to be my wedded husband, to have and to hold, for better or for worse, for richer or for poorer, to love and to cherish, from this day forward."

"Is there a ring?" the minister asked.

"Yes." He took out the ring he'd given back to Jocelyn at the hospital.

"Please place the ring on the bride's finger and repeat after me," the minister said.

Trevor took Jocelyn's hand, holding her gently and reverently, and slipped the ring onto her finger. Then he looked into her eyes again and said, "With this ring, I thee wed."

"Is there a ring for the groom?"

Jocelyn opened her palm. Trevor had given her his ring before the ceremony.

She held his hand now, slipping on the ring. "With this ring, I thee wed."

"Let these rings be given and received as a token of your affection, sincerity and fidelity to one another."

They were given and received as a token of their affection, sincerity and fidelity. Jocelyn felt it to her core.

"By the authority vested in me by the state of Texas, I now pronounce you husband and wife." The minister beamed a fond smile. "You may kiss the bride."

Jocelyn put her hands on Trevor's chest as he drew her against him. He lowered his head as she tipped hers up. He kissed her, soft, warm and long.

His brothers whistled and others hooted.

When Trevor moved back with happiness shining in his eyes, they turned together to face the crowd.

"Allow me to be the first to introduce you to Mr. and Mrs. Colton."

Everyone applauded and she and Trevor made their way down the aisle. Her chest all but burst with love and excitement—for a future she dreamed of and now finally had at her feet.

Outside, people threw confetti as they made their way to the limo. Jocelyn stopped with her bouquet of flowers. Women gathered, female officers…and Josie.

Jocelyn turned her back and threw the bouquet. When she looked back, she saw Josie holding it with wide eyes.

Trevor's brothers and sisters laughed and Sam said, "Oh, you're next, little sister!"

With people clapping and talking and laughing, Jocelyn and Trevor got into the limo. Seated in the middle, she snuggled close. When he turned to her, he kissed her.

Picture-perfect.

Epilogue

Trevor put the file down containing the latest murder investigation he'd just begun working. Jocelyn, still not showing her pregnancy to the ordinary onlooker, opened the file and began reading. She'd kept her promise and resigned, but she still took an interest in his caseload. Stepping behind her, he put his hand over the tiny mound of her stomach. He loved going through this with her. He took pictures almost every day so he knew the exact moment she began to show.

Proud father only touched the surface of how he felt.

"Trevor, let me read." She leaned over the kitchen island of their new home. They'd just moved in and had planned a delayed wedding reception so they could hold it here.

"I am letting you read."

"I'm not going to want to read in a minute." She turned her head and he kissed her. "Stop that."

He chuckled and moved back, going into the kitchen for a bottle of water. Then he went to stand on the other side of the island, a safe distance and with structure in the way so that he wouldn't be tempted to touch her.

She came to the photos and drew back at the sight. Flipping through those, she came to more of the report.

The crime had occurred three nights ago. A woman had been strangled to death in her own bedroom. No sign of a break-in. No sign of a robbery. The husband had been questioned. He denied everything and claimed to have been at a local bar during the time of his wife's murder.

"You think the husband did it?" she asked.

"Yes. His alibi doesn't check out. No one can say they saw him at the bar and he can't produce any receipts. Claims to have paid cash."

"Any life insurance?"

"Five hundred thousand."

"Any kids?"

"No kids."

Jocelyn closed the file. "That's open-and-shut."

He nodded. "Gathering evidence would be the most challenging. He was having an affair that he neglected to mention during questioning."

"And here I thought I had it so bad." She moved around the island and looped her arms around him.

"Since when?"

"Before this." She rose up and kissed him. "Do we have time before everyone gets here?"

"A few minutes. But what about the caterer and the band?"

The doorbell rang.

"Doesn't matter anyway," he amended.

She fanned her face as he withdrew with a grin. He went to open the door, and in came the Coltons.

Ethan and Lizzie entered first, Lizzie carrying their tiny newborn baby, who had begun to put up a fuss. She went to the living room and took a chair to begin feeding.

Sam and Zoe went into the kitchen.

Zoe saw the backyard decorated for the reception through the window. "It's so festive!"

Jocelyn and Trevor had rented a party tent big enough for their family. White-linen-covered tables, one with a moderately sized cake, didn't quite fill the space. Strings of lights would allow them to celebrate into the night. The caterer worked behind the buffet table, getting ready to serve gourmet surf and turf. The country-western band finished their sound checks and had just begun playing.

Ridge and Darcy arrived a few minutes later, followed by Jesse and Annabel, and Chris and Holly.

Ethan joined his wife in the living room. Trevor watched them awhile, seeing how his brother couldn't take his eyes off the infant. He'd be the same way when his own baby was born. He already felt that way. Amazing. What a miracle.

"Let's leave them alone." Jocelyn hooked her arm with his and he went with her to the back, where everyone else had gone.

Zoe the librarian in tortoiseshell glasses talked to Darcy. Trevor had told her Darcy was Ridge's high school sweetheart and her parents had split them up. Love couldn't keep them apart. They'd found each other again, now a doctor and a search and rescue hero instead of students.

Jesse and Annabel started a two-step and Chris and Holly joined them on the small dance floor.

"Where's Josie?" Sam asked.

"Right here." She held up two bottles of champagne. "Those of us not nursing or pregnant are required to share a toast with me. And, hey, I'm the only person here without a significant other or spouse, so you have to do as I say."

Trevor chuckled and leaned in to peck a kiss on his sister's cheek. "You caught the bouquet. You won't be single long."

"I don't believe in that old wives' tale. And neither do you."

"I believe it now." He winked at Jocelyn.

"Well, that will have to wait." She put the bottles down on the counter and Jocelyn took them to the refrigerator. "I'm leaving in the morning for Brush Valley."

"You're going to go look for the watch?"

Jocelyn came to stand next to Trevor, putting her arm around his waist. "As much as Matthew strung all of you along, you shouldn't feel obligated to do anything he asks."

Trevor held her, too. "If she doesn't, then I will. I want to know what's in that watch that makes it so special to him."

"Money, that's what. If the watch isn't worth a fortune, something it contains is," Josie said. "No, I'm going. Eldridge Colton is Matthew's distant cousin. I'll start with him."

"Whatever makes you happy."

"I am happy. Happy to be free of the kingpin, and happy to be out of witness protection. I finally feel safe."

How safe would she be chasing after a mysterious

watch that belonged to Matthew Colton? Trevor would worry about his sister while she went on her adventure, but he'd keep his concern to himself. One of them had to go or Matthew would never leave them alone. Until he died.

Matthew had sent him a letter congratulating him on his wedding, but in the last paragraph, he mentioned the watch and stated, "I hope you and Josie will make good on your promise." If someone didn't go search for the watch, he'd keep badgering them. The sooner Trevor could erase that man from his life, the better.

"Just be careful, Josie."

"I'll be careful, big brother. And I'll add that I'm happiest of all to be back here with all of you."

"We all are." Glad he didn't have to deal with Matthew anymore, Trevor steered his wife toward the music. "Let's give you a proper send-off tonight." And he and Jocelyn properly celebrated the beginning of a really great life.

* * * * *

REQUEST YOUR FREE BOOKS!
2 FREE NOVELS PLUS 2 FREE GIFTS!

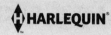 **HARLEQUIN**®

ROMANTIC suspense

Sparked by danger, fueled by passion

YES! Please send me 2 FREE Harlequin® Romantic Suspense novels and my 2 FREE gifts (gifts are worth about $10). After receiving them, if I don't wish to receive any more books, I can return the shipping statement marked "cancel." If I don't cancel, I will receive 4 brand-new novels every month and be billed just $4.74 per book in the U.S. or $5.49 per book in Canada. That's a savings of at least 12% off the cover price! It's quite a bargain! Shipping and handling is just 50¢ per book in the U.S. and 75¢ per book in Canada.* I understand that accepting the 2 free books and gifts places me under no obligation to buy anything. I can always return a shipment and cancel at any time. Even if I never buy another book, the two free books and gifts are mine to keep forever.

240/340 HDN GH3P

Name _____ (PLEASE PRINT) _____

Address _____ Apt. # _____

City _____ State/Prov. _____ Zip/Postal Code _____

Signature (if under 18, a parent or guardian must sign) _____

Mail to the **Reader Service:**
IN U.S.A.: P.O. Box 1867, Buffalo, NY 14240-1867
IN CANADA: P.O. Box 609, Fort Erie, Ontario L2A 5X3

Want to try two free books from another line?
Call 1-800-873-8635 or visit www.ReaderService.com.

* Terms and prices subject to change without notice. Prices do not include applicable taxes. Sales tax applicable in N.Y. Canadian residents will be charged applicable taxes. Offer not valid in Quebec. This offer is limited to one order per household. Not valid for current subscribers to Harlequin Romantic Suspense books. All orders subject to credit approval. Credit or debit balances in a customer's account(s) may be offset by any other outstanding balance owed by or to the customer. Please allow 4 to 6 weeks for delivery. Offer available while quantities last.

Your Privacy—The Reader Service is committed to protecting your privacy. Our Privacy Policy is available online at www.ReaderService.com or upon request from the Reader Service.

We make a portion of our mailing list available to reputable third parties that offer products we believe may interest you. If you prefer that we not exchange your name with third parties, or if you wish to clarify or modify your communication preferences, please visit us at www.ReaderService.com/consumerschoice or write to us at Reader Service Preference Service, P.O. Box 9062, Buffalo, NY 14240-9062. Include your complete name and address.

HRS15

SPECIAL EXCERPT FROM

HARLEQUIN®

ROMANTIC suspense

Finding love and buried family secrets in the
Lone Star State...

Read on for a sneak preview of
COLTON COWBOY HIDEOUT,
by New York Times *bestselling author Carla Cassidy,*
the next book in the Harlequin Romantic Suspense
continuity **THE COLTONS OF TEXAS**.

Tension wafted from Josie. "It's just like my father described—the tree, the carvings and the creek."

"Did he tell you what the carvings meant?"

She shook her head. "No, I'm not even sure he's the one who made them."

"Then, let's see if we can dig up an old watch," he replied.

They hadn't quite reached the front of the tree when a man stepped out from behind it, a gun in his hand.

Josie released a sharp yelp of surprise and Tanner tightened his grip on the shovel. What in the hell was going on? Did this man have something to do with whatever had happened to Eldridge?

"Josie Colton," he said, his thin lips twisting into a sneer. "I knew if I tailed you long enough you'd lead me to the watch. I've been watching you for days."

"Who are you?" Josie asked.

"That's for me to know and you not to find out," he replied. "Now, about that watch…"

"What watch?" she replied. "I—I don't know what you're talking about." Her voice held a tremor that belied her calm demeanor.

Tanner didn't move a muscle although his brain fired off in a dozen different directions. The man had called her by name, so this obviously had nothing to do with Eldridge.

Why would a man with a gun know about a watch wanted for sentimental reasons? What hadn't Josie told him? Was it possible to disarm the man without anyone getting hurt?

"Don't play dumb with me, girlie." The man raised a hand to sweep a hank of oily dark hair out of his eyes. "Your daddy spent years in prison bragging about how he was going to be buried with that cheap watch and then nobody would ever find the map to all the money from those old bank heists." He took a step toward them. "Now tell me where that watch is. I want that map."

Adrenaline pumped through Tanner. He certainly didn't know anything about old bank robberies, but a sick danger snapped in the air.

A look of deadly menace radiated outward from the gunman's dark, beady eyes. The gun was steady in his hands, and Tanner's chest constricted.

He tightened his grip on the shovel, calculated the distance between himself and the gunman's arm and then he swung. The end of the shovel connected. The gun fell from the man's grasp, but not before he fired off a shot.

The woods exploded with sound—the boom of the gun, a flutter of birds' wings overhead as they flew out of the treetops and Josie's scream of unmistakable pain.

Don't miss
COLTON COWBOY HIDEOUT by New York Times
bestselling author Carla Cassidy,
available July 2016 wherever
Harlequin® Romantic Suspense
books and ebooks are sold.

www.Harlequin.com

Turn your love of reading into rewards you'll love with
Harlequin My Rewards

**Join for FREE today at
www.HarlequinMyRewards.com**

Earn **FREE BOOKS** of your choice.

Experience **EXCLUSIVE OFFERS** and contests.

Enjoy **BOOK RECOMMENDATIONS**
selected just for you.

PLUS! Sign up now
and get **500** points
right away!

Earn
FREE
REWARDS
HarlequinMyRewards.com
Join
Today!

MYR16R